SACRIFICIAL WEAPON

SACRIFICIAL WEAPON

CRYPTID ASSASSIN™ BOOK THREE

MICHAEL ANDERLE

Copyright © 2020 Michael Anderle
Cover Art by Jake @ J Caleb Design
http://jcalebdesign.com / jcalebdesign@gmail.com
Cover copyright © LMBPN Publishing
A Michael Anderle Production

LMBPN Publishing
PMB 196, 2540 South Maryland Pkwy
Las Vegas, NV 89109

First US edition, February, 2020
eBook ISBN: 978-1-64202-749-5
Print ISBN: 978-1-64202-750-1

THE SACRIFICIAL WEAPON TEAM

Thanks to our Beta Readers

Jeff Eaton, John Ashmore, and Kelly O'Donnell

Thanks to the JIT Readers

Dave Hicks
Diane L. Smith
Jeff Eaton
Dorothy Lloyd
John Ashmore
Peter Manis
Tim Bischoff
Deb Mader

If we've missed anyone, please let us know!

Editor
Skyhunter Editing Team

CHAPTER ONE

Today was not a good day, and for a man who had inherited the kind of money and power he had, it should have been a really, really good fucking day.

Rod Marino stared out the window of his office and tapped his fingers gently on the golf club in his hands.

He reminded himself that people disappeared all the time. All the unsolved missing persons' cases were ample proof that it happened. Car crashes mangled the owners beyond recognition as a daily occurrence across the country, and that was the above-board and no-foul-play way they could vanish. There were a hundred different ways people could drop off the face of the planet and as a mob boss, he knew that better than most. Of course, he'd never had much to do with that side of the business until recently but still, he knew.

The issue, of course, was that his people were usually the ones who caused the disappearance, not those left wondering what had happened. It was the ordinary citizens who had that problem when someone went missing, mainly

1

because they didn't have the right kinds of resources at their disposal. They inevitably relied on the overworked and underpaid folks in local law enforcement who were well-meaning and made the best effort they could, but it was no guarantee that they would find answers.

Unlike them, he did have the right kind of resources. He had access to the kind of people who were veritable bloodhounds and could track people across continents—possibly because they knew how to hide and what to do if they didn't want to be found. He recalled some old saying about how it took one to know one and chuckled. In all honesty, he didn't care how or why. He wouldn't question their reasons as long as they continued to deliver results.

Meeting expectations was the kind of thing that was a point of pride for him. He demanded it from the people he employed in the same way his employers demanded it from him. They had entrusted him with the kind of authority they had on the assumption that he could get the job done.

While he took care not to reveal it, he had begun to doubt that he really was the man for the job. Unfortunately, his doubts would have to wait. For now, he needed to direct the frustrations that resulted from unmet expectations toward the two men who were coming up in the elevator to meet with him. He decided he would tell his secretary to hold them in the waiting room for a couple of minutes before she let them in.

The men had been lieutenants in his father's regime and he had inherited them along with everything else. Both had been around since before Rod had even been born, and aside from the respect they had paid to his father and the capos sent from Sicily, they were used to being deferred to and respected in their own right.

He had a sneaking suspicion that the fact that he'd been in diapers when they'd first met him might have clouded their judgment. They quite possibly still regarded him as "the kid" on some level—and not even the oldest son, he thought sourly—and so didn't take his authority all that seriously. It was his intention to remind them that they owed him the same kind of deference because he was, in fact, their boss. Age and familiarity had fuck all to do with it.

As if on cue, the phone on his desk rang and he snatched it up quickly.

"Mr. Gallo and Mr. Conti are here for you," his secretary said.

"Thanks, Janine. Keep them stewing for a second out there," Rod said. "Offer them water or coffee or something but keep them waiting."

"Will do, sir," she said.

No, he wouldn't kowtow to their misplaced sense of importance. He intended to make the demands, and if they didn't like what he had to say, maybe it was time for a change in personnel. People would literally kill to have their jobs, after all. He could probably use the new to get rid of the old, two with one stone and all that. Efficiency appealed to him.

A few minutes ticked passed as he put a Bluetooth earpiece in his ear and practiced his short game on a small patch of fake grass he'd set up in his office for precisely that purpose. Behind him, Janine opened the door for his guests to enter.

"No, Charlie," Rod said loudly in his pretended conversation. He rather enjoyed the charade designed to make the two gentlemen realize that they weren't at the top of his priorities at the moment. "No, you don't tip the floor manager...that's crass, honestly. Besides, they make enough money as is, trust me. No, you tip the dealer. Always tip the dealer. That way, they know you're the one who gives them a little extra when you win money, see?"

He turned and gestured for the two men to sit and continued his act.

"Right...like when you tip the waitress, she'll be a little quicker on the draw when you want your drink refilled... correct." He leaned the club against the wall and strolled to his desk. "Keep the money flowing and it will come back to you. Now, I have to go. I have a business meeting... Yeah, you have a great afternoon, Charlie. I'll see you at the magic show at nine, okay?"

He pretended to hang up, tossed the earpiece casually on his desk, and settled into his chair. "Gentlemen, thanks for coming in so quickly. Did Janine offer you coffee?"

Gallo, the taller and leaner of the two, nodded. "We prefer to keep the pleasantries until after business has been handled, however."

"No, that's weird." Rod pressed the button to call Janine, not because he particularly wanted something but because it was a small way to assert his authority. "Hey, can you get us two espressos and a latte for me? Thanks."

"Right away, Mr. Marino," she replied crisply.

"Okay, right to business, shall we?" he asked, clapped,

and ignored their slight frowns. "Two mercs on my payroll have disappeared. I've sent you the details, so why don't you two go ahead and share what you've found with me?"

Conti, stouter than his companion and sporting an elegant beard, stood from his seat and placed a file on the table. The mob leader picked it up and glanced through the pages before he replaced it on the desk.

"Why don't you guys give me the broad strokes, huh?" he asked brusquely. He knew what they would say and didn't see the point in beating about the bush.

The two exchanged a glance before Conti spoke. "Well, Ro—Mr. Marino, the long and the short of it is that there is no sign of where the two mercenaries went. They bought no plane tickets or train tickets and the car they rented was found abandoned alongside Boulder Highway. None of our connections have seen them over the past few weeks. They haven't been drinking, eating, or gambling anywhere in the state and they haven't used any of their credit cards."

Rod knew all that—his other sources had already told him as much—but he was careful to keep his expression neutral as he tapped his forefinger on the mahogany desk in front of him.

"So, all that to say you two have fuck all, is that right?" he asked when the man said nothing more.

A hasty glance was exchanged between the two before Gallo spoke. "That's not entirely accurate. We know they didn't use any of the regular ways out of the state, and from that, we can extrapolate—"

The mob boss raised a hand imperiously to interrupt him in mid-sentence, and he smiled inwardly at the gratification it brought to see the man go silent immediately. "I don't pay the two of you to extrapolate data or make any guesses. I need you to understand that I have two men walking around with twenty grand of my money and nothing to show for it."

"If it's about the money, I'm sure we could—" Conti began but fell silent when Rod glared at him.

"It's not about the money, okay?" he said and although he started quietly, he deliberately let his volume build slowly with every word. "It's incidental. Seriously, I net twenty grand every couple of hours on the gambling floor downstairs alone. I don't give a shit about the money. That's why I was happy to pay it in the first place. The problem is the services I'm not fucking getting!"

His tone became a yell at the end of his sentence as he pushed from his chair and pounded his closed fist on the desk for emphasis.

As suddenly as his display of temper had appeared, it faded and he dropped into his seat as Janine stepped in with their coffee.

"Look, this is not simply about me being an asshole here," he said, his tone coldly reasonable once the secretary had left the office again. "My father trusted you two to help run things for him, and I need to trust you too. It's very simple. I need you to find these two guys and at least give me a definitive answer. Are they still working the job? Did they blow all the money on coke and hookers? Did they overdose on said coke and are currently lying dead in a motel room in a puddle of their own vomit and piss? I don't care. Get me a location or get me a body."

He fixed each of them with a hard glare and noted that neither of them met his gaze. They weren't cowed but they were at least cautious. Satisfied, he continued. "Now, did you guys talk to the cops about this yet? You have connections in the commissioner's office and with the DA, so if anything went through them, you should know about it."

His tone remained patient and reasonable now. While he was happy enough to do away with them if it came to that, it would be more expedient and far simpler for them to simply do their jobs with a healthy respect for him and his position. He preferred not to work with idiots who groveled in terror so held back enough to encourage their willing participation rather than reluctant acquiescence out of fear.

"Nothing has come from contacting local law enforcement," Conti said. "Those who looked into the case have noted, however, that when they tried to investigate previous cases involving McFadden, they were consistently stonewalled by the feds. And not simple interference either. We're talking serious stonewalling, the kind they would need warrants from a federal judge to overcome. It would appear that the man has serious connections."

Rod shook his head. "I have serious connections," he reminded them. "The kind that have been in place before the FBI even existed, if my father was to be believed. It stands to reason that we should have people in the agency who could give us a lead into who the hell is backing McFadden. Not only that, they should be in a position to find out where the two mercs are."

"Well, we don't necessarily have any people in the FBI itself." Gallo sighed. "The ATF, sure, but the FBI tends to be very particular about the people they hire—"

The man cut off quickly when his boss leaned forward,

his expression hard and unyielding and his hands clasped tightly on the desktop. "Don't give me that bullcrap, Gallo. I pay you to find solutions, not problems. There's always someone who needs a little more cash, even if it's for good reasons like a sick kid or whatever. And if not, they have something to hide we can exploit. If you don't have a reliable contact, you're not doing your fucking jobs. I learned many things from my father, gentlemen. One of those was that people who don't do what they are paid to do...well, let's say someone else is always willing to do it and leave it at that, shall we?"

The implied threat seemed to have the desired effect. Both his employees shifted uncomfortably and exchanged a not quite panicked but definitely uneasy glance

"Maybe some of our friends in New York or Washington might have better luck," Gallo responded quickly. He obviously attempted to buy time and move quickly past the issue of their competence, but at least some kind of effort was now visible. "We could always contact them to see if they have a few rocks to turn over."

Rod leaned back in his chair and nodded. "You do that, Gallo. I think my dad had friends in the FBI too so I'll look into that and see if I can't put you onto someone there." The subtle reminder of his father's power and the possible resources that might easily supplant them had the desired effect and the men froze for a moment before they nodded vigorously. "I'll send you the details later. While you find out what the hell happened to my two mercs, you can also hopefully sniff out who's protecting this quack."

"That sounds like a good plan, Mr. Marino," Conti said and hastily finished his espresso, which he'd largely ignored until this point. Perhaps, his boss thought grimly, he was careful to not offer any semblance of disrespect, even if it was simply coffee he'd essentially refused in the first place. "We'll contact you when we have more information."

Rod smiled, stood as well, and walked around his desk to where the two looked both relieved that the discussion was over and hopeful that they would be let off the hook. "Well," he said cheerfully, "I believe in giving people the chance to make things right—at least once, anyway. After our nice little chat, I think you'll find a way to get the job done. When can I expect to hear from you again?"

"We should have updates before the end of the week," Gallo asserted, took his boss' extended hand, and shook it firmly.

"The end of the week it is," he agreed, his smile affable but still with an edge that warned them not to miss the deadline. "I won't keep you gentlemen. You have much to accomplish, so I'll understand if this time, you don't stop at any of the bars or restaurants downstairs for a drink or a meal and tell them to send me the bill. As my lieutenants, it's part of your perks, of course, but I won't be offended if you decide you'd rather set a good example and focus on priorities."

Conti chuckled nervously. "That's...uh, very understanding, Mr. Marino. We would definitely prefer to... focus on, uh, priorities."

"You two have a productive afternoon, you hear?" Rod said as he opened the door to let them out.

Carrots and sticks were important when pushing people to give him their best work. That was a rule that applied both to running casinos, as his father had taught him, and applied equally to the mob activities as a whole. These men would hopefully give him their best work—at least for now. He had no doubt they'd push for information. There had been enough reminders of the power he had inherited and that he was, in fact, his father's son and might well be capable of the same types of punishment the old man had shown no hesitation with.

Frankly, he didn't give a rat's ass how they felt about him. While he'd prefer honesty, if they only pretended respect but did what was expected, he could live with that. It was possible they would keep reality in mind and realize that he was both able and willing to replace them by whatever means were necessary. He hoped his message had been sufficiently loud and clear.

If it hadn't, they could expect a few personnel changes. He had even managed to show them that the simple question of why he spent so much time with what should have been a simple smash and grab was irrelevant. The guy owed much less than what he'd paid to the two mercs and his persistence would hopefully highlight another important point to his employees.

They now understood that it was less a matter of money and more about sending a message that while authority had changed hands, it had lost none of its power.

Rod sighed, shook his head, and returned to his desk. It was one thing to expect them to deliver, but he had similar responsibilities. He needed to move on those and sooner rather than later.

He lifted the phone off its cradle and punched in a number he knew by heart by now. There was no need to go through secretaries or assistants. A direct line was so much simpler.

"Madam Mayor," he said and forced a smile on his face to make his tone more agreeable. "Rod Marino. How are you doing this afternoon?"

"How nice to hear from you again," she replied and laughed. "How long has it been?"

"Well, I would say I'm not counting the days, but I would be lying." He chuckled. "It's two weeks now to the day. Anyway, I wondered when you would join our poker table? You still owe me a rematch. It's only fair to give me the chance to win my money back."

"I don't know about that. I've played since you were knee-high to a grasshopper but sure, you'll have your chance. What do you think about tomorrow night?"

It had been a long-standing tradition of his family to have the mayor in their pockets, and the best way to accomplish that was to pay them. In a city where gambling was legal, it was expedient and wonderfully simple to invite them to a very exclusive poker game and let them win. No one could really question that, of course. It seemed perfectly logical that the mayor of Las Vegas would be really good at cards—almost, he thought with sardonic amusement, like it was a requirement.

They both knew the tradition and there was no reason to abandon it.

Rod checked his watch. "Tomorrow night sounds fantastic. Remember to bring your checkbook."

He'd added that both for appearances and as code, his way to remind her that payment implied an exchange of other less tangible services. She knew more about what law enforcement was doing in Vegas than the DA did since she was the kind to stay on top of situations, both on the state and federal level. If anyone knew about what the feds were busy with in Vegas, it was her.

"I look forward to it, dear. You take care now," the mayor said and hung up.

To anyone else, that would sound like an average conversation between two acquaintances and occasional poker buddies. He replayed it in his head to assure himself that it contained nothing the people who would inevitably listen in on her discussions would be able to use against her.

Or him, for that matter. While people emphasized how his family's business operated on the kind of honor and strength of character that was absent from most other organized crime syndicates, it didn't provide any real protection. There were numerous people who would be more than willing to turn him in for the equivalent of a pat on the head to those who would no doubt like to destroy the family empire.

"Fuck me." Rod sighed heavily. "I should have turned this position down and stuck to running the casinos."

He didn't mean it, but in his saner moments, he really, really did.

CHAPTER TWO

Vickie still could not see how this was a good idea.
People had pushed her to get a college degree for
a while so it would be nice to have them off her back for
once. While it didn't mean they would leave her alone, it
would remove one thing from the seemingly endless lists
of their complaints.

That alone almost made it worth it. Besides, with her
brains, college should be something of a breeze. That was
the theoretical assumption when it came to learning insti-
tutions, but things never worked out in practice the way
everyone seemed to think they would.

Rather than a simple and painless process, people in
college wanted her to be outgoing and sociable. They
expected her to be a part of school projects and be involved
in non-studying-related activities—groups and sororities
and protests and things like that.

That, essentially, had been her experience in her last
attempt at college and she saw no reason why it would be
any different this time. It had been part of the reason why

she quit. The other part had been that none of the professors actually taught her anything she didn't already know. If she wouldn't learn anything, there really wasn't any point in hanging around.

At that particular point in her life, walking away had been an easy decision. She had wanted to push ahead and if something didn't help, it was discarded.

Her life was different now, though. Taylor and Bobby were practically family, by this point, and her boss had told her he wanted her to be the one with letters after her name. His little shop paid her well and she was happy about that, but the future wasn't guaranteed. He wanted her to have as many options as possible if his endeavor ever went under, and she could appreciate that.

It was difficult to admit but she actually cared what her colleagues thought of her and what they wanted for her future. Despite all appearances, it was something she held close to her heart. She would die before she admitted it out loud, but those two dummies were as close to her as she would ever let anyone be. Her own family kept her at arm's length and even Niki—who had put her own career at risk to keep her from being shipped off to hell on earth—still looked at her like she was a ticking time bomb.

As it turned out, the two men she worked with were cut from the same cloth and they took her in as one of their own.

The campus almost overwhelmed her with its "excited to learn" vibe. It grated on her nerves but a hasty deep breath and a fake smile took her through it.

People said that forcing a smile was a way to trick one's body into feeling a little better. She didn't know if that was based on scientific study or simply on insight derived from personal experience. Of course, there were many things in human bodies she had no clue about and didn't want to know.

Besides, the smiling actually did work. It was also supposed to help if one felt nauseous, but she'd never had the opportunity to test that theory.

Well, she had, but she'd never remembered to use it. Drinking wasn't something she did often, but when she did, she tended to overindulge. Nausea inevitably followed, which left her unable to think of trying the trick until she was already an hour or so into having a deep and intimate conversation with the nearest toilet.

Vickie locked her car and walked through the campus, following the directions that had been sent to her phone for the acceptance interview. The administration building wasn't difficult to find and the administrator in charge of her case waited in the lobby for her.

It was immediately obvious that the tall, lean woman who had former cheerleader written all over the perfect blonde ponytail had not expected someone like her. There was a reason for Vickie's appearance, of course, and while she actually liked the shock and awe it brought her, she wondered if the short hair, the tats, and the piercings might hurt her chances to enroll there.

Her experience was that people liked to say they weren't about appearances but they were mostly full of shit. Still, she reasoned, even if she was rejected, she could return to Taylor with an "at least I tried" badge and she would be able to focus on what she really wanted to do.

Either that or he would guilt her into enrolling into

another college with another impassioned yet surprisingly down to earth speech about how this was her future they were talking about. She had a feeling it would be the latter over a couple of drinks later at Jackson's.

She had wondered why they liked that watering hole so much, but when she met Alex the bartender and saw the way she looked at Taylor, Vickie could at least understand why the red-headed giant liked going there. The woman wasn't her cup of tea but she would be lying if she said there was nothing there to like.

"Victoria Madison?" the administrator asked and proffered her hand tentatively.

With another fake smile, she took the woman's hand and shook it firmly. "That's me. My friends call me Vickie, though."

"Vickie, how nice." Her chuckle seemed a little forced. "I'm Cordelia Williams, the administrator in charge of admissions at the University of Nevada. We were so pleased to receive your application and really, it made for some interesting reading."

A little curious, she inclined her head as Williams gestured for them to walk down the hallway and deeper into the building. "Interesting, huh? Interesting how, exactly?"

"Oh, nothing too complicated, don't worry," the administrator said with a laugh. "It's only…well, we don't usually see people with your kind of recommendations and the high aptitude test scores you achieved. Suffice it to say that people with your qualities usually make applications for MIT or Stanford."

"Okay, uh…how do I put this?" she responded. "Folks at

MIT and Stanford like their geniuses to wear suits, ties, and dress like they're applying for a job at a bank. That's really not me. I understand there are rules to be followed here too, but…well, the whole point is that UNLV had the most attractive computer sciences program that was the best fit for me, I think."

The woman obviously hadn't expected that. Vickie had practiced the speech and even the pause on the ride over. She knew the questions Williams would ask and her reactions and had even chosen the scores that would look the most impressive and the recommendations that would catch her eye.

Some of them were even real, although her scores were mostly bullshit. She had studiously avoided the aptitude tests and honestly believed she was too good for them. While she could have taken them later, she had always assumed that the ability to fake the scores on the databases was equally as impressive. Or, if people didn't realize she'd faked them, it was still as impressive, although no one would actually know it.

"Well, the…we don't hold appearances too high in our alums," Williams said and held the door to her office open for her to step inside. "Although I do have to say you have a very unique look about you. Is there a story behind it? You don't need to answer that, of course. I'm merely curious—okay, and maybe a little nosy."

"No story," Vickie said and took the seat that was offered. "Some of the piercings are functional, some are for show, and ditto the tattoos. The hair…well, that's from a recent bout with chemotherapy."

The woman's eyebrows raised at that last statement,

exactly as she expected them to. "Oh, my God. I'm so sorry."

"It's okay, I actually got my remission diagnosis a few months back," she replied with a small smile. "The treatment carried on for a little while longer, though, which is why I'm a week late with the application. I…well, all of this was in the application I sent you."

Williams looked startled, then a little embarrassed when she realized she was on the hook for that. It was like Taylor said. The best way to ace an interview was to make sure the person conducting it was on the back foot since it allowed the interviewee to dictate how it would go.

Taylor probably wouldn't have approved of her lying this much to get the interview, in the first place, but what the ginger giant didn't know couldn't hurt him or her.

"Well, then, why don't we get started on what you expect to learn in the courses you'll take?" Williams asked, desperate to move past the awkwardness that still hung over the room.

"I hoped to be able to continue with computer science and engineering," Vickie said, withdrew a file from her backpack, and placed it on the table so Williams could look at it. "Obviously, my grasp of the coding aspects is advanced enough, even though I could benefit from refresher courses. My interest is more toward the physical construction of hardware with a focus on the digital electronics domain more than anything else, I think." She paused and studied her companion's face for a moment, relieved that she seemed willing to simply let her continue without interruption.

"If there's any weakness in my current knowledge base,

I would say it's in the construction of algorithms, data structures, and database systems. Many of the people who go into IT these days have a working knowledge of the basics, but when it comes down to it, if you run the systems that process trillions of operations every second, you need to have more than a grasp of the basics. Look at all the trouble they had last year when Nasdaq shut down because squirrels had become a little too rowdy with the power lines. You need to be better than that in the world we're living in, am I right?"

She talked fast and kept the conversation moving while Williams' eyes glazed over. The ex-cheerleader likely had a social science degree or something similar required for her position that was basically only human relations. She didn't know for sure, but she suspected that a quick check into the woman's computer history would reveal that she needed to Google a search engine.

Still, she made sure to let nothing of these thoughts show in her speech or manner. There would be no point in being mean. What she wanted to convey was that she was enthusiastic about a field Williams knew nothing about and that she was far from a beginner in said field.

When the administrator realized that her visitor had stopped talking for a full five seconds, she chuckled nervously. "Well, that all sounds very interesting and incredibly impressive. I would need to run your proposed projects pasts the professors, of course, since they have full control of their courses here at UNLV, but—"

"I would really like to talk to them about that," Vickie said and leaned forward. "I've wanted to put a couple of upgrades into the Python model that has been taught in the course here over the past couple of years. Of course, I would need input from the professors since they probably know better than me, but I think it would be a real advantage to the university to be the one that works with cutting-edge technology. As you can see right there, I interned extensively with the folks at the Department of Defense and they are actually already implementing some of my upgrades into military software."

"That can't be rig—" Williams started to say but stopped herself and leaned forward, only to find that it was, in fact, in the application. Her paperwork included a certification that she had worked with the DOD to develop new software and a glowing recommendation from one of the generals under the Secretary of Defense. That one was, ironically, actually real.

"Oh...wow, that's quite impressive," Williams said. The woman looked like she had thought about how she might be able to refuse her application but had become more and more accustomed to the idea of accepting her.

The cogs could almost be seen in her head as she paid real attention to the application this time. It was easy to guess what she was reading from the expressions on her face until she put it down again with a kind of decisive gesture.

"Well, I can give you a fairly definitive answer right now that we'll be happy for you to study," Williams said finally and slid papers to Vickie to sign. "I'll need a couple of signatures from you here—standard policy stuff. Oh, and when the acceptance is made official tomorrow, you'll also have the option to use some of our on-campus student living facilities if you need them."

"Well, I do have living arrangements," Vickie told her. "But they're not the best, so maybe I'll actually take advantage of the student living."

Williams smiled broadly, likely relieved that the interview was drawing to a close, stood quickly, and shook her hand. "Well, let me be the first to welcome you to the University of Nevada. I know you'll have one hell of a learning experience here."

"I think you're right about that," she said as she stood. "Thank you so much for taking the time to talk to me."

"Please, it was my pleasure." If it was a lie, and Vickie believed it was, it was at least gracious. "My assistant will show you out."

She thanked the administrator, turned, and headed to the door where a young man stood. He seemed to belong there so she assumed he was one of the students who worked part-time in administration to help fund his college costs.

It surprised her a little when he fell into step beside her but she said nothing and he waited until they were out of earshot before he spoke. "I can't say I've ever seen anyone make Miss Williams that uncomfortable before. It was fun to watch."

"So she's not very popular around here?" she asked and turned to face him. He'd obviously been interested enough to watch the exchange through the open door of the office, and it startled her that she'd been so focused that she hadn't noticed him.

"Well, she's a former alumnus and a cheerleader who thinks she owns the campus because she dated a quarterback ten years or so ago," he replied with a shrug. "I can't say she's ever been as popular as she thinks she is. I'm Myles, by the way. Myles Hendricks."

She tilted her head and smiled at him. "I'm Vickie Madison. Nice to meet you, Myles."

"I know it's a little forward of me, but I don't suppose you'd like to go out to dinner with me sometime?" he asked when they reached the door. "You know, once you're settled in and don't have all the pressures of starting a new course hanging over your head."

"I'd like that, Myles," she replied. "I'll give you my number and we can find a time that works for us both."

He grinned. "That would be awesome."

CHAPTER THREE

P eople talked about the Zoo like it was hell on Earth. By all accounts, it was the absolute worst place to find oneself in, where everything around you attempted to kill you, even the trees. It was located in an area of the world that had done all it could to tell humans to find another place to live. As if a desolate desert region wasn't bad enough, a jungle had sprouted from alien goop and proceeded to make the location even more hostile.

At any other time, Jon would have told himself they were overly dramatic. The media attempted to drum sales up for the next movie, TV series, or video game. They tended to do shit like that, which included ignoring or exaggerating the truth.

In this case, however, he could say with absolute certainty that they had been one hundred percent correct. If anything, they had undersold how terrible it was.

He and Mike had trekked through the jungle, which was too rough and dangerous to traverse with the popular Hammerheads or any other kind of vehicle that might normally be used. The heat was overwhelming, even taking into account that they had been flown in from the Mojave fucking desert.

The mech suits they had to wear to protect themselves from the dangers they would face were the kind that had been made by the lowest bidder. Of course, it was better than heading in with nothing but your skin, but barely. Besides, with the unaccustomed weight and having to learn how to actually use them, they posed additional problems for anyone who had no training or experience. That potential vulnerability encouraged more sweat than normal simply through nervousness, and with the fact that the suits had been designed with very little airflow in mind, they rapidly degenerated to a sweaty, stinky mess.

And like any vicious circle, it naturally returned to the simple reality that they couldn't take anything off. They had to remain in the fucking things lest one of what felt like hundreds of thousands of monsters that lurked decided to come in for a snack.

Yeah, hell on earth covered it damn well.

"I've stayed away from damn jungles all my life," Jon said once he connected with Mike on a private commlink.

"Yeah?" his companion asked and turned slightly to look at him. "Why's that?"

He barked a mirthless laugh. "Mosquitoes, if you can believe it. I visited Florida once in my life, near the Everglades. When I had one peek at those clouds of insects hovering all over the damn swamp, I said 'hell no' and got away from that place as fast I could. From that moment on, I vowed never to go anywhere else that was hot and humid and had insects that could practically pick you up and carry you off."

"Well, I'd say that vow is broken," the man said and shook his head. "I'd say there are probably insects around here that can quite literally pick you up and carry you off, although they won't settle for sucking you dry of blood. These fuckers will probably see that mech you're wearing as a crunchy outer shell that makes the squishy inside all that much tastier."

"Yep, I'm fairly sure all these critters see is a walking, talking spring roll." He shook his head in disgust as they continued to move through the jungle.

"How much fucking longer do we have to do this?" Mike asked and shifted in the suit to try to ease his discomfort.

"As long as we fucking have to," their CO shouted and strode down the line to the two newcomers. "If you think you're here to put your feet up and relax in the sun, you're in for one hell of a surprise. Now keep up with the rest of the group or you'll be left behind."

Both men were quick to pick up the pace. They had been away from the military for a long time before they had been shipped off to the Zoo, but some things never went away. Immediate response to the snapped orders from a CO was one of those. They obeyed with alacrity.

"They said this was only a routine patrol to inspect the sensors that had been set up on the borders of the Zoo," Mike grumbled.

"Well, you're new to this place so I'll give you a pass on that," the CO replied. "We're heading in to find one of the old sensors they put on the borders of the Zoo periodically."

"We're nowhere near the border," Jon pointed out.

The man snapped his fingers. "Penny for the smart guy," he said sarcastically. "In case you didn't know, the borders of the Zoo constantly grow, spread, change, and in short, get bigger. We need to retrieve one of the sensors and the data it collected while inside the jungle and take them back to the smart guys at the base. Their job is to tell us what new fresh horrors will kill us next time we're here. Understood?"

"Yes, sir," Mike shouted as they continued to move.

"It's weird how this shit comes back to you, right?" Jon said as they kept up with the ten-man team they had been assigned to.

"Like riding a fucking bike," his companion agreed. "A bike with no seat."

He laughed. "You know what I fucking realized? And I feel stupid because it's only come to me now. McFadden— the guy we were tasked and paid to take care of and who is the reason why we're here... Well, I thought he wore some kind of body armor like most military folks do these days with maybe a couple of power functions to help with the weight distribution. But I realize now I was wrong. Given the way he moved, how he attacked, and how he beat our asses without even trying, he could only have worn a mech suit."

Mike looked down at the armor he currently wore. "I don't know, man. The guy was big but he wasn't seven and a half feet tall and he sure as fuck didn't weigh tons."

"You're thinking of the big-ass one we saw at the base. I

know he didn't wear one of those," Jon retorted brusquely. "Not even the military has many of those, and most of the mercs don't either. They all use the light to medium versions, I assume, or the basic armor suits like they've shoved us into."

"Is there a point to this?" Mike asked irritably.

"Well, there is, but you distracted me before I could get there."

His companion snorted and he could imagine him rolling his eyes impatiently. "Okay, I saw a couple of the hybrids on sale in the shop at the base, and they were much smaller, lighter, and faster than even the light armor some of these guys are wearing. I bet you someone has found a way to camouflage those to work in an urban environment. If so, it's easy to look at almost anyone who walks around in bulky clothes and think they might be wearing a hybrid mech beneath."

"Okay, but you have to assume the shit would trigger the hell out of a metal detector," the other man pointed out, his tone one of weary patience.

Jon shrugged. "Sure, but in the end, you could have an army of these dudes, maybe give them a motorcycle helmet to work the HUD system, and bing bang boom, you have a dude who's a walking tank who looks like he might simply be your average motorcyclist. With that said, it has to be incredibly illegal or at least heavily regulated. That's assuming our country is ahead of the curve on people owning what can basically be considered tanks people can wear."

"It's not a great assumption," Mike said, once again the voice of reason.

"Nope, but my point is—"

"Jeez, finally, the man has a point."

"This guy had serious connections that Marino never told us about." Jon sensibly chose not to respond to the sarcasm.

"Which makes me feel much better about taking the man's money and not giving him shit," Mike grumbled. "How does your leg feel, by the way?"

"Thankfully, I won't need the mad hopping skills he mentioned," Jon said.

He still limped from the shattered kneecap McFadden had left him with but honestly, he didn't really blame the guy for it. They had been on track to do the same thing to him so it was merely self-defense. If he had wanted a way for them to not survive this, he would have put a couple in their spines or maybe damaged both knees.

One kneecap had been more than sufficient to get the point across and the chances were they would at least have a fighting chance in this fucking jungle.

"Stay focused, rookies!" the CO shouted when he noticed they were still talking to each other. "We have movement on the perimeter of our sensors and you can bet your bottom dollar it ain't going to be friendlies. Guns out and lock and load, people!"

"Where'd they get this guy from, the eighties?" Mike asked.

"The seventies, I think," Jon responded. "That's when people still had no idea how boot camps were run and even before the days of my personal hero, R. Lee Ermey."

His friend laughed. "He was a fucking legend, that guy."

"I mean it, rookies. Form the fuck up. We have hostiles!"

It seemed obvious that the CO was unaware that both men had prior combat experience. To his eyes, they were probably as green as a buck private kicked out of boot camp and technically, he was correct. Nothing could prepare them for the Zoo. But they did know a thing or two about combat and how they were supposed to fight.

The team formed up quickly and made no attempt to seek any cover for the moment but simply maintained a line and continued to move as the motion sensors went crazy. Movement caught Jon's attention and he turned and fired at what looked like a giant locust with a scorpion's tail. The volley eliminated it immediately.

It was difficult to describe but it felt like the entire jungle suddenly came alive at the sound of gunfire and surged toward the group of men who stood their ground and began to shoot.

He kept his eyes on the targets. For a brief moment, he reminded himself to ignore the fact that they were an unholy abomination of mixed earthly and alien DNA and treat them like he would any other target. None of this was personal. It was all very much a professional disagreement.

All the humans wanted was to live and the aliens didn't want them to. It was merely necessary to fight it out and whoever was left alive in the end was right.

Hastily, he ducked under a claw-slash from one of the black six-legged panthers and managed to avoid the venomous fangs. His assault rifle needed to reload but he drew his pistol hastily and it was more than sufficient to fell the beast.

Mike had issues of his own with a group of the locusts. These didn't have the stinger tails but were a dangerous threat nevertheless. They jostled for position ahead of him and tried to break through the line. He stepped forward, thwarted their attempt to flank him, and drew his sidearm to kill two of the creatures before he holstered it again.

Jon glanced at their CO and wondered if the man felt even slightly surprised. He was the type who deliberately withheld his emotions and only pointed out the negative and had shown them scant respect when they had been assigned to his team. It would be gratifying to see him pleasantly surprised, even if it was only momentary.

The group assembled and took a moment to hurriedly reload their weapons and ensure they were ready to keep fighting if they needed to. The beasts had begun to back away, however, having taken enough damage for the moment.

"Not bad, rookies." The CO actually laughed as he jogged closer to them and patted their shoulders. "You might actually make it out of here alive."

"We appreciate the vote of confidence, sir," Jon said with a small smile, his attention on a couple of their team members who seemed to have located one of the sensors. The device was hard to see at first as it had been overgrown by roots and even encircled by a couple of smaller trees and vines. It took a little effort to cut and hack through the vegetation before they managed to pull it free.

"Is that all we're in here for?" Mike asked.

"We'll head out now and to the Hammerheads we left," the CO said. "Take five minutes, then we'll move."

No one really wanted to hang around, so it was less than five minutes before the team set out back the way they'd come. They moved faster now that they didn't need to monitor for the sensor and almost broke into a jog by the time bright sunlight filtered through the trees in front of them.

Jon grinned as excitement pooled in the pit of his stomach. He wanted to get out of this fucking place and back to the semblance of civilization they now called home. The location wasn't the best, obviously, and wasn't one he would necessarily have chosen voluntarily. Still, after they'd been given the material to read up on what they would have to do, it became clear that they could make far more money there than they could ever expect to earn in the States.

The downsides were still massive, but Jon liked to think of himself as a glass-half-full kind of guy.

He looked around when a few chips of bark landed on his shoulder and brushed them off before his motion sensors went wild.

Something extremely large moved above them at unbelievable speed.

"Oh, shit!" one of their team members shouted. "Killerpillar!"

Logic told him that wasn't the actual technical name for the creature, but as more and more of it was revealed, he had to conclude that it was actually accurate. It looked like a centipede but was the size of a small car, and when the soldiers responded with an immediate fusillade from every quarter, it screeched loudly and dropped on top of them.

A couple of their team members were crushed under the weight of the monstrosity, but any hopes that it might have been killed in the fall were dashed when the creature twisted quickly onto its feet.

The head—or what looked like the head—swung to the side and into Mike as he tried to shoot it. The bullets bounced harmlessly off the carapaces and the jaws snapped shut around his midsection.

Metal bent and gave with a loud crunch and Jon muttered a frantic oath when the jaws literally cut his friend in half. The man's screams ended abruptly as the lower half of his body fell away and the upper half was drawn into the jaws for consumption.

"Like fucking hell!" he shouted, aimed his weapon at the jaws, and fired in an attempt to find some vulnerable target that wouldn't simply deflect the bullets. The monster immediately pulled back and shrieked as green blood spattered in a wide radius.

He took a step forward to press his advantage when more bark drifted onto him and drew his gaze upward. Another beast loomed over him, its jaws already extended and ready to strike.

"Oh...fuck me," he whispered and attempted to bring his weapon to bear as the massive jaws closed around him.

CHAPTER FOUR

There were a couple of places where Taylor didn't mind spending extended time that didn't involve living, working, eating, and drinking.

Going to the movies was acceptable from time to time, although it was better to simply watch what was released for a quarter of the price on the radio waves or online. Still, if you wanted to be in the know immediately, it was sometimes worth it.

Another place was the gym. He preferred to do most of his exercise on his own. Jogging, weight-lifting, and anything else he chose to do were usually more effective when he didn't need to focus on potential threats in his peripheral vision. The only time he was willing to lift weights and exercise outside his comfort zone was when there was someone there to help him out—a spotter like most snipers used.

Except, in this case, he and Bobby were each other's spotters.

"Could you fucking focus?" his friend asked.

"I don't know why we can't simply set something up do it at the strip mall and take our turns while working," he replied and shook his head. "You want to come out here to testosterone and steroid city to what, check out the hot dudes?"

"It helps to have nothing to focus on but the exercise. And that's better done in a place where there's nothing to focus on but the exercise."

"It would help if we did cardio." He moved to the head of the bench as Bobby lay on it and grasped the bar with both hands. "Weights have their place but it's a good thing to keep your lungs and heart working properly."

"The way I see it, weightlifting is the best way to stay in shape," his companion countered. "I don't believe in cardio. Weights burn more fat and give you more muscle mass, which in turn burns even more fat. That's the way to go, trust me."

"Yeah, tell that to your gut," Taylor grumbled under his breath.

The other man scowled at him. "What did you say?"

"I said it's your turn to lift the weights so get to it already." He patted the bar. "We aren't paying this place an exorbitant amount to lift things up and put them down again only to not lift things up and put them down again."

"Whatever." Bobby grasped the weighted bar a little tighter, lifted it off of its hook, and began the repetitive bench presses. "I'm still not sure why you don't open a gym at the strip mall. A proper gym, I mean. It's not like you don't have the space there. You could use one of the abandoned locations, set everything up, and even take memberships."

"I don't know if you've noticed, but our location doesn't exactly overflow with the kind of people who can afford a gym membership," Taylor responded and kept a careful eye on the weights the man lifted.

His friend growled as he went through his fifth repetition. "It would mostly be for the two of us, but memberships could be for sale. If it takes off, you could always hire folks to clean and maintain it. Gyms run at a high profit, especially because most people who sign up for memberships don't even show up."

"I'll think about it." He chuckled and helped Bobby a little when he started to sag. "But I think we're already fully committed on the whole business side of things. We have our work cut out for us to push the orders out on time, and they're coming in faster than ever before. That's probably where our focus should be right now. Seriously, even with Vickie on board, we might need more help simply to keep up."

"She's made good strides," the other man noted, finished the last rep, and relaxed against the bench. "And she's taken on a fair amount of work. Even with her starting college, she'll still be a huge asset in this."

"You're not wrong. Like you said, she's made huge strides. I don't think we'll be able to keep her as an intern for much longer. With the progress she's made and her education, we might need to elevate her. With her skills in getting us better-paying work, I think it might be in the field of sales. You know, taking calls, making calls, and convincing people to pay us as much money as possible. Maybe after a while, we could extend that to marketing too."

"I think she'd be good at that." Bobby sat and took a sip from his water bottle. "But if she'll focus more on the sales and marketing side of things, I think you're right. We'll definitely have to find new meat for the business."

"But that's something to be discussed at our next quarterly meeting," Taylor said. "Once we have a full taste of what particular brand of business we'll be."

"What do you mean?" The mechanic looked a little bewildered as he prepared for another round.

"Well, we are a business and I took a loan to start it," he explained as his friend resumed training. "I need to show that we've had a profitable quarter to the bank that made me the loan so at the end of the quarter, once I make sure they're paid with profits from the shop and not from my own money, we can talk about upping salaries for you and for Vickie and possibly hiring someone else. It's sustainable growth, you know?"

"I actually don't," Bobby said with a small frown. "But again, I keep forgetting how much work and thought you put into this business. But wait—you want to give me a raise?"

"Of course. You've been with me the longest and will be my head mechanic, so of course you'll get a raise. I don't have the exact numbers yet but that'll come out during the end of the quarter meeting."

"Oh. Well, it sounds like I'd better be there for that shit."

"Well, you'll get your raise whether you're there or not but yeah, attendance will be appreciated." He helped him through the last few reps before Bungees stood.

Taylor took a moment to clean the bench before he took his place on it. He liked to rib his friend about the additional pounds he had around his waist and stomach, but there was never any doubt about the man's upper body strength. The weight currently on the bars was about the limit of what he could bench, and he settled himself and took a couple of deep breaths.

"Of course, I still appreciate you giving me a job so I could get out of that garage," Bobby said and spotted him as he went through the same reps, although a little slower. "The six-figure salary is nothing to sneeze at and the work...well, working with mechs is really the only thing I miss about the Zoo. Besides, having coworkers like you and Vickie is always a good thing. But you knew that yourself since you hired us, right, Taylor? Taylor?"

"Help me out, moron," he all but snarled as he struggled with the last rep.

"Oh, right, sorry." Bobby helped him finish it and placed the bar on the hook. "Are you sure you don't need to take a couple of pounds off?"

Taylor flipped him the bird. "I'm fine."

"You didn't look fine in that last rep," the man pointed out.

He scowled. "That's because instead of being my spotter, you expounded on how awesome your life is now. Which, yeah, you're welcome for that, but it's still a business and we need to run it like one."

"What's that supposed to mean?"

"Nothing bad, I promise," he assured him. "For now, we should probably start to look into the people we might want to hire for the business and maybe find some names and arrange interviews. We won't be able to actually hire until the end of the quarter but it would be a good idea to get the process out of the way."

"Do you have any ideas?" Bobby asked.

Taylor settled onto the bench again and readied himself for another sequence. "Not really. Maybe one or two."

"Are you considering that bartender at Jackson's?" his friend asked.

"Why would I be thinking about her?" He lifted the bar off the hook. "It's not like there's a part of our job that requires the pouring of spirits. That usually comes afterward for our own safety."

"Well, you hire people you like and let's be honest, you do like her," Bobby pointed out cheerfully.

He grunted as he went through the first few reps and his chest and arms burned with each. "You don't shit where you eat, Bungees. And you certainly don't fuck where you eat. Well, I guess there are people who are into that kind of thing but..." He paused and his companion helped him with the last couple of reps. "The metaphor stands. Actually, why don't we take a couple of pounds off the bars?"

"What, you feel like a warm-up instead of a workout?" Bobby asked with a grin.

"Bite me, Jet Li." Taylor growled, stood, and removed the weights.

"So, where do you fuck if it's not where you eat?" his friend asked.

"It doesn't really matter," he responded. "Someplace where you catch and release, you know?"

"Catch and release?"

"It's a fishing metaphor, Bungees," he said with exaggerated patience. "You know, where you can hook up with women who are looking for a little self-esteem boost and not much else. Bars are generally a good place. Or strip joints if you're up to parting with some money."

Bobby tilted his head. "Online?"

"No, never online," he corrected him and settled in for his last set. "The women online are looking for something a little more permanent. I have nothing against that, of course. If that's what you're looking for, all power to you. But if what you're looking for is a little more like mutual stress relief, it's better to do that in person."

"I'll take your word for it," the man replied as he stood ready to help. "What about here?"

"Here?"

"You know, the gym," he clarified. "There are tons of people looking for a little ego boost and rushing with hormones from working out. It seems like the kind of place where you could eat or fuck without it becoming a problem."

Taylor still needed help to finish the set and grimaced as his arms and chest burned when he stood again. "Well… I've never thought about it but yeah, you're right. We need to get you out of that place and into the world. You know, show you off to the ladies, and I guess here is as good a place as any to start."

"Please don't pretend this isn't about showing your goods off to the ladies." Bobby laughed. "Like baiting a hookup, if we're doing fishing metaphors."

He nodded and looked impressed. "Nice wordplay."

"Thanks."

"Well, you know it's easier to hunt or fish in pairs," he said as they moved to the weights where they could work their shoulders. "You know, in case they bring a wing woman. They like to work out with friends and they don't like to abandon those friends because some sweet piece of Asian ass shows up. Enter me, the friend to the friend, and if it works out between me and the friend and you and the girl...well then, all four of us win, right?"

"It sounds like you know what you're talking about, but it doesn't sound like what you're talking about makes sense," Bobby responded.

"You don't have to overthink it," Taylor said. "Women are humans, not some mystical creature from the beyond. What they want is genetically designed to be the same thing you want, more or less. It might be a little more complicated, but it doesn't have to be. Many people like to think of them as different—the whole men are from Mars and women are from Venus crap—but when you think about it, all they really want is to have a good fuck as often as possible and with as few consequences as possible. You only need to make sure they know how much fun they'll have."

His companion laughed. "It's weird how you managed to make that sound both enlightened and incredibly misogynistic at the same time."

He shrugged. "Look, you don't need to take it from me. Learn from experience, okay? That's why some people have this kind of mythological view when it comes to women. They assume that because they have boobs and nothing hanging between their legs that they're a different species. They're not. They merely have higher standards, is all. There's a case in point."

He nodded his head toward two young women who

strolled toward the treadmills. Both looked to be in incredible shape as evidenced by the skin-tight leggings and tank tops they wore and they laughed and joked loudly.

"You'll think they're strong and confident with a wide range of friends and even a couple of boyfriends each they keeping on the hook, right?" he asked.

"Sure?" Bobby seemed dubious.

"If that were the case, how come they're here at the gym and not hanging out at someone's pool party? They're here because they need a break from their regular friends but they don't want to do it alone. They can't stand to be alone, but they also can't stand each other. At the first chance they have to break ranks, they will, as long as there's no hard feelings or guilt involved. Observe."

He moved away from Bobby and over to where the two girls took their time around the water fountain.

"Hey, sorry to bother you ladies," he said. "I don't suppose either of you would be personal trainers, would you?"

The brunette turned and inclined her head when she realized that she faced his chest and needed to look up to meet his eyes. "How did you know?"

"I could tell you that I'm a mind reader but honestly, you have the site to a personal trainer finder written across your leggings," he said and nodded. "I'd say I wasn't looking at something else, but...yeah. Sorry. At least I wasn't leering."

Both women laughed.

"What do you need a personal trainer for?" the blonde asked with genuine curiosity. "You look like you're in great shape."

"Thanks." Taylor laughed and lowered his head like he was abashed. "Actually, it's for my friend behind me. Don't look right now but...and you're both looking. Okay."

Another laugh followed.

"Anyway, he has a problem with cardio and I've tried to explain how it's good for him but he won't take it from me," he continued. "I have the feeling he'll take it better from one of you two lovely ladies and since you have your credentials on you, would you mind going ahead and supporting my argument?"

"No problem," the brunette said. "I'll go on over and see if I can't talk your friend into a better workout."

"His name is Bobby and I really appreciate it." He winked as she moved away and turned his attention to the blonde.

"How about you?" she asked and took a step closer. "Do you need any help with any of your workouts?"

"Well, I think I've lost my spotter for the afternoon," he commented. "If you need one, that would actually be a great way to spend the afternoon."

She grinned. "I'm sure we can think of some way to spend the afternoon. I'm Candi, by the way. With an I."

"Of course you are." He chuckled and checked to make sure Bobby was hitting it off with her friend. "I'm Taylor. With a Y."

CHAPTER FIVE

She took another deep breath and tried not to shift uncomfortably on her seat. No matter how she felt, she didn't want to make it obvious that this wasn't the kind of place she tended to frequent.

It wasn't only a matter of budget, although that certainly did play a part. People said the fancier locations were an acquired taste but she'd never been able to acquire it. As far as Niki went, she liked the establishments that served good burgers, good fries, and had cold beer on tap.

Some people liked wine and said it was more refined, but she wasn't at all that way inclined. Even as a kid, she'd never conformed to the norms of girly things. People had called her a dyke and many other things, none of which were pleasant, and a few that were deliberately insulting.

In all honesty, she'd never really cared. She never let anyone tell her what she could and couldn't like or what her preferences said about her.

Still, this was the kind of place she could get used to if she came often enough. But, given that it was her first time there, she inevitably felt like she had ants under her skin. They had four different menus—one each for wines, entrees, main courses, and desserts. She wasn't even sure which order she was supposed to use them in.

Okay, she decided, that was simply nerves talking. She at least knew that entrees came before main courses, which were then followed by desserts, but she had no idea when she was supposed to order the wines.

"I really shouldn't have arrived early," Niki mumbled quietly, shook her head, and noticed the waiters eyeing her closely.

At least she could be sure she had dressed the part in a pantsuit most businesspeople wore to the meetings they held in a restaurant like this. That wasn't the problem. Her discomfort stemmed mostly from the fact that she had asked for a table for two and her guest was running late.

"I don't know why Jennie picks these places," she said and studied the menus for the umpteenth time.

Her sister did finally arrive, thank goodness. She had fashionably late down to a science and arrived precisely fifteen minutes after they had agreed to meet. A waiter showed her to the table where Niki was seated. She wore a red dress that ended at her knees. It was both attractive and expensive and very flattering in a loose, flowing style.

She'd always managed to look good in a "don't even know it" kind of way that made guys go crazy over her.

"Hey there, sis. It's nice to see you again," she said and wrapped Niki in a hug. "And after such a long time too. How have you been?"

"It's not been that long, but I guess that's part of the

joke, right?" she asked as she sat again. "How have you been, Jennie? Are you still working at the lab?"

Jennie took her seat as well and picked up one of the menus while the waiter hovered a little closer. "Yeah, they had me trapped there for a while. I actually needed to drag myself away otherwise my bosses would have kept me there all night."

"It's not a problem," she responded with a smile. "Since you were the one who wanted to meet, after all. I don't think I would ever choose a place like this on my own, which means you'll be a doll and pick up the tab for this one. I would offer, but given the kind of money I make working for the government compared to what you make working for a private firm, there really is no reason to play any games, right?"

"Well, if there was ever a person for you to play games with, it would be your sister, right?" Jennie retorted.

Niki shrugged. "True. Still, I'm not sure what the appeal is of a place like this. Even the judge-y looks I get from the waiters is enough to put me off my appetite."

"Well, that's because you're dressed for work," her sister said. "They expect people coming in for work not to tip well, so they want to make sure you know they disapprove. Maybe they think you'll tip more to get their approval. I don't know."

"It's simply puts me off any enjoyment I might find in the food," she insisted.

"Well fine, then. I'll pick up the tab." The other woman grinned. "You should know that you still owe me for all the work I've done for you pro bono."

She laughed. "Well, you should know that your government thanks you heartily for your service. You're a true patriot, a real American hero."

"And does the gratitude come with a good paycheck?" Jennie countered and raised an eyebrow. "Well, let's go and ask your paycheck."

Niki laughed again and shook her head. "Low blow, little sis. Low blow."

"Are we ready to order?" the waiter asked deferentially.

"Hi, yes." Jennie smiled at the man. "I'll have the smoked duck breast carpaccio with the pine nuts and veggie chips, and the beef tenderloin with the roasted asparagus, mushrooms, and choron sauce."

"Excellent choices, ma'am," he said and jotted the order down. "Will you order something for dessert now or later?"

"Now, I think. Your chocolate lava cake with vanilla ice cream was to die for. All with maybe a bottle of your 2016 Chianti Classico."

"Excellent." He finished noting her choices and turned to Niki. "And for you, ma'am?"

"I'll…have what she's having," she said. "Although maybe a Riesling for the duck? The 2020 vintage if you still have it."

"Oh, that's good. I'll have that too," her sister said quickly.

"Perfect. I'll be right back with your drinks." The server nodded to them and moved away toward the kitchen.

Jennie tilted her head. "Riesling for the duck?"

"I Googled which wines worked best overall for first courses on my phone, then double-checked the menu to see which one was recommended by the sommelier on the menu," she said with a broad grin.

"Good tricks!" Jennie responded approvingly.

"You're still picking up the check, though," she pointed out. "This is your kind of place, not mine. Give me a burger or a pizza over someplace this fancy any day of the week. It's like people with money want to be judged on their food and clothing choices."

"Well, it is why they always spend so much on clothes and food," her companion concurred and shrugged. "This dress, for instance. Take a guess as to how much it cost."

Niki narrowed her eyes and inspected the garment. "Three, four hundred dollars? Any more and you were cheated, sis."

"Seven hundred and ninety-nine big ones." The woman patted her dress smugly. "Okay, it was a Christmas present but still, who drops that much on a dress?"

"That does seem like a ridiculous amount to spend on an item of clothing. Who bought it for you—some guy with a crush?"

"I think so," Jennie said. "It's the project supervisor at the lab. He said it was to celebrate a job well done—which yeah, we had a great year—but then I looked around and saw he bought everyone else a bottle of scotch. Even Dr. Henry, who had issues with alcoholism in the past. He didn't really pay attention to anyone else's gifts, but he did to mine."

"Ew, creepy." She shuddered visibly.

"Right? But yeah, sometimes, you have to take the good with the bad. We've had three CEOs kicked out for harassment, so we've had five or six harassment seminars to make sure these guys know to keep it in their pants."

"Well, make sure that if it becomes more than buying

you presents to ask for a raise the very next day," Niki told her emphatically.

"Is that what working for the government has taught you, big sis?"

She shrugged. "Okay, it might not be completely honest, but the guy perving out on you isn't honest either. If they don't keep their supervisors in check, you might as well squeeze them for every cent you can get your hands on."

"You know, I wouldn't have to if I had someone with me to keep the handsy folks at bay," she pointed out as the waiter returned with their entrees and white wine. "You know, someone I can show up with to those parties who looks good in a suit. Someone big and tall with muscles that show even through the suit."

She rolled her eyes and knew exactly where this would go.

"A beard wouldn't hurt," Jennie continued once the server had brought their first course. "It would give off the feeling that he might be classy but he's not afraid to throw down if he sees someone getting handsy. And bright red hair too so that the point is really driven home, you know?"

"I will not introduce you to Taylor," she said with a no-nonsense scowl.

"You know, I really thought you would bring him to our table at the bar," her sister said. "But no, he had business to get to and an early start to head back to Vegas. As if I don't know how you make excuses. I've beaten you at poker since we were teenagers."

"It's weird, then, how you seem surprisingly unclear on what 'I'm not introducing you to him' means," she said, her eyebrow raised in a challenge.

Her companion grinned and took a mouthful of her meal. "I know what it means but I'm really, really insistent."

"Then maybe you haven't taken enough away from those harassment seminars you're supposed to attend," Niki told her caustically before she took a mouthful and followed it with a sip of wine once she'd chewed and swallowed.

She wasn't much for cold foods for dinner and the carpaccio wasn't really her thing, but she wouldn't go so far as to say it was terrible. The pine nuts and chips did add some texture and it was definitely better than she had expected. The only downside, of course, was the fact that it was a tiny portion and gone too soon.

The plates were cleared almost immediately and the waiter assured them the next course would be there momentarily.

"It's been a month and a half since that time at the bar," Niki pointed out. "Did you intend to hold onto that grudge until Christmas? Is that how this will be now?"

"I merely think you should tell him why you put so much work into hiring him," Jennie said as their second course arrived, together with the red wine. "It's only fair, given all the work you send his way and the number of life-threatening situations you've put him through lately."

"He knows why I hired him," she retorted and her mouth watered when the size of the tenderloin steak was all she could see for a moment. "Okay, a few details of the why might be a little hazy, but he knows I hired him because he's simply the best available in the business. All the rest are in the Zoo, getting their asses killed. Was I completely honest? Maybe not, but the lie—if omitting some of the truth is a lie—was convincing enough. Either that or he doesn't really care about the truth right now."

Jennie took a moment to enjoy her first bite of the tenderloin before she spoke. "You know, I don't see how it won't blow up in your face later. I might not have the big-picture view you have, but I honestly don't see it."

"Until it does, you need to stop thinking about him," she insisted and attacked her meal as she spoke. "You need to find someone who won't cheat on you and won't get himself killed in a battle with some weird monster and get shit out."

"That sounds like a Taylor-like thing to say."

Niki grunted, chewed the food in her mouth, and swallowed before she replied. "So what? Even Cro-Magnon man can come up with a valuable explanation at times. You can't suggest it isn't a highly likely scenario."

"Or you merely don't want to admit that he might have a brain," her sister countered. "You don't want someone that big to be anything but a grunting and growling prehistoric excuse for a man."

"Can you really blame me?" she asked, her mouth full again.

"No, I guess not," Jennie admitted. "It only…"

She paused and dug in her purse to retrieve her phone. It continued to buzz like she was receiving a call, but she didn't answer and instead, pressed a couple of buttons and stared at it.

Niki knew her sister well enough to know that whatever it was that she'd been alerted to immediately took her attention away from their discussion of her crush. There weren't many things in the world that could do that.

"Niki, I think you should check in with your task force immediately," Jennie said after a moment of silence and looked at her sister. "If they haven't heard about what's happening in Wyoming yet, they soon will."

"What the fuck is in Wyoming?" she asked and took the last mouthful of her steak. The waiter stepped in to take the plates.

"You'll see. It's the kind of thing best seen for oneself," the other woman replied. "And I think it can wait until after dessert anyway. Seriously, the chocolate lava cake is to die for. Oh, and don't think that I've forgotten your efforts to keep me from riding Taylor all night long."

She rolled her eyes. Some things simply didn't deserve even an attempt at a response.

———

Jennie hadn't actually lied. Niki had, in fact, killed people for less than what that chocolate lava cake had been.

Thereafter, a short drive returned her to her hotel room, but it was only once she was finished washing up for the evening that she remembered what her sister had said about Wyoming.

"Damn my immature hormone-addled brainiac sister," she said to herself. "That man will not ruin your life, no matter how bad your million-year-old lizard brain hormones make you want to find him and screw his brains out."

It was a quick connection, thanks to Desk, who had put up a couple of servers or something to ensure she was always as connected as she could be. Jennie had explained the process three or four times by now, but it simply made no difference. Most of the brains in the family went to others, at least when it came to computers.

The details of potential jobs came up with one highlighted in red at the top of the list. Even before she looked closer, she knew it was Wyoming.

"How the hell did she know about that?" she grumbled and clicked on the device to see exactly what was happening. "That girl is a little too involved in my business. She and I need to have a talk about boundaries, a nice, long—holy shit..."

It definitely wasn't the average job. She needed to see this for herself.

All thoughts of her laying into her sister for abusing their family bond vanished as she hastily began to make arrangements to fly to Wyoming. Everything else could wait.

CHAPTER SIX

"I'm honestly not a big fan of these newer tank mechs," Bobby said, his head tilted dubiously. "They're so heavy that something's bound to break down and all you're left with is a big fucking coffin to climb out of while you're being attacked. I'm really worried about anyone who heads out in one of these and forgets to make sure that the hydraulics are all top-of-the-line."

"Yeah, I have to agree with you," Taylor replied and shook his head. "With that said, it's probably comforting to head out into the field with this much armor between you and the Zoo and this much firepower to carry in with you. Look at the Gatling on the shoulder, two different rocket launchers, and almost all the guns a suit like that can carry."

"Still, the bigger something is, the slower it is, so if one thing goes wrong, you're fucked," the mechanic countered and continued to peel the layers of armor off to get to the electronics beneath.

"Well, yeah, but planning for something to go wrong—hold up." He looked up from his work on the software when his phone vibrated in his pocket. "Huh. There's an unknown vehicle pulling up."

Bobby put his tools down. "Trouble?"

"It could be," he grumbled and scowled at the phone. "I don't think anyone would attack us in a Tesla, though. Still, we're not exactly a hot spot in the area, so there's really no reason for anyone to come here."

"You'll never find answers if you don't head out there and ask," Bobby pointed out.

Taylor looked sharply at the man. "And if they are here for trouble?"

"Well, better you than me." His friend shrugged casually. "You're the boss, after all. I'm merely a humble employee."

"Yeah, I'm the boss who'll remember that come bonus time. Just saying," he replied and grinned as he stood from his seat and headed to the garage door as the Tesla in question pulled to a halt.

It was a 26, one of the newer models released a couple of years before, with the number displayed in bright silver letters on the back.

The question of whether there was trouble or not still wasn't answered until Vickie stepped out of the driver's seat.

"Morning guys," she said, a broad smile painted on her face as she removed her sunglasses. "What do you think about my new wheels?"

Taylor seemed less than happy and looked a little suspiciously from her to the car. "Assuming they're yours."

"Hush, you," Bobby snapped, moved closer to the vehicle, and ran his gloved fingers reverently over the curves.

"He doesn't mean it, baby. He's a mean old grump but he knows he loves you too."

The red-headed giant laughed. "Cool it a little there, Bungees. You don't want to gross Vickie out and you certainly don't want to make that girl whose number you walked away with jealous."

"I wouldn't worry about me, Tay-Tay," Vickie said, still grinning. "I know a thing or two about the pure, physical delight that comes with seeing a beautiful machine. Not necessarily sexual, but still."

Taylor came closer and tilted his head as he inspected the vehicle. "I do admit, it is a nice machine—one of our friend Musk's best with that powerful electric engine and some of the best efficiency converters in the market, not to mention the solar power cells distributed across the whole surface of the car."

"Yeah. They say it can go for five hundred miles without recharging," Vickie said.

Bobby shrugged and looked a little doubtful. "I don't know so much...that's probably in a controlled environment with all kinds of sun. Which, admittedly, you will get out here in the middle of the Mojave Desert. A more realistic call would be three hundred and fifty miles before a recharge."

"It's a top-of-the-line model, no doubt about it," Taylor agreed. "Which, of course, begs the question of where you got this vehicle because I sign your paychecks. While I pay you well, I don't pay you that well."

She scowled at him. "I didn't steal it if that's what you think."

"Then how did you get it?" he insisted. "And stealing

wasn't what I thought, but you have to cut me some slack for asking, all things considered. You're all kinds of awesome, but I would like to know if there's any trouble coming our way."

Vickie nodded. "Well, all the trouble you'll encounter is if my bank finds out that I've faked my credit score for the past ten years or so."

"Wait—I thought you said that you were twenty-two," Bobby protested.

"I did." She rolled her eyes. "Anyway, that probably won't be an issue and even if it is, they'll most likely ignore it since it would make them look bad to the IRS. The point is for you to hakuna your tatas. The car salesman almost fell over himself and I got a brand new car for a monthly payment I can afford. That's all you need to worry about. It's totally legal. People do this shit all the time."

"You know criminals exist, right?" Taylor asked and scowled at Bobby, who was too preoccupied drooling over the vehicle to support him. "People who literally do illegal things all the time?"

"Well, what I did was legal," she insisted. "I can give you a PowerPoint presentation if you want."

"I have the feeling I should worry about this a little more, but that's a problem for another time." He sighed and his head. "Anyway, it would be nice if we could make a living yapping all day but we have a job to do. Vickie, since you're here, you might as well get in on it too."

They turned to return to the work area while Vickie parked her new vehicle inside.

"I thought you were supposed to be in college today." Bobby handed her a couple of the tools she would need from his own box. "Learning and finding out how to create a better tomorrow and all that crap."

"The professor canceled classes for the day," she said and sat where a pile of parts needed to be taken apart and cleaned. "He said one of his cousins or something in Wyoming died and he needed to head out to attend the funeral. Anyway, it was a choice between spending the afternoon with people who might be my own age but are nowhere near my intellectual peers and spending time with you two dumbasses. I elected people who are a little older and know how stupid they are instead."

"Okay, I know you started out wanting that to be a compliment, but it turned out terribly," Taylor told her. "I do love to hear me some modesty, though."

She stuck her tongue out at him as the phone rang. He had invested in a landline, one that would make it cheaper to make and receive the international calls they dealt with more and more frequency.

"That's for you, rookie," he called without looking up from his work. "You man the phones, remember? That and make sure our shipments come in and head out on time so we have a steady but not overwhelming stream of work to deal with."

"Ugh, fine, but if I wanted to do spreadsheets, I would have stayed at the campus." She hissed annoyance but stood and strode to the desk where the phones and most of their computers and laptops were set up to snatch the phone from the cradle. "McFadden's Mechs, how can I help you today?"

Taylor shook his head. "Seriously, I need me a better name than that."

"You've said that for months now," Bobby said yet again. "You might as well settle on using that same old name forever."

"Until inspiration strikes me, anyway," he replied gloomily.

Vickie rolled her eyes as she put the phone on speaker so the men could listen to the conversation.

"No, I'm still not the secretary around here. I'm the manager," she said and pointed at the phone, a disbelieving expression on her face.

"I'm sorry, I didn't mean to offend you," the caller said.

"I know that, but you assuming I'm the secretary simply because I have a feminine voice is as annoying as fuck," she retorted sharply. "For all you know, I could be a guy. What do you think of that?"

"Can we maybe talk about the order now?" the man asked. "I swear I won't assume you're the secretary. I mean...you're not, right? I never did get the answer on that."

She scowled. "It doesn't really matter what I am or am not. The only thing you need to worry about is what I can do for you today."

"Give me your number?"

"In those lonely, pathetic dreams of yours," Vickie snapped tartly. "What was that you said about talking about the order again? Because I have half a mind to over-charge you for wasting my time, which you should know is quite valuable."

"Well, we obviously don't want that," he said hastily. "I need a rush order on the two suits we sent a couple of days ago and which should arrive there before the end of the week. We're heading into the Zoo and we need those suits back or we'll go in there in our skins."

"Uh...sure, what's the number on your order?" she asked and immediately sounded less sassy and more like a businesswoman as she typed into the computer in front of her. "Oh, right, you're Y-7645, right?"

"Correct."

"Well, you guys already have a rush order on the five-day turnaround, so if you need it to be faster than that, it'll cost you even more." She leaned back in her seat and studied the screen.

"You guys are bleeding us dry on this already," the merc complained but sounded like he was joking.

"Look, you'll have your suits repaired for literally a quarter of the price you'd be charged for repairs there," Vickie reminded him. "If you want the suits to be finished quicker, you need to pay half of what you'd pay there. It's still a friggin' bargain. But if you want it even faster, you need to pay for the extra work we'll have to put into it—you know, to cover things like overtime and extended hours to get the job done. Or do I need to spell it out for you in...what's your preferred nerdspeak? Elvish? Klingon?"

"Okay, fine. If we put an extra rush on the project, how much will that cost us?" the man asked with a laugh.

"That'll be an additional ten thousand per suit added to the Y-type report," Vickie said and rubbed her chin thoughtfully. "I'll have to come up with a whole new kind of report for that, I guess. Anyway, you'll find out when the invoices are sent out. Have a nice day."

"It's night here," the man told her.

"It's day here, but who gives a shit?" she grumbled. "Okay, expect to get the invoice with an additional ten thousand per suit as long as you approve the document I'll email you now. Once that is signed, you'll get the rushed order plus the heftier bill. If you don't sign, the paperwork won't grant you the additional priority. Do you understand the terms as I've laid them out to you?"

"I do," he said. "Sorry, I'm practicing for our inevitable wedding."

"Do you think I'm the kind of guy who would get married?" she asked. "Yeah, that's right, you still don't know if I'm a guy with a really girly voice. Keep that in mind for later. Bye!"

She hung up and looked at the two men, who tried not to be distracted by the conversation and instead, focused on their work.

"So, what do you think?" Vickie asked as she turned in her chair to look at her two coworkers.

"I think you've added another cool two grand to your paycheck this month," her boss said without looking at her.

"It's like they don't even care that I'm ripping them off for every dollar I can get," she exclaimed and rolled her chair to the table she had previously worked at. "Were you guys that starved for female attention in the Zoo? Was it that bad?"

"Not really," Taylor said thoughtfully. "Not in my experience anyway. Women did serve in the military and also worked in the research positions there."

"I'm fairly sure it's become something of a game for them," Bobby said with a chuckle. "They'll tell stories about it at the bar. The chances are that while you're ripping them off, you're also making sure they won't have to pay for drinks for the next couple of days. Believe me, out there on the edge, that bill can run up well over five hundred bucks."

"Yeah, that does sound about right," Taylor grumbled and glanced at her disbelieving stare. "Interaction with folks outside the Zoo is always a story to tell."

"Wait, so he comes away with a profit too?" she asked. "Even the guys I charge more? The ones we send Y-forms to?"

"Well, maybe not a total profit," he replied. "But he could if he's an alcoholic, of course, and can stretch the story long enough. The other guys would have to spread their earnings over a couple of days, so whether or not they come away with a profit depends on how good the story is."

"I'd say it's safe to assume they're all alcoholics over there," Bobby stated with no hint of sarcasm.

He nodded. "Yup."

Vickie scowled for a moment, but once she'd thought about it, she shrugged and turned to her work again. "It sounds like a win-win to me. Still, am I like his...booze whore?"

"I think the better question is if that makes us your booze pimps," the mechanic retorted.

"If that's true, you guys owe me far more than what you pay me on each upsell," she retorted without looking at them.

"I think it's best for all of us to not pursue that line of thought," Taylor said.

She looked quickly at him, her eyes narrowed. "I still think I should get more on my upselling. Like...at least twenty percent sounds fair, you know?"

"We can talk about that at the end of the quarter," he told her. "But spoiler alert, yeah, you'll get a raise. I need to talk to an accountant about our earnings, which will happen when I talk to the bank about our loan to see if it needs restructuring. Still, if my calculations are correct, both of you can expect an improvement on your paychecks."

"Awesome," Vickie said and grinned. "I might be able to afford that car after all."

He looked up sharply from his work and scowled at her.

"I'm kidding. Jeez." She laughed.

"You'd fucking better be," he warned.

CHAPTER SEVEN

There were certain things the modern world required these days. People who lived in the cities needed everything to come to them as quickly as possible. Food had to be fast. Information should be transmitted instantly. With anything less, you would have something like a revolution on your hands.

Kyle Francis IV understood why. It was how the world worked and if you didn't keep up with it, you were left behind. That usually meant you were left without any money or job prospects and, in other words, in a whole world of shit.

Thankfully, the entire world wasn't like that. There were pockets where time appeared to stand still and everything was essentially unchanged from what it had been for the past few thousand years. Northwestern Wyoming was one of those places.

He honestly didn't think the area had changed at all and that the sweeping plains had been around since Noah's time. In his mind, that was more or less how it should be.

No one wanted to settle on a wide, empty plain and certainly not in any great numbers. Large cities wouldn't be built this far away from the original train tracks that crossed the country or from the tributaries to the major rivers in the country. Admittedly, the vastness of the once untrammeled plains had shrunk to fairly small areas in comparison to their original grandeur. Still, in one of those forgotten areas, a man could look out and see nature as it had been intended—wild, free, and untouched by the instant-generation.

No one wanted land like this except for the massive beasts that grazed on the grass that grew wild and the men who watched over them.

Of course, everyone across the country—with a handful of nutty exceptions—still wanted the steak they provided. Some of them didn't even mind the kind that came from the cruel barns that gave the cows six square feet to live in for their entire lives where they were overfed and finally slaughtered.

People who knew their meat, though, could taste the bullshit. Those who knew what they were buying would always choose the meat from the Herefords Kyle and his team now herded and reject that which was raised in inhumane conditions.

Unfortunately, circumstances had changed. He came from a long, long line of cattle ranchers but in the end, it was time for his family to move away from the business. His son was already a well-established lawyer in Chicago, and his two daughters were in college, studying to be doctors. They had no desire to be a part of the business and wouldn't do it unless he asked them to.

He had come to terms with this and didn't want to force them into anything. Unfortunately, he wouldn't be able to manage it all on his own any longer. He could either bring in people who knew what they were doing to do the work or simply let it all go and live off the profits of what he'd worked at for most of his life.

The ranch—all twenty thousand acres of it—had been sold after a bidding war that had left him with almost five times what it was actually worth. All that remained was to sell the cattle. The buyer had elected to take most of them and wanted to maintain the herd, but those he didn't buy had been snapped up by another Hereford ranch farther north.

Which was why he now helped his team to move the ten thousand head across the wide expanse of grassland. It wasn't practical to move such large numbers by truck or by train so they simply did it the old-fashioned way cowboys had for the past couple of centuries.

The long, slow journey gave him too much time for introspection. It was a family business and had been for generations, and it felt wrong to leave it all behind like this. Despite the fact that he'd seen no other viable alternative, it simply didn't feel right. The Francis family had worked cattle since people still explored this area and before it had ever been brought into the fold of the good ol' US of A.

Sometimes, he couldn't actually believe it was gone and all that was left of it was the herd that now trundled to another ranch. It was why he had elected to work the trail instead of delegating it to the men he'd hired for the job. He sure as hell was paying them enough for it.

He rather felt that it was part of his process of closure

to have one last ride before he became yet another old guy with an investment portfolio.

And damned if it wasn't worth it. He shifted in his saddle and took a swig from his canteen, which contained only water. Jennifer had tried to convince him to quit drinking all through their marriage and when she died, he decided he owed it to her to at least give it the old college try.

His gaze drifted over the cattle as they grazed and moved slowly across the grasslands, guided by a group of men on horses. There was no need to rush the beasts, of course. Guiding them was all you could really do. If they started to run, panic would set in. Kyle's father had always said that when cows started running, they assumed they were running from something and panic was inevitable.

It didn't really make sense, at least not in human terms, but people forgot that cows were living creatures with brains that didn't quite work the way humans wanted them to.

As he gazed over the moving herd and into the sun that was setting over the mountains in the west, it was impossible not to feel nostalgic. He hadn't done much cattle moving himself and usually left the work to the hands he hired. But he had occasionally, and while there were certainly all kinds of downsides—the smell of literal bullshit, the sweat, the heat, and the dullness of it all—he couldn't deny that there was certainly an allure to living this life.

When a man rode out in the open with the wind and sun in his face and no cities or roads for miles, it was hard not to feel free.

Dusk approached, though, and it wasn't wise to try to drive the cattle at night. The chances were one of them would find a hole to trip into, break a leg, and be trampled by those behind.

The hands had already begun to set up the temporary fences to keep the herd contained and happy. Cattle weren't difficult to keep happy, even in these kinds of numbers.

Kyle dismounted and moved to help them to put the electric lines up and settle the poles in with them. They didn't expect him to do much work, being the boss and all, but every hand out here would eat and every hand would help with the work.

This was another thing his dad had taught him. Even when you were in charge, you needed to keep yourself busy. If folks saw you in the saddle watching them work their hides off, they started to think you weren't worth the money you made.

Sometimes, he thought he wasn't worth the money too.

"Let's get this done before dark, boys," he said and rubbed his mustache gently. "The trucks should get here with our dinner soon so let's get this buttoned down before they get here and then set up camp and relax."

It was good honest work and kept them busy until the vehicles arrived with the paraphernalia for their camp. The group immediately set up the sleeping area and the portable stoves to prepare the food that had been packed. It might have seemed overkill to outsiders but it wouldn't do to underestimate how important it was to have good, hot food to eat. Coffee, too—ranchers would murder folk if they didn't have their coffee as strong as possible.

Once the camp was set up and those on first watch had wandered away to their various positions, the remainder turned their attention to the food. Soon, the camp smelled tantalizingly of biscuits baking and bacon frying to be added to the beans they were cooking. In addition, there would be rice and even a couple of steaks. Kyle was the one paying for the whole thing and damned if he would let his boys go hungry and especially not on their last trip together.

Sunset came quickly in the plains and without any city lights to keep the darkness at bay, it would descend fairly rapidly to cocoon them in black velvet night. They would hopefully have a fairly bright moon later, which always helped, but flashlights would light up like beacons as those on guard eased the cattle closer together to keep the herd secure for the evening.

Kyle turned when a couple of the hands rode over to where he stood. A glance at their faces revealed that they didn't look happy at all.

"Mr. Francis, sir," Logan stated in what sounded like an accent straight out of Texas. "I been looking for Gerry and West but can't find them anywhere. Maybe they went out to find strays but they've been gone a while now."

When they herded this many head, they were bound to lose a couple along the way. That was merely the price of doing business, but they always needed to make it look like they at least attempted to look for the strays. It wasn't possible to find them all, so those who spent too much time looking for them wasted both his time and his money.

"Try to call them on the sat phone and see if they can't give you their coordinates," he replied.

"I already tried with no answer," Colby, the younger of the two, said. It was never the older hands who decided to call someone when you couldn't find them so the young men played a useful role. He'd learned to include a couple to fill the ranks alongside the old-timers.

"Shoot." Kyle scowled his displeasure. He had really looked forward to kicking back at the end of a long day. "We'll need to find them before we turn in for the night," he muttered. "I'll mount up and the three of us can look for them. The rest can stick with what they're doing but they need to stay alert in case we need to call for help."

"I'll spread the word." Logan guided his horse closer to the camp to fill the rest of the hands in as the boss walked over to where his horse grazed contentedly.

He didn't like it when Brady ate anything while he had his bit in his mouth—which made it more difficult to clean —but sometimes, you couldn't stop a horse from doing what it wanted to. Brady was an older beast, still a stallion and a cantankerous old bastard, but Kyle loved him. They'd grown old together and he was one of five horses he hadn't been able to part with. A buddy of his had agreed to give them a good home at his ranch where he could visit when he had a mind to.

But it was best to only think about that when he had finished moving into the house he'd bought. It was closer to the city than he usually cared to be, but it also made it easier for the kids to visit if they ever cared to. He wasn't the kind of father who would hover over them when they wanted to live their own lives, but a little appreciation was acceptable. Come Thanksgiving, they would expect him to cook for them too.

His brief distraction soon ended when he joined his men to begin the search and his responsibilities took precedence. The hands had already retrieved a couple of the high-beam flashlights but hopefully, they'd find the men before they needed them

"Did you see where they headed out?" Kyle asked as they moved into the grasslands and the gathering dusk and tried to make something—anything—out that might provide insight into where the two men had gone.

"They was headed out to the east where you can see them pastures still untested," Colby said and pointed away from where the sun had begun its final slide behind the horizon.

"It's not possible that they would run off without a thought when the meal's being prepared," he said and shook his head. If there was anything he knew about all hands everywhere in the world, it was that they were always hungry. That aside, he'd worked with these men before and they'd never been even remotely unreliable.

His mount jerked his head warily, suddenly a little unsettled, and attempted to pull away from the direction they moved in.

"Calm down now, Brady," Kyle mumbled softly and patted the horse's neck. "Ain't no wolves or coyotes going to come close to you and me, not with this gun of mine." He patted the rifle tucked into the saddle's holster for emphasis.

The beast didn't calm and grew more and more restless as they moved farther from the herd.

"What's that smell?" Logan asked and looked around warily. "It's...uh, raw meat is my guess."

Kyle could smell it too. Despite the fact that the air cooled quickly, the odor was pervasive. That particular kind of smell would draw the wolves and coyotes he'd reassured Brady about.

A darker smudge against the grass a little way ahead drew his attention and became more noticeable as they moved in closer.

"What the fuck is that?" Colby asked and leaned closer, his face scrunched in concentration.

"Watch your language, boy," he snapped out of habit but in all honesty, he could understand the sentiment. It echoed a growing sense of unease deep within his gut.

In the distance, the lowing of the cows seemed louder but he decided it was his imagination, a reaction to his unease.

"That there's a body," he said when they covered the final distance. He yanked his rifle clear of the holster.

"It's kind of big for a body," the older hand pointed out.

"It's a horse—or what's left of it." Kyle tensed, every sense alert, and studied the darkening terrain in an effort to catch a glimpse of what had done this.

"It's been picked to the bone," the younger man said. "Or near to, anyway. What the f—uh, hell could have done that?"

"I'm not rightly sure," he replied. "Maybe a bear or a mountain lion."

"Ain't nothing I've ever heard of can clean a carcass like that," Logan stated unequivocally and grunted.

Gunshots from the direction of the camp made them all turn quickly. The horses trembled visibly and pulled at the bits, evidence of their growing nervousness. The muted lowing of the cattle transformed to frantic bellowing and another volley of gunshots was clearly audible over the growing din.

"Let's get back and see what has them all excited," Kyle instructed and urged Brady into a gallop through the grass. He needed to get back as quickly as possible. They might be shooting at wolves, but the cows were obviously already in a panic. It wouldn't take much to push them over the edge into a terrified stampede.

It seemed the darkness encroached more rapidly now but he was able to catch a brief flash of movement. Brady did too and neighed as he fought for control, which his rider refused to relinquish. He'd not been thrown from a horse since he was fifteen years old and wouldn't break that record now.

Another flurry of movement drew his attention and he aimed in the general direction and pulled the trigger. The rifle kicked comfortingly but there was no sound of impact or any sign of the creature.

It would help if he knew what the hell he was looking for.

A scream from behind made him turn and he craned his neck to try to see was happening in the gathering gloom. A low growl—a snarl, really—was immediately followed by the scream of a horse and a solid thud. More snarls and growls suggested a pack of some kind, but nothing in his experience provided any insight into what they might be.

Brady shied on his hind legs and neighed loudly, and something warm splashed across Kyle's face as the horse fell back. He was barely able to jump free but his ankle twisted when he landed.

"Damn it!" he shouted and grimaced in both pain and frustration. He'd let go of the rifle and it was somewhere in the grass. Frantic, he dropped to his knees and felt for the cold metal while in the background—as if from some muted other place—he registered the fact that Brady had fallen and hadn't moved. The unmistakable sounds of flesh and tendons being ripped and flesh devoured had a surreal quality, something real but distant and incomprehensible.

His hands closed around the cold steel of his weapon and a wave of relief washed over him as he tried to pick it up.

Something stopped him when it stepped on the barrel and held it on the ground.

The gunshots in the distance were more sporadic now against a low rumble he immediately recognized as the distinctive soundtrack of a stampede. At least, he told himself dully, some of the cattle might escape.

A low growl yanked him back to reality. It was too close and his weapon was still trapped beneath something he couldn't identify. The air was suddenly filled with the stench of rotting meat.

"Oh, fuck." He gasped as a large mouth opened to bare its fangs in the almost-darkness not two feet from his own head.

CHAPTER EIGHT

I t was possible that she'd never seen this much open, uninhabited space in her entire life.

That struck Niki as odd since she traveled across the country a fair amount for work and for her personal life. For some reason, Wyoming had always been one of the flyover states people conveniently ignored. It probably had something to do with the fact that there weren't many people there and not too many strategic resources either.

But there was land—so much land as far as the eye could see. Of course, it wasn't like it had been in the old days. Ranches were visible and fences had carved out the individual portions from what had once been endless miles of untrammeled grassland. Even then, they seemed to be large, sprawling properties that were unlike anything in her experience. They had flown in the helicopter for two hours now, heading roughly northwest, and while the Rocky Mountains loomed in the distance, they didn't look any closer than they had when they'd started out.

It was almost hypnotic in a way, although she wasn't

sure why. Given both her life and her preferences, the landscape should have bored the absolute hell out of her. Instead, the longer she stared out at the grasslands below, the harder it was to pull her gaze away.

She was almost relieved when the helicopter finally came in to land. It settled on the open plain in what appeared to be the middle of nowhere a few hundred yards away from field tents that had already been set up. A couple of trucks were driven to and from what she assumed was the closest field base they could use, but the absence of real roads made travel both inconvenient and probably uncomfortable. She was thankful she'd had the chopper to spare her the arduous trip along rough ranch roads, even in a four-by-four.

Niki scrambled out of the helicopter and kept her head low as her hair was whipped in the wind that was generated by the spinning blades behind her. One of the agents in charge strode toward her and didn't look too happy about her arrival.

Either that or he was pissed about being in the middle of fucking Wyoming this early in the morning.

"Special Agent Banks?" he asked.

"That's me," she replied, took his hand, and shook it firmly.

"I'm Special Agent in Charge, Richard Eifert," he said and hurried her away from the noisy chopper. "We were told to expect you and provide you with anything you might need." He guided her to a four-by-four that waited with the engine running and they scrambled aboard. She grimaced as it lurched over the grassland toward the field headquarters and reminded herself that at least it wasn't hours in the damn vehicle.

"You don't sound very happy about me being here," she said bluntly. It was better to bring the politics out in the open and deal with it before it interfered with what had to happen.

He shrugged and brushed his thinning hair back over his head. "Normally, I would be pissy over having to share my jurisdiction with a task force I've never heard of, but in this case—honestly, I'm really glad to have the help."

She started at him for a moment, then grimaced. "Shit, this place must be one hell of a mess for you to say that."

"With all due respect to what might or might not have been done over the past couple of years that gives you precedence in my jurisdiction, I feel safe in saying you have no fucking idea," Eifert said, his tone edged with might have been both fear and disgust. "Even for your task force —which, if you were called out here, I have to assume deals with all kinds of weird—this is some fucked up shit."

"Well, don't leave me in suspense, Special Agent in Charge Eifert. Why don't you fill me in about the situation?" Niki prompted.

She sounded a little more annoyed than she meant to. While she'd had some coffee, it wasn't nearly enough to cover the night flight and the couple of hours of sleep at a small motel before they had a helicopter available to fly her all the way there.

"It's really hard to put into words, actually," the man said with a brittle laugh when the vehicle stopped with a jolt behind the tents. "Maybe it's best to simply show you and let you have your own reactions. I don't really want to color what you might see."

It was odd to hear an agent talk like that. Eifert didn't look like an ordinary agent, of course, and even though she'd only known him for about a minute, she could tell he was out of sorts. His hands tapped at his coat pocket and the yellow stains on his nails told her that he was aching for a smoke but didn't want to offend the new arrival.

As they moved closer to the scene, she really couldn't blame his need for nicotine. She actually had a sudden hankering for a smoke of her own and it had been years since she'd officially put that habit behind her. She'd slipped once or twice as everyone did, but it was usually at times like these when stress levels soared and the weight of responsibility sat heavily on her shoulders.

The grass had been heavily trampled, the damage very clearly from something other than the result of the people who worked the scene. It wasn't difficult to tell what was new and what was old, though, since there was still a light film of dew on the grass and…well, everything else.

A few human bodies could be identified, although they had been literally torn to pieces. There was no sign of internal organs and most of everything that wasn't bone had been stripped away to leave only bright red streaks on the white. A couple of horse corpses had been similarly shredded and dismembered.

Everything within her recoiled instinctively, yet Niki's gaze was riveted on the grisly scene. The ground had been churned and the grass trampled in a wide area, and those responsible all appeared to have been felled while they attempted to flee their attackers.

With her emotional response firmly clamped under iron control, she assessed the carnage. Unlike the human and horse remains, the cattle carcasses seemed intact aside from the very obvious fatal injuries. What really shocked her to the core was the fact that these extended as far as the eye could see.

"Holy shit." She hissed a sharp breath as she covered her mouth and continued to stare.

"That was more or less my reaction when I saw this fucking nightmare," Eifert concurred and his fingers tapped his coat pocket with renewed vigor.

"How many?" she asked and turn to face him. "You can go ahead and smoke if you like."

He smiled apologetically, drew the pack from his pocket, and lit one hastily. "Thanks. It's a dirty habit but I've had a hell of a time kicking it, and... Well, things like this don't help. Do you want one?"

Her hand twitched toward the extended pack but she shook her head. "No thanks. So, how many?"

"Twenty-five men, mostly hands and helpers, but one was the former owner of the herd," the agent explained and exhaled a lungful of smoke. "Their horses, of course, and hundreds of cattle. Herefords."

"How do you know that?"

"Oh...the owner had sold them to a ranch further north. They were a couple of days late, so the buyer rode down to see what the holdup was. Most of the herd had stampeded, from what I understand, although what I know about cows wouldn't fit in a fucking matchbox, so yeah, I took his word for it. He located them a good distance from here and they still looked spooked and behaved oddly, and some were slightly injured, so he pushed on to find the rest and... Well, yeah. He called all the law enforcement he had a number for to get here to see what the hell happened to his cattle. We're still not sure."

"Wait, this happened days ago?" She scowled and looked around as if to verify what she knew she'd seen. "There's still meat on those carcasses. Shouldn't this place reek all the way to high heaven? Where are the buzzards? Carrion, wolves...whatever picks corpses clean around here?"

"That is actually a really good question," Eifert said. "Even the dogs that were brought in wouldn't go close to those bodies and seemed to hate the smell of them. We've taken samples, obviously, and all our lab geeks can really say is there's something on the meat that... Well, for lack of a better word, it keeps anything that might decompose the meat away, including the bacteria. I know this sounds weird and even impossible, but it's being preserved somehow."

"That's new, even for me." Niki rubbed her cheek and mentally reviewed her very limited knowledge of predators. "Creatures don't usually preserve their meals. They eat what they want and leave the rest to rot, from what I know."

Her companion tapped the ash from his cigarette and took another drag. "I had a bad feeling you'd say that, honestly. Like I said, I have never seen anything like this and whatever it is, I don't like."

"We need this solved quickly." She scowled when her gaze settled on what definitely were way too many people on-site. "And we need to keep this contained—even the buyer, although we'll have to think of a smart way to convince him to keep quiet until we have answers and this resolved."

"It's a good thought but already virtually impossible," Eifert said. "I imagine the cops who arrived before us will have already posted pictures on social media as soon as they were within spitting distance of a Wi-Fi connection."

"Yep, and with them will come a horde of those ZooTubers to try to catch a glimpse of something that'll earn them views." She pursed her lips like she'd bitten into something sour. "We had an issue with a couple of them a few months ago when they stumbled across the remains of a few monsters. At the time, we managed to spin it as a fake, a forgery made to get views, but that won't work forever."

"What do you suggest?" She noticed he didn't pursue her mention of monsters and decided to let him learn slowly. He already seemed way out of his depth.

Niki sighed and resisted the urge to ask for a cigarette. "I have connections who deal with this kind of problem—freelancers who kill the creatures that do this kind of thing."

She moved to one of the tents that had been set up, drew a laptop from her bag, and connected it quickly.

"How do you get signal out here?" he asked. "We're stuck using sat phones and Stoneage tech."

"Well, I happen to have a...something," Niki typed in the password to connect her to Desk's server. "Not a guy in the strictest sense so 'something' is about right. Anyway, it's all about who you know and what they can do for you."

"What can they do for you in this kind of position?" Eifert asked released another lungful of smoke out the tent.

"I actually have no idea," she admitted. "They'll arrive, have a look, and tell me what we're dealing with. Thereafter, they'll kill it, bring me proof, and I'll pay them. It's a good system if you can tolerate the kind of asshole who's drawn to making a living by killing all kinds of monsters."

"It sounds like a tough gig," the agent commented. "And here we were thinking you were lucky to have your own task force."

"Oh, it has its perks, I'll admit," she said. "But it also comes with…issues."

"Issues?"

"Budgeting issues," she explained and held a hand up to tell him to wait while she talked to Desk. "Taylor won't be in the budget for this, not if I bring more people in. Bring… Yes, get them out here as quickly as possible—"

The AI interrupted to tell her that she was connected to them but none were answering their phones.

"Fuck… No. Message them and tell them to pack as much gear as they might need to deal with a large problem," Niki instructed, sure that Desk would take the necessary notes and alert the three freelancers they had selected. "They need to come prepared to find what did this, kill it, and bring it back and they can look at the best payday they've ever seen from us. Time is a factor here, though, so I'll send helicopters to pick them up—make sure to give them these coordinates so they don't waste time. They need to be here by tomorrow at the latest."

"Who are you talking to?" Eifert asked, flicked the cigarette butt out the tent, and stepped closer.

"My something," she said and closed the laptop again. "The task force comes with a connection to my freelancers so I can get them to emergency situations when I need them."

"What if they say no?" he asked.

"I've never had that problem. They like their jobs of killing monsters for pay. It's not for everyone, of course, so the penny-pinchers in DC don't mind paying a little extra. Ordinarily, anyway. We've had to spend too much lately, so I can't use my main man for the job."

"Let's hope the sloppy seconds can get the job done," Eifert said.

"Amen to that."

CHAPTER NINE

He didn't like to be up this early, although he was used to it given his history. The work was all he needed, or so he liked to say, but once in a while, he needed a little more. Food was a good way to start the day, and if food was the idea, there was really only one place to go.

While he wouldn't go so far as to say he was addicted to the place, there was a certain something about the food that constantly drew him back. There were others who were regulars too, so he knew he wasn't the only one.

Taylor had persuaded Bobby to add it to his list of preferred venues, although the man was more a fan of their lunch and dinner menus. He enjoyed the pasta too much, which was why they had also increased their gym attendance.

Bungees was his friend and he needed the man to stick around, something that wouldn't happen if they were one day faced with one heart disease or another. It wasn't necessarily something to be said outright, but he would definitely do what he could to keep the two of them in business for as long as possible.

All that notwithstanding, there was no need to deprive himself of the simple pleasures of life. A trip to the New York New York Casino had almost become a daily habit, one he saw no real reason to curtail.

As he stepped inside Il Fornaio, he paused and realized he had already been identified. One of the waitresses came over to him almost before he stepped through the door and smiled brightly.

"It's nice to see you back, Taylor," she said.

"Well, I'm glad we're on a first-name basis," he replied and checked her name tag. "Terri. It's nice to be back."

"Will you order the regular?" she asked as he headed down toward the bar.

"You know, I would, but I've tried to get a friend of mine to cool it on the carbs so it would be a little hypocritical of me if I don't do the same," Taylor replied, sitting down.

"Your friend, Bobby, right?"

"Damn, you do have a good memory," Taylor said. "Yeah, Bobby. So I think I'll load up on proteins instead. I have a feeling I'll need it."

"Okay, that sounds good. How about I get you an iced tea to get you started?"

"That would be fantastic." She headed behind the bar to get his drink. "Oh, and if you could get me a to-go version of the order too? I'm doing a delivery run."

"I'll get right on it." She placed the chilled glass in front of him.

"Taylor, nice to see you gracing us with your presence

again," a familiar voice said behind him. "You know, you're starting to come here more often than Niki does, and that's saying something."

He turned to see the manager, Marcelo, coming forward to greet him.

"Well, you should know it's hard to stay away from this place," he said and shook the man's hand firmly. "And I probably come more often because she's out of town. She'll be back here when she can, I guarantee it. I'm fairly sure you guys put a little something in there to make us keep coming back, but until I can actually prove it, I'll simply run with it."

Marcelo laughed. "Well, you let me know if you find something. Until then, we'll really enjoy your patronage."

Taylor shook his head and sighed. "I won't lie, that's exactly the kind of thing a villain would say. Do I need to call a superhero team in to deal with you?"

"Well, if you do, I think our kitchen will need to work overtime to keep them fed," the manager pointed out. "Do you know how many calories go into keeping them as fit as they are?"

"No."

"Me neither," Marcelo admitted. "But I'll bet you it's considerable."

"Yeah, I won't take that bet," he said with a chuckle.

"Well, let me know if you need anything else." The man patted him on the shoulder.

"I do want to leave Terri a good tip," he replied. "And maybe leave a good word for her. She's good at her job."

"One of the best," Marcelo agreed as Terri returned with the order.

"The take-out order will be out in a second," she said set the plate in front of him.

"I appreciate it," Taylor said.

Damned if the low-carb option wasn't as good as the French toast and pancakes. It was finished only too soon and almost at the same time that the packaged order was being placed on the bar.

"I'd ask if you enjoyed your food," Terri said and laughed. "But I guess you were hungry, huh?"

"Damn straight." He dabbed his lips with a napkin. "Can I get the bill?"

"Coming right up."

He paid and headed out to where he'd parked Maddie, the four-by-four, after he'd left a generous tip for Terri. People who did their jobs well deserved to be rewarded for it and the excellent service was of the many, many reasons why he returned so often.

A quick drive brought him to one of the apartment buildings in the city, where he parked once more, made his way to the front door, and pressed the buzzer to one of the apartments.

There was no answer right away, but he didn't really expect there to be one. Alex tended to work late, which meant she usually slept in. It was why he had allowed himself the time to eat before coming over. The chances were she wouldn't want company anyway, and he could simply leave her with breakfast before he went to work himself.

"Who is it?" the woman's tired voice said through the intercom. "If it's the Jehovah's witnesses, I don't want what you're selling. I'm headed to hell and I'm happy about it."

That was one way to greet the morning.

"Breakfast delivery," Taylor said simply, not wanting to piss her off further.

"Oh...well, come on up," she said and sounded surprised as she buzzed him in.

He stepped through and into the elevator and only minutes later, knocked at her front door. It felt like it had been a while since he'd been there. He knew she wouldn't like his place—you need to be in a special frame of mind to like it—and if their trysts didn't lead to hers, he simply took a hotel room for them.

It was simpler that way and they could both use simple in their lives.

Once again, she took a couple of minutes to come to the door, and when she answered, she kept it on the chain as she opened it a couple of inches and peered out with one eye closed.

"Breakfast?" she asked once she had confirmed that it was, in fact, Taylor.

"If you want it," he replied with a small smile.

She leaned in closer and sniffed the package in his hand. "Is that Il Fornaio?"

"That's a good nose you have there. And yes, it is."

She stared at him for a moment, shrugged, and closed the door to take the chain off before she opened it fully. "You know how they say that the way to a man's heart is through his stomach?"

"I know from experience that it's easier to find it between the fourth and fifth rib, actually," he said and stepped into the apartment. It wasn't the fanciest but it was clear that considerable effort had gone into making it a home.

"You're hilarious." Alex took the package from his hand, opened it, and inhaled. "Oh, damn, that's the good stuff. Suck it, kale, you bush-league superfood."

"What was that?"

"Nothing," she said quickly. "Anyway, they say the best way to a man's heart is through his stomach. It's a saying so don't overthink it or get all technical on me. But they neglect to say that the best way to a girl's heart is through her stomach too. It's not as traditional, I know, but I'll tell you something—show up with food for almost anything you have in mind, and the chances are you'll get what you went there for."

Taylor's eyebrows raised and he nodded as he sat at the small dining room table while she took the seat across from him. "That's good to know. You never know when I might need to bribe you. Is chocolate the go-to food in this instance or is that merely a myth?"

"Chocolate is one of the classics and should not be ignored," she conceded as she selected a piece of bacon. "But you should never underestimate the power of fried foods. Warm foods. Pastries. Breakfast foods in general. Obviously, steak or chicken and stuff like that will never get a nose up from me, but your go-to should always be the guilty pleasures. The kind we would usually feel guilty buying for ourselves, you know?"

He nodded and leaned back in his seat. "Guilty-pleasure foods, so sweets make sense. Breakfast foods?"

"They are generally a good bet too," Alex admitted. "The power of bacon should never be underestimated. Eggs are kind of iffy. Hash browns are good. Stay away from the healthy stuff, though. The chances are she's already spent a good amount of money to buy better healthy stuff than you do."

"Noted."

"Again, always choose the guilty-pleasure stuff, the kind we would feel guilty about buying for ourselves but would feel more guilty about not eating when given freely as a gift. We like to make excuses for ourselves like that."

"Would it surprise you to know that guys make excuses like that too?" he asked.

She shrugged. "It sounds about right so isn't really surprising. I can't say you are the kind of guy to binge on unhealthy food, though. You have the look of a guy who is religious about counting his calories and spends time at the gym, mostly flexing for yourself in the mirror."

"Well, I don't count the calories that religiously," he admitted. "Mostly only to keep track of intake and outtake. If I eat a little more or eat something a little unhealthier, I keep track and I make sure to put a little more intensity into my exercise. And as for flexing in front of the mirror, I mostly do that when no one else is looking. You know, like after a shower in front of the bathroom mirror."

"I don't know. I think I'd like to catch that show," she said and leaned back in her seat.

"Well, you'll have to be around after I shower to find out," he said with a small smile and stretched his hand toward the meal he had brought.

She was quick to intercept him, however, and darted her hand across the table to give his a slap before it could even reach the container.

"Another thing to note is that we don't share food." Alex growled in warning.

"Even if I'm the one who brought the food?"

"Especially if you're the one who brought the food."

Taylor retreated quickly and rubbed the small red splotch on his skin where she'd smacked him. "Well, that's good to know. Is there a reason why? Also, are there ever exceptions?"

"Well, again, the reason is because this is a guilty-pleasure indulgence and there's no sharing when it comes to indulgence." She grinned at him. "If you want to indulge with us, you have to bring your own—which you might be required to share as well. Is that hypocritical? Maybe, but if you want something in exchange for the food, some sacrifices need to be made."

"That does sound hypocritical but it also makes sense," he said and made mental notes.

She smiled and tilted her head. "As for the exceptions to the rules...well, there are always exceptions, but you need to know when to take your shots."

"My shot before—"

"Not a good time," Alex said and shook her head firmly. "But if you're really interested in getting in on some of my breakfast—"

"Which I brought."

"My breakfast," she insisted. "If you were really interested in getting in on it, you would have to offer something that would take my mind off the food and turn it to something else. Another pleasure, guilty or no, to convince me that you're offering more than only food."

"More than only food, huh?" Taylor muttered. "Do you

have anything particular in mind? Like a little peek at that post-shower flexing, for instance?"

She grinned. "Now you're getting the idea. For instance, I don't suppose the breakfast comes with a little side of sausage?"

"It could, but it should be said that I didn't expect it to," he said, unable to contain a small smirk. "And while it might be a side in this particular circumstance, you know better than most that it's by no means little."

"Now that's what I like to hear," she said, leaned forward, and shoved the paper bag out the way. "Do keep going and tell me more about this side of big sausage."

He had never been much good at dirty talk and always preferred to do rather than say, but he was willing to learn from Alex. Better yet, she always seemed up to teaching, which usually brought satisfying results.

"Well, unlike the regular kind of sausage one might expect from breakfast, it does require some degree of nudity," he said. "And while putting it in your mouth is allowed and in fact encouraged, chewing on said sausage—"

"A definitive do not chew. Understood." She pushed from her chair and moved to his side of the table. "And since you did bring the food and everything else, I suppose I should adhere to your rules."

Taylor opened his mouth to speak but paused when she stopped in front of him, pulled her pajama shirt off, and tossed it somewhere that he couldn't see and didn't really care to discover. She straddled his lap and her hands slid behind his neck to pull him in closer so she could press a firm kiss to his mouth.

"I hope that food reheats well," she whispered and licked her lips. "And I really hope you ate your Wheaties this morning because I'm about to abuse the shit out of you."

"No, no Wheaties," he said with a small smile as his hands settled on her hips and pulled her in closer while her thighs squeezed him. "A good breakfast, though."

"It's only a saying," she mumbled and leaned in to press a kiss to his neck. "It simply means you'll need extra stamina for what comes next."

"Stamina?" he asked and bit his bottom lip. "I have that covered."

CHAPTER TEN

Bobby looked up from where he worked on the chest piece of one of the mechs, then scowled and shook his head as he checked his watch and the garage door in turn.

"Say it, big guy," Vickie said, her attention still focused on the electronics she was helping to rewire. "If you constantly check your watch and sigh like that, you're bound to give yourself an ulcer. That's what it did to my dad."

"Let me guess—you were the one he checked his watch and sighed about?" he countered.

"The whys and the wherefores aren't really important right now," she replied and shook her head. "But yes, I was. Again, it's not really relevant to my point, which is that he got an ulcer from keeping it all in. Playing the passive-aggressive guilt game only really works when the person is present to be guilted, and even then, only when they really, really care about what you have to sigh and shake your head about. It's always better to simply get it out when they're not around."

"I'm only thinking that it's not like Taylor to be late, is all," Bobby said. "Yeah, sure, he's the boss, so we don't get to dictate his hours. But at the same time, he's also the one who has the most to lose if this goes badly. You and me lose our jobs and that's big enough for us, but for him, there's a huge amount of investment into this he stands to lose."

"Do you think he doesn't know that?" She turned to eye the mechanic with a little displeasure.

"No, it's only—"

"Do you think he doesn't care about the hours he's putting in?" she continued. "Because I know for a fact that he stays late to keep working and picks up any hours he missed. I know because I hear him clanging around long after we've closed shop and it's a little annoying, to be honest."

"I get it," he responded, clearly annoyed. "And I'm not saying Taylor doesn't care about the work. I'm only saying that...well, it's not like him to be late. We can work on our own, obviously, but we do more quicker when all three of us work in tandem with each other, so...yeah."

Vickie shrugged and returned to her work. "The chances are he went to that breakfast place the two of you love so much."

"It's called Il Fornaio, and it's not only a breakfast place," the mechanic replied and resumed his task. "Actually, the fact that they serve breakfast is incidental. They're an Italian place, so they serve Italian food for all three meals of the day. And a couple more meals too if you're a hobbit."

"You're Korean, though, so why don't you go more for the Asian food?"

"I'm Chinese-American, thank you very much," Bobby said. "And it's not a trait that defines who I am or what I eat. I happen to like me some authentic Italian food, so there."

"Sorry, I didn't mean to offend you." She sounded genuine in her apology. "Still, your guys' obsession with that place is a little unhealthy, both for your bodies and your minds."

"Hey, don't knock it until you try it," he snapped. "Head on over there for the breakfast special and you'll see what all the fuss is about."

Vickie raised an eyebrow. "Breakfast special, huh? Is that what you older guys call Netflix and Chill?"

He turned away from his work again and looked at her with his eyes narrowed and a confused expression on his face.

"Oh, come on," she said. "Don't tell me you don't know what Netflix and Chill is code for. It's been around since before I was born. People have used it literally for decades."

"Not where I come from," the heavyset mechanic said.

"Where is that, the fucking Stone Ages?"

"Explain it already."

She rolled her eyes. "Ugh, fine, but could you be any more stuck in the mud? Anyway, Netflix and Chill is the term for a booty call cleverly disguised as an invitation to have a nice little fuck sesh, you know? When a girl texts someone to come over to 'Netflix and Chill,' it means she'll be on her knees before the first commercial break in the Friends marathon, her mouth full of—"

"Okay, okay, I got it, thanks!" Bobby said a little louder than he needed to. "Yeah...stop talking, please."

Vickie laughed. "I'm sorry. Did I offend your delicate sensibilities?"

"I don't think it's an appropriate topic for the workplace."

"It's only the two of us, man. Calm the hell down."

"I think that only the two of us should talk about the breakfast instead," he said and shrugged in an attempt to regain his nonchalance. "I'm not sure how we got to the point of Netflix and Chilling."

"Come on. It can't be that good. It fucking can't."

"You say that," he replied and shook his index finger at her, "but only because you haven't tasted it. The pancakes are served nice and fluffy but the butter and real maple syrup add weight to the taste. All together, it melts in your mouth. But if you need something more, there's no need to look further than the thick, hefty strips of bacon served with it. The salty taste fills your mouth and contrasts with the sweet and savory pancakes perfectly, and all coalesce together in a delicate, mouthwatering crunch that reminds you of how your parents used to make breakfast."

He looked at Vickie and knew immediately he had a captive audience before he continued. "Maybe not your parents specifically, but it's what you always wanted your parents to be like. You always wanted that picket-fence childhood when there was nothing more complicated in your life than worrying about getting to the bus on time because your mother would always be there, serve you this breakfast, and let you know that everything would be all right."

Vickie swallowed as her mouth suddenly filled with saliva. That did sound absolutely delightful but damned if she would give the man the satisfaction of knowing it.

"It sounds like it was a borderline religious experience for you, my man," she said once she finally felt able to speak again without giving herself away.

Bobby shrugged. "I've said it before and I'll say it again —good bacon is a religious experience for anyone."

She was about to respond but stopped when the computer on her desk beeped. A quick glance at the screen confirmed that the cameras were trained on a dark-purple four-by-four that turned into their parking lot. "Well, your fears need not be realized. It looks like Taylor's back so you can sigh and shake your head at him in person."

"Don't be shitty," the mechanic grumbled. "I'll only ask him where he was and what he was doing, he'll explain it, and that'll be that. There's no point to all that passive-aggressive bullshit. Real friends will be open and honest with each other. Hint, hint."

"I still won't tell you who I'm seeing, old man," Vickie said. "Mind your own business."

The garage door opened, the vehicle entered, and Taylor got out. He didn't look tired as they might have expected after he woke up early enough to not have alerted her when he left the strip mall. Coffee would do that to a person as well as a good night's sleep followed by a good breakfast.

As well as a couple of other things.

"Hey, Tay-Tay," she said. "Nice of you to join us. Are those scratch marks on your neck?"

"Yep," he replied but didn't elaborate. "How's the work

going? Did those deliveries come in yet?"

"Uh-huh. I'll go this afternoon to pick them up from customs," Bobby replied. "I assume you got those forms cleared, right?"

"They're in the desk," his boss said, walked over to the desk in question, and opened a couple of drawers before he located the paperwork. "Don't forget them or they won't be released to you. Oh, and maybe think about taking Liz with you? We need to ease her back into things. I don't think she likes being on reserve this long."

"We still have repairs to do," the stout mechanic replied. "Only on the outside, though. The engine's fine and she does handle better than my truck with that kind of weight."

"Let me know if you need gas money. I'll clear it on the corporate credit card." He glanced at their surprised expressions. "Oh yes, we have a corporate credit card, thank you very much."

Vickie laughed as the phone rang and immediately stood to answer it, but Taylor held a hand up to stop her.

"I'll take it," he grumbled and lifted the device from the cradle. "This is McFadden of McFadden's Mechs. How can I help you?"

She scowled. "It's a terrible, terrible name."

"Shut up," Bobby hissed.

Taylor waved at them to tell them to quiet as he listened. "Yeah, she does work here. While she's still on an entry-level basis, that is looking to change... Yes, I would say she's vital to the operation of the business."

He paused to listen to what the person on the other side said. "Well, it's a fairly new business and we repair mechanical combat suits that are used by the military, mostly in the Zoo area... Yes, she has a great deal of specialist knowledge and I do think she is learning a great deal that would apply to the courses she's in... Yes, I can send you a generalized list of the operations of the company... She has your email? Fantastic. Expect it within the hour."

When he hung up and settled the phone on its cradle, he turned to Vickie, who worked studiously on the wiring.

"So, that was an administrator from UNLV," he said and watched his employee closely. "What the hell did you do to their computers?"

"I don't know what you're talking about," she said and Bobby barked a laugh in the background. "Hush, you!"

"Vickie, come on. This is a judgment-free zone here," Taylor said. "They talked about how your work here would count toward college credit. I need to know what they're talking about so that I can nudge that report they asked for in your favor."

"Oh, well...no problem, in that case." Vickie stood quickly. "I made a few calculations and I saw that only working the courses I was doing wouldn't give me enough credit to graduate in three years, so I needed a little more. I looked through their programs and nothing really caught my eye until I saw that they count certain jobs toward credit, but only as long as the job in question is applicable to the course I'm working on. Given that my course mostly deals with software, my work on the suits and their cutting-edge software does apply in this case."

"Okay, it sounds good to me," he said, settled into the office chair, and pulled the laptop closer to himself. "I have to ask, though—and this is merely to settle my personal curiosity—are you actually secretly a genius of some kind?

For being as sharp as your average socket wrench, you actually do come up with good ideas."

"But socket wrenches are—oh, you asshole." Vickie growled annoyance, snatched the nearest socket wrench, and threw it at him.

Taylor ducked quickly to avoid the thrown tool. "Hey, watch it with my tools over there. If you break anything, it'll come out of your paycheck, Missy."

Vickie tried to look like she was angry but a small smile betrayed her. "Call me Missy again. I dare you—I double-dare you, motherfucker—call me Missy one more goddamn time."

"See, now that's a reference I do get," Bobby said, still hard at work.

"Everyone gets that reference," his boss retorted as he stood. "Pulp Fiction is a fucking classic that will last the ages. The real question is what exactly do you think you're threatening me with, Missy?"

She stepped forward and punched him in the shoulder as hard as she could. He remained unmoved but she fell back, her expression pained as she rubbed her wrist, and made another attempt. This time, she delivered a punch to his chest and another to his stomach before she retreated again.

"God fucking...what the hell are you made of—granite?" she asked and massaged her aching hand as she glowered at him.

"Uh...no, but I would say your punching skills are about on par with your throwing skills," Taylor said and looked for the wrench she had thrown at him.

"What the hell are you talking about?" Vickie raised her

arms and bounced the way that she thought a boxer would. "I'm one hell of a scrappy fighter. I know all about…uh, chi interruption and nerve points. Plus, I kick and bite like a motherfucker."

"Well, kicking and biting won't do you much good," he said, reached out faster than she could move, and caught both her hands firmly. He forced them open, leaned in, and tapped his head gently against hers. "Not if you're down with one hit, which I guarantee will happen if you don't defend yourself properly. Keeping your hands up only does so much. Stop bouncing around like a monkey on cocaine and make sure you move on your hips a little. Keep your head in motion and shift your stance."

"What are you talking about?" she demanded. "You simply stood there and let me hit you."

"She is right," Bobby interjected.

Taylor sighed and shook his head. "Fine. Come at me and throw those punches."

She didn't hesitate, moved in closer, and aimed the same punch at his head this time. He intercepted the strike, grasped her hand by the wrist, twisted, and tapped her in the gut with his fist.

"With that, you're doubled over, trying to breathe and not able to think about anything but that," he said. "There'd be no biting, no kicking, nothing. Don't over-commit on your punches and keep your core and your head protected. Tuck your chin in, clench your teeth, and keep your hands up but loose with your shoulders bunched."

She did everything she was told to and although she exaggerated somewhat for effect, she still demonstrated his instructions.

"Now, I'll throw a punch," he said. "In slow motion. You have to block or dodge, whichever feels more natural to you, then counter. Countering is your best friend since they will likely be open. Never strike the head with a closed fist."

"Wait—what?" she asked.

"Stay in position," he remonstrated. "The head bones are much harder than what's mostly cartilage in your knuckles and wrist, so don't aim for the head unless you can hit the jaw. Otherwise, target the gut or don't be afraid to take the dirty route and hit him in the nut sack. If it's a her...well, stick with the gut."

He swung first but slowly and let her guide his punch to the side and slide a clumsy uppercut into his midsection.

"Well, a little lower—between my abs and my ribs—you'll find the solar plexus, a cluster of nerves and ganglia that when hit, immediately contract the diaphragm. That makes anyone exhale and double over."

"Right, it's a chi center," Vickie said.

"Nope, that's bullshit," he retorted. "It's a nerve cluster. Don't think about chi, okay?"

"Okay," she said, nodded, and aimed a little lower. Her blow connected with his stomach and she adopted a pained expression again. "Seriously, you need to teach me your ab workouts."

"Actually, I think you might benefit from a self-defense lesson," Taylor said and rolled his shoulders. "After work, do you have any school?"

"Nothing I can't blow off."

"Great, we'll figure out what to start you on then," he said. "For now, back to work."

CHAPTER ELEVEN

Not many people in the world hunted for a living. There was a time in human history when you either hunted, gathered, or both, but those were phased out by the farmers, who produced regular food to compete with the delicate balance between hunter and prey.

These days, some people still did it for fun, sport, and entertainment, but it wasn't quite the same thing when you didn't do it for your survival.

This was as close as Clarke Terrence thought anyone could ever get to those old ways. He was part of a small and possibly dwindling group of people, most in the wilder areas in the world, who still hunted for a living. There were, of course, the people who hunted in the Zoo and dealt with that particular brand of danger, and he respected them a great deal.

He still felt he belonged in the elite group of men and women who qualified as hunters in the true sense of the word, but this was something a little different, a kind of crazy space somewhere between the past and the future.

He had been with Banks' task force for almost two years and used his skills to track and kill monsters that would have been seen as nothing more than science fiction not that long before. Most of the prey he hunted now would qualify as the daydreams of mad scientists and people who needed more excitement in their lives.

For him—and for humanity, although most had no clue —it was a reality. An entire jungle flourished in the Sahara Desert and like a disease, it had begun to spread across the world, either as something to be feared or something to invigorate the minds of humanity as a whole.

Once or twice, the predators he had pursued had been nothing more than serial killers, and on one occasion, it had been a pack of wild dogs on a rampage. The rest, however, had paid well and gave him the experience in this new type of hunting he needed.

This was the first time he had been teamed with other members of the task force. Most of the time, Banks had simply called him or texted him a location and credentials to use to deal with the local authorities.

This time, it was different. Two others had been called in to form a team and it soon became apparent that it was the kind of mission that carried a substantial price compared to previous jobs. While it wasn't a write your own check situation, it was definitely more lucrative than other opportunities he'd enjoyed.

Ryan Teller looked like he had just flown in from Kansas and had a mustache and a fedora. Even without the obvious build and the kind of weapons he used, Clarke recalled that the man had a military background. They had met before, although he couldn't claim to know him well.

He hadn't said much since they had been told to meet on an airfield in Wyoming, but he didn't need to. The past wasn't a concern in this kind of situation.

Wade Jensen was an altogether different animal—a veritable chatterbox who almost never seemed to stop talking. He claimed it was a condition and that he would settle once they were on the job but it didn't seem likely. Lean, well-armed, and packing the power armor that had only recently begun to be released for civilian purchase, he looked like he knew a thing or two about what was required under these circumstances. Perhaps that was enough to outweigh his propensity to talk shit constantly.

Overall, Clarke felt rather confident about their chances to come away with the win and a better than usual payday. None of them looked nervous or overly thoughtful about what they were doing, and that was a good sign. He didn't have much in the way of traditional training with weapons, but his father had been a Navy SEAL and had become something of a paranoid recluse. While this had many negative implications, the advantage was that the man had made sure he knew everything there was to know about combat.

It hadn't been useful in the real world, where people wanted fewer knives to throats and more time spent behind a desk when it came to qualifications. All that had changed when he'd been contacted by the FB freaking I to work on a special task force after some research showed his qualities as a deputy police officer would be better-used hunting monsters.

Now, they'd been called to a military airbase, where a

helicopter waited to carry them to the site where the hunt was supposed to start.

How awesome was that in a world populated by suits and dead-end paper shuffling?

"What do you think we'll face down there?" Jensen asked and looked at the two of them. "I know they'll have all the details when we get there, but maybe we should put bucks down and see who makes the better guess, right? I think something like those spiders they had in Maine but not exactly the same, you know?"

"Do you ever fucking shut up?" Teller growled irritably, unwrapped what looked like a strip of nicotine gum, and popped it into his mouth.

"Not while I'm awake, no," the man replied with a small grin. "Like I said, I have a condition. I talk most of the time. I've learned to tune myself out and you will too, eventually."

"That's assuming we don't accuse you of being the monster and shoot your ass for the reward," Ryan said and shook his head.

Jensen smirked. "Yeah, good luck with that. I mean, no disrespect, I'm sure you're one hell of a shot even with that lip toupee weighing you down, but there is something to be said for the guy who knows how to keep his calm. And despite the sheer number of words coming out of my mouth, I am incredibly calm and the quickest and sharpest draw you'll ever find."

"You do seriously need to clam up when we're in the field, though," Clarke told him firmly. "We won't be able to look and find much of anything out there if all we can think of or hear is you listing the fifty kinds of birds that can be found in your hometown."

"Oh, I can shut up on demand, no problem there," the garrulous man said and scratched the blonde bristle on his jaw. "It takes focus—or medication if I can. Not in the field, though. If I take the medication, it usually means I'm no good to anyone and more of a drooling mess. On the other hand, with the focus, it can get a little tiring for me so that's usually better done when we're actually in the field, you know?"

"I say we throw him out of the chopper, tell them he didn't show up, and take his money," Teller grumbled.

Clarke nodded. "I second that motion."

Jensen laughed. "Once again, I'd like to see you mother-fuckers try. Maybe I simply shoot you, take the job on my own, and say that you bitches simply slowed me down."

He was about to retort, but his gaze froze on the man's 1911-style pistol, which was already in his hands and aimed at Teller's head. Admittedly, he was quick on the draw. Clarke hadn't even seen it happen and he flinched instinctively when the man pulled the trigger.

Of course, logic dictated that the guy wouldn't fire on his fellow hunters, but it was simply reflex. You didn't treat your weapons like that, not unless you wanted the kind of unpleasant accident that inevitably happened because you had forgotten to put the safety on or something.

It was asking for something bad to happen, in his opinion. When you mistreated your weapons like that, they tended to mistreat you in return. That was what his father always said, anyway. Respect when handling firearms was of paramount importance.

Wade grinned and slid the weapon into its holster. "Don't worry. I wouldn't shoot you ladies in the chopper. I'd have to clean the mess up myself. It'd be best to wait until we land and the two of you are facing away from me."

"Yeah, that's a great way to inspire confidence in the folks you'll work with." Ryan chuckled. "Threaten to shoot them in the back at the first chance you get."

"You guys threatened to kill me and toss me out the flying chopper because you didn't like how much I talked," Jensen countered and tilted his head, his smirk unfazed. "I'm merely making sure you know that you'll both be dead before you're even out of your seats. But again, I'd rather not clean the mess."

The rest of the chopper ride passed mostly in silence, at least on Clarke and Teller's parts. The low roar of the rotors overhead was only matched for pace by the man who continued to waffle on about…something. Clarke had no idea what, by this point, and realized that the guy had been right. They had learned to tune him out.

Maybe this whole job would actually work out after all.

It was a gentle landing, given that there was no sign of any landing pad and only grasslands as far as the eye could see in practically every direction. Mountains formed the horizon out west and a line of poles with wires extended to the south, but aside from that, green and brown grass defined the sprawling vista.

They moved away from the spinning rotors with their heads down. Teller clutched his fedora, his scowl indicative of the effort required.

Banks waited for them with her arms folded over her

chest. The man in a suit beside her appeared to be another agent.

She didn't look happy but then again, she hadn't on the other three occasions when they had met face to face on a job either. When he considered that now, each time had been when things had been at their most dire, so he couldn't really blame her if she wasn't in the best of moods.

"Morning, boss," Jensen called and jogged ahead of the other two. "I heard you were looking for someone to deal with a monster problem in the area."

"Yeah, that's why I shipped the three of you out here," Banks said, still dour. "Now that you're here, we might as well get on it. I assume you have read through the dossiers I sent you?"

"Why don't we go over the details for those who didn't?" Clarke suggested.

She sent him a sharp look as they moved closer to the tents that had been set up. "I assumed that would be the case. To be honest, we don't actually know much about the critters you have to deal with anyway, so the information was fairly brief. All we know is that they killed and moved on, leaving one hell of a lot of bodies."

They stepped beyond the line of tents and the three hunters stared at the carcasses still left out in the sun. Clark's jaw dropped as he looked out onto what could only be described as a massacre—of cows, mostly, but still.

"What the fuck?" Jensen exclaimed.

"How long ago was this?" Teller asked the real question, although it seemed instinct rather than considered thought.

"A few days now," Banks responded. "And yes, we

weren't sure why the bodies hadn't decomposed either, so we had our lab folks take a look. From what they can discover, the meat is coated by what seems to be saliva but it keeps anything that might be able to decompose those carcasses—from bacteria to regular carrion—away for some reason. We're not sure how many of them there are but given the sheer number of killings contained in a relatively small area, we can assume there is a fair number and they are probably fast."

"Fun times," Jensen said. "When do we get to kill the fuckers?"

"There's no time like the present," she said. "You three now know about as much as we do, give or take. Provided you're ready to get going, there's literally nothing stopping you."

"Fan-fucking-tastic." Clarke grunted and turned to his two comrades. "Are you boys ready to rock and roll?"

Teller spat on the ground. "Let's get this over with."

"It sounds good to me," Jensen said as they strode across the grass and carefully avoided the dead bodies.

After a few minutes of moving across the grasslands in silence, Jensen turned to the other two. "Do you guys think Banks was a little different?"

"That didn't last too fucking long," Teller said, shook his head, and toyed somewhat irritably with his mustache.

Clarke shrugged and decided to engage the kid anyway. "Define different. It's not like she's ever been the easiest person to read under the best of circumstances."

"That's what this kind of view does for you," Teller said and gestured to the field of corpses they walked through. "There aren't too many people in the world who can see this kind of shit and not be a little off while that image lingers in your head."

Wade sniffed the air. "I don't know... When you see that many bodies, you really expect to smell something, don't you? Like that smell meat gives off when it's been out in the open for a little too long? Not quite rotting but it's very clearly not fresh?"

Clarke nodded. "I assume something in that stuff they found on it is keeping it fresh."

"Fresh meat smells too," Teller pointed out. "There has to be something in it that makes it not smell at all. All I can pick up is wet, trampled grass—like it's all a mirage or something."

Curious, Clarke moved to the closest carcass, gave it a light tap with his boot, and wiped the clear liquid that came off of it on the grass. "This shit's real all right. Maybe it's only your sense of smell that's fucked from all that smoking."

"I quit almost a year ago." Teller tugged the corner of his mustache. "It doesn't mean I don't still crave the occasional smoke, and I like the gum. But after that long, you get your smell and taste back and I'm telling you, there ain't no smell out here. I'm sure the stuff they left behind is what's doing it but I can't for the life of me think why."

"There's only one reason why you'd want to preserve meat like this," Jensen said, dropped into a crouch, and gingerly inspected the body in front of him.

Clarke waited for the kid to say his piece and realized that the silence had begun to annoy him more now. "Well, don't leave us in suspense, kiddo. Do tell."

"Oh, I thought it was obvious." Wade looked at them as

he stood. "The same reason why we preserve meat—because they're coming back for it. Anyway, it's easy to track the fuckers on grassland like this, so let's circle the carcasses, see where the tracks start, and follow them."

"That's…actually a good idea." Clarke shook his head. It was also obvious, and if they hadn't been so distracted, they'd have thought of it themselves. Tracking was a basic part of a hunter's skills.

Teller laughed. "The kid talks so much, he's bound to have a good idea eventually. It's the law of averages. He's bound to say something intelligent simply through statistical possibility."

"What do you know about statistics, Burt Reynolds?" Jensen retorted.

"I teach a course on statistics for business and economics at a local college when I'm not killing monsters," Wade said cheerfully.

Clarke had no idea if the man was telling the truth but shrugged. It didn't really matter. What was important right now was to find those tracks.

CHAPTER TWELVE

"I'm not saying I don't like the work," Bobby said. "In fact, this is the kind of work every mechanic dreams of."

"Then what are you saying?" Taylor asked as he helped to put the pieces together again.

"I don't know. I merely feel a little concerned about repairing the suits and sending them off," the other man said. "I know we test them, but that's still not the best thing ever, right? We send them back, something breaks, and it turns out we're the guys who sell faulty product. It only needs one, you know?"

"Don't you trust our work?" his boss asked, picked the pieces of the chest plate up, and handed them to the mechanic to screw in.

"I know we're good, but there's no point in being arrogant," Bobby said and shook his head. "We're bound to fuck up somewhere or miss something."

"Well, that's why we have an instant money-back policy," Taylor said. "It's written up in the contracts."

His friend shook his head, still working to seal the parts in place. "What happens when someone dies inside one of our suits?"

"Well, it's not like they'll go out there without testing it themselves first," he pointed out. "They have the opportunity to make sure and they know their suits better than we do. If there's something wrong, they send it back on our dime. And so far, no one's sent one back. Not only do they like the repairs, but they also love the upgrades you and Vickie are responsible for. So it's really not our problem."

The mechanic laughed. "I love how you say that like it'll calm me down."

"Doesn't it?"

"Not really."

He shrugged. "Well, it's as good as we'll get. Now come on. We've been at this all day."

"That's what I was worried about. Your business runs on word of mouth. We need a plan for when that word turns a little sour."

"I'm all over that," he said but paused when his phone rang. "Hold that thought. I think this is Desk."

"How do you know?"

"She always makes sure it's not a number I'd recognize," Taylor replied and pressed accept on the call. "This is McFadden."

"Hi, is this Taylor McFadden?" said a voice that was decidedly not Desk.

"That's what I said," he replied and scowled. "This is the part where you introduce yourself before I hang up. My mommy taught me not to talk to strangers."

"This is Jennie," the woman said. "I won't share anything

else but suffice it to say that I've worked with Niki's task force for a while now."

Taylor raised an eyebrow. "Niki?"

"Niki Banks," the woman confirmed. "Special Agent Niki Banks."

That was all he really needed. He'd never heard anyone at work refer to her by her first name except Desk. That wasn't enough on its own but introducing herself as Jennie, the same name as Banks' sister, clinched it for him. He also knew for a fact that she didn't work for the FBI, which begged the question of why she had called him and tried to pass herself off as a member of the task force.

He couldn't ask her outright, of course. It would scare her away and make her feel defensive, and he wouldn't get anything out of her. He needed to play this smart and safe.

"Right, Jennie," he said and took a deep breath. "You were the one Banks met at the bar in Portland, right? She never did say how she knew you."

"She wouldn't," the woman huffed. "Anyway, I'm afraid this isn't a social call."

"How can I help you?" he asked.

"Well, first of all, yes, that was me at the bar in Portland," she admitted. "And...well, if I'm honest, I hope you don't mind me saying that your reputation precedes you."

Taylor raised an eyebrow. "I have a few reputations, so I'm afraid you'll have to be a little more specific."

She laughed. "I guess you're right. But the reputation I'm talking about is the kind that has you hunting and killing all kinds of monsters and being fantastic at it, by the way."

"Oh, that rep," he replied and shook his head as Bobby

raised his hands to ask silently what the delay was about. "Well, yes, you are right about that. I am darn fantastic."

"Well, I needed to contact you because Niki...Banks is busy," Jennie continued. "She's got herself into a fair amount of trouble and she won't admit that she needs your help. Anyway, she's busy, so—fuck, one sec. I'll call you back."

The line went dead and Taylor stared at the screen of his phone in confusion.

"Who was that?" Bobby asked, still working on the suit.

"I think it was Banks' sister, Jennie," he said. "First, she tried to pass herself off as working for the task force but I'm not sure why. She said Banks was busy, complimented my hunting skills, said her sister was in trouble, then panicked and hung up. So honestly, I'm not sure what that's about. I'm a little confused verging on pissed. How do you feel?"

"Like you should help me with these suits," the other man said. "But it does sound weird."

"Right?"

"Maybe you charmed her so much that she hung up for a little personal time," Vickie said and stepped from behind the desk she was working at.

"Shit—" Taylor hissed in surprise. "I need to put a bell on you."

"What?"

He shook his head. "Nothing. What did you mean?"

"Come on, I don't need to explain to you the kind of danger you pose to all womankind," she said, laughed, and ran her fingers through her short hair. "Well, the straight ones, anyway. I can't allow you to have that kind of information. Merely having the skill is bad enough on its own but having the knowledge behind it is asking for bad juju."

"Well, you'll have to be careful about that because you might not want to know that I'm learning," he retorted. "I now know that bringing girls guilty-pleasure food is a good way to get them in the mood to do almost anything you want them to."

Vickie made a face. "Ew."

"Not the dirty kind of stuff." He snorted, paused, and nodded. "Well, not only the dirty stuff."

"Yeah, we saw the scratches," Bobby called from his side of the shop. "By the way, anytime you guys want to stop talking about sex, would you help me here? We have an order to finish and ship off. Remember the business we're running here?"

Taylor laughed. "Relax, Bungees, we're ahead of schedule."

"Yeah, no thanks to either of you," the man grumbled.

"Hey, you guys both said you didn't need me for this," Vickie said and raised her hands defensively. "That's why I was over here, working on scheduling these orders to make sure we don't have a horde of broke-ass mechs piled up in our garage."

"Well, yes, and I direct my shit to Taylor," Bobby said and focused on the mech he was working on.

"Fine, fine, I'll get back to it," his boss grumbled and returned to work himself. "Don't you forget, though, Vickie. Later today, you have a date at a shooting range where we'll talk about how you'll protect yourself better. Not that I really expect you to need it, but it's one of those things it's better to have and not need than to need and not have. Like when you two had your asses kidnapped."

Bobby looked up from his work and took the piece Taylor handed to him. "Because people were gunning for you. Let's not forget that little piece of trivia."

"I can't control the people who want me dead," he protested. "If I could, they wouldn't want me dead so it's neither here nor there. All we can really do is make sure that the next time they attempt anything in my place of business, you know how to leave them dead in their tracks."

"How literally dead in their tracks are we talking here?" the mechanic asked.

Taylor paused to think about his answer. "Well, as literally as you need them to be. Banks would probably clear up any issues that arise, but if you guys are too enthusiastic and the cops are called on you tearing them fifteen different assholes—"

"Ew!" Vickie shouted from the other side of the room.

He nodded and continued. "If you guys are caught in the middle of it, I'm not sure there's much that Banks or the whole of the FBI can do. So, as literally as you need to but not much more if that makes sense."

"Not perfect sense, but I'll take it," Bobby replied. "Pass me the socket wrench, would you?"

Taylor did as he was asked and handed him the tool Vickie had thrown at him earlier in the day. It took only a moment to bolt the final couple of plates in.

They finished putting the suit together and gave themselves a moment to take a step back and admire their work.

"Well, that's one mech done," Taylor said and tapped it

gently. "Do you think we have time to test it, or should we call it a day and drink a couple of beers to celebrate?"

"As much as you're in the running for boss of the decade, I think we should probably have all our I's dotted and our T's crossed before we call it a day," Bobby replied firmly. "Just to make sure."

"Okay, load her up and let me take her for a spin."

Vickie rolled her chair closer as they toyed with the adjustments to adapt the suit for someone Taylor's size.

"So, when will you guys let me try one of those ?" she asked and bit into one of the doughnuts from the breakfast Bobby brought.

"Not soon," her boss said. "Don't get me wrong. It's not because we doubt your ability, but suits like this one cost around twenty million dollars apiece. They're expensive, and it usually requires at least some experience to handle one. Take Banks, for instance. While she was training to use some of the older models, she barreled into one of the walls of her training facility. The FBI doesn't like their walls damaged, and especially not by one of their own."

"And I'm sure we aren't a fan either," Bobby added. "These mechs are expensive, sure, but they're one hell of a lot more durable than the walls we have up around here. Seriously, you could literally walk through one and not even notice it with this one in particular."

Taylor patted the suit's shoulder. "He does have a point. Even worse, you could walk through one of the structural supports and have a building fall on you for your troubles. Not even this baby was built to have a whole building attack it."

Vickie rolled her eyes and folded her arms. "Okay, fine,

I don't get to ride the big mech thing. I get it. But I think... well, we all talk about me being able to defend myself, and that would work so much better if I could climb into one of those babies and be safe from damn near anything."

He nodded. "Sure, but there's always the risk that you might be killed by the mech. If you don't have it calibrated to your particular specifications, it won't be about wearing a suit of armor. There are all kinds of software in here that are primed to act based on your movements inside the suit. On your first time out, you usually wear something light or a hybrid, and you're told to move very slowly and very deliberately. Otherwise, you could adjust your arm and have the suit break it. Or you reach up to scratch your nose and accidentally give yourself a concussion."

"Wait, did that happen for real?" She laughed. "Which one of you gave yourselves a concussion."

"I told you that shit in confidence, Taylor," Bobby grumbled.

Taylor laughed. "Yeah, that was your mistake, although it should be noted that we've all had our little mishaps that taught us to respect these things. Banks had her wall incident, Bobby almost knocked himself out—"

"What was yours?" his friend asked. "Come on. You shared mine with the kid so it's only fair that you give yourself the same treatment."

He took a deep breath, looked at the ground for a moment, and nodded. "True, fair is fair. My case happened on my third trip into the Zoo, I think, and the first time I manned a fully-equipped combat mech. I felt like the absolute shit, right until I sneezed and faceplanted into the mud."

Vickie laughed and Bobby joined her as Taylor's pale face grew steadily redder by the second.

"Yeah, well, laugh it up," he grumbled and focused on calibrating the mech.

"We are!" Vickie replied before she turned to the computers. "But in all seriousness, I do appreciate you guys being all protective of me and trying to get me to protect myself and shit. That said, you should know I have a date with something other than a gun range tonight."

"I don't think you can call what you do in the dark with your computer a date," Bobby pointed out.

"You're hilarious." She scowled at him. "Wait, or do I mean gross? Eh, we'll call it both. Anyway, I have a date. With a guy—a college guy. I have a date with a cute college guy."

"Well, you know what they say, don't give it up on the first date," Taylor said, slipped into the mech, and closed the hatch behind him. "But if you feel like you're going to put out anyway, you might as well make it worth it and order the lobster."

"I'm not a big fan of lobster," she retorted. "Can I make it the steak instead?"

"Make it a good steak," Bobby said. "Like a filet mignon. But anyway, it should be said that I have a date tonight too."

"The gym girl?" Taylor asked as he took control of the mech and powered it up.

"The very same," the mechanic confirmed.

"Nice." He chuckled. "I would fist-bump you right now, but I don't want to pulverize every bone in your hand. I don't think our bottom line could take that hit."

"Well, I guess it's true what they say," Vickie said without looking away from her screen. "There's no accounting for bad taste."

"Fuck you." Bobby growled in mock annoyance. "I'm a catch."

"Damn straight, big old cuddly bear." Taylor took a couple of tentative steps.

Vickie flipped them both off. "I'd say fuck you too, but I guess I'd have to get in line, wouldn't I?"

"Now who's gross?" Taylor asked.

"Still the two of you bozos."

He laughed and rolled his shoulders slowly. "Well, let's not get caught up in the fun stuff. I have some Netflix to get to while you're off getting it on."

"Only Netflix?" Bobby asked and proffered his fist to Vickie for a bump. "No chilling?"

She laughed and bumped it—hard.

Taylor guided the mech into the open area of the garage, moving a little more freely now. "Nah, I had me some of that this morning. You saw the scratches, remember?"

The mechanic shook his head. "Am I seriously the only one who didn't know about Netflix and Chill?"

Vickie patted him on the shoulder. "I hate to say it but yes, Teddy Bear Bungees. But hey, don't worry, we all have glaring gaps in our knowledge. Like Tay-Tay here unable to sneeze without kissing the dirt."

Her boss didn't reply and simply flipped them off, the gesture more impressive using the sheer size of the mech's middle finger.

CHAPTER THIRTEEN

Nothing in this entire clusterfuck could be said to be going well.

"I'm really, really, really starting to wish I'd stuck to running casinos," Rod Marino muttered and rocked gently in his office chair.

It wasn't only the stresses of his role as the head of an entire branch of a criminal empire. He'd had to deal with various pressures his whole life and while it wasn't necessarily a good thing, it had prepared him for life in his father's shoes. People had made demands of him that he had attempted to live up to since he was a teenager so that wasn't a new and unfamiliar challenge.

What really wore at his patience and pushed him beyond his limits was having to deal with people who had different instincts from his own. His buddies in the business were well-known as ruthless assholes who would do anything to get ahead. They had even been known to engage in violent behavior themselves, but that was generally the kind of last resort they could avoid if they played their cards right. There were all kinds of financial and unsavory persuasive tricks one could use to leverage others into compliance.

His peers were the kind who had been raised in an underworld where they expected to have to deal with violence on a daily basis. While there were always the customary negotiations, they had to have a deadly reprimand primed and in hand in case it was needed.

It wasn't like he disapproved, of course. He'd seen what his father had done, but there was really no equivalent for it in the world of traditional business—a semblance of which he'd enjoyed to a large degree when all he'd done was manage the casinos. Now, however, these people expected him to be as inflexible and ruthless as his father had been. At any sign of weakness, they would pounce and make sure it was his head on the chopping block next.

Rod had, in fact, run the business side of things rather well and turned a hefty profit. He'd also made up his mind that he would become the man he needed to be— the man he was expected to be—because he really had no other choice. When he'd accepted the responsibility passed to him on his father's death, he'd accepted everything that went with it. The real stress came from the fact that he had no idea how his superiors would react to what had happened with McFadden and his missing mercs.

It had been relatively easy to convince himself that things would be resolved and he'd emerge stronger than before. Now, however, they were sending someone who was precisely the kind of person Rod had hoped not to have to deal with. One of the Cosa's caporegime—simply shortened to capos—had been sent to investigate the situation firsthand and report to the family in Sicily.

These peoples were captains, ranking members in the family who wouldn't hesitate to cut him down if they felt that it was necessary.

"Mr. Marino, a Mr. Luca di Stefano is here," his secretary said through the intercom. "He said he has an appointment with you?"

"He's my five o'clock," Rod said quickly. "Let him in."

"Of course," she replied and a few seconds later, the door was opened to reveal the secretary first and his visitor second.

The capo didn't look like much at first glance. Darker skin and olive-colored eyes lent him a faintly Mediterranean look and he was a little shorter than his host. He was considerably better-built, however, and his muscles could easily be seen through the understated yet clearly expensive three-piece suit he wore. The gray contrasted rather nicely with his skin and suggested someone who was used to money but didn't like to show it.

The silver Rolex on his wrist and the golden wedding band on his finger were a little flashier, though, likely gifts he couldn't afford to be seen without.

"*Ciao, Signor Marino,*" the man said and inclined his head slightly. He took Rod's hand and tapped his forehead gently against the knuckles. "*È un piacere conoscerti. Grazie per aver dedicato del tempo per incontrarmi.*"

It was a standard greeting and one he had heard offered to his father many times before—how it was a pleasure to meet him for the first time and thanking him for meeting with him. Later meetings would only involve the second half of the greeting. It was meant as a show of respect since he did technically outrank the man.

Rod inclined his head in return and replied with what was expected, even if it would be laden with a heavy American accent. "*Grazie per essere venuto fin qui, Signor Di Stefano.*"

The man smiled and patted him on the shoulder. "Please, call me Luca."

"And you can call me Rod," he replied. "How was your flight here?"

"Flying has never been a favorite form of travel," Luca replied in perfect English. "If it was an option, I would drive here from my home but unfortunately, it is not."

"There isn't much in the world that feels better than being in the driver's seat with your foot pressed on the accelerator, knowing you won't need to ease up anytime soon. Anyway, would you like to walk with me? I find sitting in the office for these kinds of talks a little stuffy and boring."

"Of course. I would like to see more of this casino of yours," the shorter man said.

He gestured toward the door. "Follow me, then. I'll give you the tour."

They left the office and he told the new secretary—whose name he couldn't remember for the life of him—to cancel the rest of his appointments for the day. He didn't have any others, given that it was the end of the workday, but it always made him look important and the person he "canceled" for felt suitably important.

When they stepped into the elevators and the doors closed, Luca turned to face him.

"Mr. Marino, allow me to be frank and a little blunt before we begin our talk," he said firmly.

Rod nodded. "Of course."

"You should know that the family knows you were not raised to be in this position," the man continued. "The position was thrust upon you with the sudden and unfortunate death of your father, and while better arrangements would have been preferred, you were the best choice in the urgent situation. I mean that as no disrespect to you, of course."

He narrowed his eyes but maintained a calm expression. "I appreciate your candor."

Luca nodded and smiled. "So, while we appreciate you stepping in to fill the gap and doing so better than we would have expected, we do not expect the transition to go without any...hiccups, you could say. There have been bumps, yes, but there is no need to be alarmed. The family still supports you fully in all your endeavors and are prepared to help you to establish your position as the representative of the family here in Las Vegas."

Rod narrowed his eyes as the elevator came to a halt at the ground floor and they stepped out but remained silent as they began to walk through the hallways of the casino. He certainly hadn't expected that assurance. Some people would be insulted with what might be considered condescension, but the fact that they were willing to support him and help him through the steep learning curve that came with the job was encouraging.

Well, maybe not encouraging but at least a little less terrifying than thinking that they would simply kill him and move on to the next candidate.

"With that said, I was told to tell you of the commendations that the heads of the family have extended to you," the capo continued almost without missing a beat. "Never before in our history has a transition of power gone so smoothly and with comparatively little bloodshed and tension. Not only that, but you have actually managed to organically increase our profits in the city since your father's death. They are truly impressed by your business acumen."

"Well, as you pointed out, I wasn't raised to manage the...let us call it the more colorful side of my family's business," Rod said and kept his voice low. "The business side is what I was groomed for, so I thought I would put my efforts toward making sure it was a little more stream-lined. Increasing efficiency and reducing spending has been the goal."

"And you have done that impressively," Luca assured him. "Don't think it hasn't been noticed or that the family will fail to recompense your labor."

"I didn't think that," he replied, but the man might as well have not heard him speak as he continued quickly.

"Of course, word of other difficulties has spread and cannot be ignored. It's not something to be worried about, however. Challenges are a staple of any change in power and honestly, we expected far more with you taking your father's place. But they still cannot be ignored. The situation with one of the local businesses disrespecting your authority—and repeatedly so—is an issue. Not for the money's sake, of course, but rather because word might spread and our position might be challenged. The Camorra are not forgiving of displays of weakness, as you well know."

Rod wasn't sure how he was supposed to "well know" something like that but he nodded anyway. The Camorra was a name that rang only the vaguest of bells in the back of his mind and he would need to look up who and what they were. For the moment, however, he could play along.

"If you don't mind, could you lay out to me what it is that you have done to rectify the situation?" Luca asked.

He paused and took a deep breath before he responded. "Well, at first, I thought it was better for the local muscle to handle the situation. For someone in my position to be involved in something as petty as that would be seen as an overreaction, but when things began to escalate, I decided it was both necessary and a good time to get involved. I felt I needed to make sure that those who work for the family knew who was in charge."

His companion nodded briskly. "That seems reasonable, but I was not sent here to handle reasonable."

"Well, no," he replied. "As it turns out, our friend—who goes by the name of Taylor McFadden—had connections we were unprepared for. It isn't anything we haven't dealt with before, mind you, but you don't expect your average small business owner to have connections in the fucking FBI."

"Federal connections should not be a problem," Luca said. "Well, not usually. Is he a state witness? Is that why they protect him?"

"I don't think so," Rod replied as they paused near one of the Casino's bars. The waitress recognized him immediately and she hurried behind the bar to collect a couple of drinks for him and his guest when he raised his hand.

"How so?"

"Well, they usually move witnesses to keep them out of trouble," he explained. "No, there's something else involved here, but no investigations into the man are permitted at all, and even trying to find the people who were sent to deal with him merely results in serious stonewalling too. I've sent some of my connections to determine who's bankrolling the guy and I'm still waiting to hear from them. Even the mayor has attempted to find out more from her network, but has run into the same problem."

"What other action have you taken against this McFadden?" Luca asked as two vodka martinis arrived.

"Well, I allocated funds to two outside hires," he admitted and suddenly felt he could trust this man for some reason. It was probably a bad idea but the reality was that there was nothing he could even try to hide from the family that wouldn't eventually be learned. "I elected to go with an outside hire since I didn't want word of the difficulty with the man to spread among our ranks. It seemed like a good idea at the time. I paid them a portion of the money upfront and the two began the work. They delivered daily reports while they conducted surveillance. From their reports, his office premises—where he also lives—were defended like a damn fortress, so they asked for more time but not more money. About a month and a half ago, they dropped off the map. Simply disappeared."

"Both of these men were aware of whom you represented?" The capo's expression was grave.

"Of course, although they were very insistent to have it on record that they weren't," Rod replied.

The shorter man rubbed his smooth chin pensively for a moment. "Well, I think we can safely assume they're both dead. If not already, they will be soon. You said McFadden had connections with the federal government, so the chances are that he entrusted all issues with hiding any bodies to them. Finding out if anyone was shipped out by federal order might produce better results than finding the men themselves."

He nodded. "But the chances are they are dead by now, right? So I don't have to worry about them anymore?"

"You didn't need to worry about them in the first place, but yes," Luca confirmed and paused to take a sip from his drink. "They are most likely dead. The fact that you have not been able to trace them is the message."

Rod frowned, a little startled by the statement. "The message? Surely it would make more sense to deliver the bodies—"

Luca smiled and raised a hand to effectively stop his protest. "Think about it. What he is saying is that he has more power than you think—the kind of power that can make people vanish without a trace. It is something we are familiar with, yes?" He waited until the younger man nodded, albeit reluctantly. "While the bodies remain unfound, you continue to wonder what happened to them, what the man is capable of, and when he might choose to retaliate."

"I hadn't thought of it like that," Rod confessed, a little shaken. "But yes, you are right. The worst part is not knowing."

"This McFadden—what do you know about him personally?"

"Most of his records are sealed, which was surprising in and of itself," he replied. "He was in the military but most of what he did while in service has been redacted and classified. Do you think it's important for us to look into that too?"

The man sighed and leaned back in his seat. "Well, in the words of Sun Tzu, know your enemy. It's better to have a good idea of what he is capable of since, by your telling, he was able to deftly handle the local muscle without too many problems before the feds were involved. What is the business that he's running?"

"Mostly mechanical from the orders," Rod said. "What we've been able to see is pieces for a wide variety of mechanical armor, and his hiring a mechanic does seem to confirm that."

"Keep digging," Luca advised. "You want to know as much about the man as possible, especially since he is holed up in what you described as a small fortress."

Rod smiled. "Will do. What do you propose we do when we have all the information available?"

"Well, you must forgive me for being bold, but I have already commissioned the services of two men the family has used in situations where violence was needed," his visitor said. "They are professionals and have worked on the orders of the family for decades. Anything we cannot find about McFadden, they will."

"But what will they actually do?"

The man leaned forward. "Well, you have two options, really. The peaceable route is where you meet him, all smiles, and tell him all is forgiven. You let him know that you do this out of the kindness of your heart because otherwise, you would tear into him. Maybe you even offer him a position on your side. The second is a great deal less diplomatic and involves making an example. Kill him and everyone he's ever cared for or will care for and burn the business to the ground while you're at it."

Marino knew which option he would prefer. Making allies instead of enemies had always worked for him in the past, but he had the feeling that, despite the soft words offered by the man, he would report everything that was said to the heads of the family.

"I have a feeling the option you'd prefer is the one that involves making an example," he said and finished his drink. "And I agree. Burn that fucking shithole."

Luca smiled. "I'll let the men know of your decision."

CHAPTER FOURTEEN

The three hunters set out confidently without even the slightest suspicion that things might turn ugly.

The tracks were easy to follow. As Banks had told them, there was a large group of the creatures and they tended to leave a mess of churned earth and grass everywhere they went. It would be hard not to find the trail.

The only problem, of course, was the sheer numbers they would have to deal with. Jensen, for all his time jabbering, had proven himself to be a valuable asset to the team with his tracking skills. He had stated with a great deal of certainty that they could expect a group of creatures that numbered about thirty or so, although some might have hidden in the tracks of those that had gone before.

It wasn't a number to sneeze at, given that by their conservative estimates, the monsters were about the size of a smaller mountain lion with large claws that tore easily into their prey. Despite this, the three were still confident they could eliminate the mutants, especially in the open grasslands where hiding was a little difficult for such a large group.

Clarke grimaced and hoped their deductions weren't merely wishful thinking that wouldn't pay off in the end.

His doubt was hastily set aside when Teller raised a hand abruptly. The man hadn't been lying when he said his senses were finely tuned and he gestured quickly to warn them that he could hear something following. As impossible as it seemed, something was tracking them now.

The three team members paused to study their surroundings but couldn't locate anything that might indicate where the creatures were. Clarke assumed they had doubled back, circled, and now followed the hunters, hidden in the tall grass.

He wondered if the entire horde was together or whether this was a smaller group. Logic suggested that to sneak up on the three men couldn't have been an easy feat for thirty-odd fair-sized monsters. If there were less of them gathered for a sudden attack, it should make them easier to handle. Piecemeal was always better than taking a bite out of the whole thing.

Of course, that could again simply be wishful thinking and they needed to maintain a worst-case scenario mindset. Underestimating the enemy was a guaranteed death sentence.

Ryan's silent warning was enough for them to draw their weapons and ready themselves for a fight.

"I don't like this," Clarke grumbled quietly and checked and double-checked his weapon as they moved on and attempted to circle and return to the camp.

"Why the hell not?" Jensen asked and looked around.

"It's not the best situation, sure, but when you look on the bright side, it means they've come to us. They could have forced us to track them to a cave or worse."

"I have to say that's not really the greatest silver linings," Teller retorted, spat his gum out, and primed his weapons. "Something not right about these monsters. They're unnaturally intelligent and seem to go about this with too much clever behind their actions. I don't like hunting something like that. It feels like killing sentient creatures."

"Wait, the problem you have with being surrounded by a horde of beasts that wiped out a herd of hundreds of cattle is a philosophical one?" Jensen sounded incredulous.

"I'm a college professor," the other man reminded them. "I'm allowed to have a deep thought or two, even though I take money to kill monsters for a living. Have you thought about what they might be doing on this planet, why they act so aggressively, and if we might not be somewhat to blame for that?"

"Hey, I'm all for discussing the meaning of alien life on our planet when we're not surrounded by a group of blood-crazed monsters determined to kill us," Clarke said. Low growls issued, seemingly from all around them, and the hackles rose on the back of his neck. They were closer, obviously, and might even have encircled the hunters and merely waited for the right moment to strike.

Most mutants wouldn't realize that the weapons the humans carried were lethal, but these were no ordinary creatures. Like Ryan had said, they were too intelligent. Prey didn't circle to flank someone when they were hunted.

Not ordinary prey, anyway. The three-man team

needed to determine exactly how deadly these creatures could be now that they appeared to be able to think for themselves. Most animals out in the wild only thought about a finite number of things.

Food and water were always at the forefront of their minds. Reproduction came in at a close second and sometimes moved to first. Protecting their young usually came in third, although mothers of the young tended to make that their top priority. Some species, anyway, although not all mothers in the wild were helicopter parents.

These creatures did appear to be capable of higher thought, although he wasn't entirely convinced of that. They were smart and knew how to turn from prey to hunter in a matter of minutes, but did that constitute higher thinking or sentience?

He grinned with dark humor when he realized how absolutely foolish that particular train of thought was at this moment. It was better to leave the deep thoughts to the professor and focus on not only staying alive but also doing the job he'd come to do.

Clarke caught movement out of the corner of his eye. Something flickered in and out of his field of vision before it darted away. He wasn't able to get a solid look at it so could identify no details, and by the time he turned his head, it had completely vanished.

"I don't like this," he said again, took a deep breath, and checked that he held to their formation and hadn't moved away. It felt like the beasts were toying with the hunters as if to tempt them out where they would be vulnerable. It was, he realized grimly, like they tried to find weaknesses in their defenses.

He ducked quickly when gunfire erupted from one of his teammates. Smoke drifted from Jensen's assault rifle.

"I...there was something there," the man said in his defense and hastily exchanged the mag with one that was full.

"Did you hit it?" Teller asked.

"I...no blood, so no."

Clarke couldn't see anything either, although he could identify completely with the urge to shoot. If the younger merc hadn't done it, he likely would have.

"Then let's keep moving," he said.

"What the hell are they waiting for?" Jensen asked and looked around quickly. The sun had already begun to set in the distance, and that alone was cause for concern.

"They know they have us cornered and surrounded." Ryan kept his voice calm and low. "They're taking their time. There's no need to take any unnecessary risks when they'll get the better of us eventually."

"Yeah, unlike us, animals in the wild don't have medical help that can save them from life-threatening injuries, so them playing it safe does seem on par with what they'd usually do," Clarke pointed out. He had something of a fascination when it came to animals, the kind that didn't usually go away. That essentially meant that him taking money to kill them probably wasn't the best thing ever, but he had never really claimed to be a good man.

"We could do something they can't stop us doing," Jensen said and looked at each of the two men in turn. "We can call for help."

"What kind of help would they be able to send that wouldn't get killed in the process of helping?" Teller asked quietly. "Oh, and might actually make it here in time to get us out of this particular frying pan?"

"They have the chopper," the younger man reminded them. "It'll take it less than fifteen minutes to reach us, drop down, pick us up without landing, and take off, and Robert's your mother's brother."

Teller narrowed his eyes and looked confused.

"Bob's your uncle," Clarke explained, took the sat phone from his pocket, and dialed the number that would connect him directly to Banks.

"This is Banks," the woman said when the line connected.

"This is Clark," he replied. "You can confirm our position from this phone, can't you?"

"I can, why?"

"Because shit's about to go down around us, and a quick getaway would not go amiss," he explained. "Is there any chance you could send a helicopter to our location for a quick getaway? Tonight looks to be a bust, but we'll be able to track the fuckers down tomorrow."

"Shit." Banks yelled something he couldn't make out before she returned to the line. "Okay, the chopper's scrambled. You guys stay alive long enough for it to get there, understood? Keep the line open so we can continue to track your location."

"Gotcha," he said. "It looks like we'll have a ride out of here, boys."

"Not a second too soon." Teller yanked his pistol clear and held his assault rifle on his hip to have two lines of fire. "I'd say our creatures are closing in."

"Do you think they understood that we called for help?" Jensen asked as he looked around nervously.

"Don't be ridiculous," Clarke said and tried to convince himself that he was being ridiculous too for thinking the same thing. The growling drew closer, to the point where they could see the tall grass bend and displace, although it hadn't yet revealed the mutants themselves. Ryan was right, though. Something was approaching steadily and whether or not the creatures understood the sat phone and the call they had made, it seemed attack was imminent.

"Fuck." He grunted when a heavy shape struck him in the chest and hurled him back. He couldn't see much as his assailant was shrouded by the long grass. Panic surged but he fought it back and focused on the violent movement within the vegetation and pulled the trigger. He fired blindly in the hopes that he would hit something—anything—but the only visible results were tufts of dirt and grass kicked up as each round missed.

His attacker moved again and a claw dug into his shoulder and dragged him a few paces. He twisted frantically and the creature released him and rushed past. His gaze found Teller, who hadn't yet seen the blurred approach as he was fighting something else. It was impossible to see clearly with the speed of the movement as the beast suddenly found purchase in his teammate's back. His brain struggled to take the image in, let alone understand it, and he desperately wanted to look away. A violent flurry of muscled limbs, heavy paws, and fangs was all he could really make out.

Powerful jaws snapped around Ryan's head. The sickening crunch was strangely much louder than the cacophony of snarls and growls as the fedora disappeared inside the mouth before the man's head was severed completely.

"Oh, God," Clarke whispered and turned away. The rhythmic thump-thump of the chopper in the distance seemed lifetimes away.

He knew he should fight, but what was hard to see was equally hard to shoot. Hell, he couldn't even tell if they'd hit any of them at all, and all three of them had opened the engagement with a steady stream of fire from the beginning.

Jensen continued to shoot, yelled something incoherent, and fired again. Even in the middle of combat, the guy wouldn't stop yammering. There was something tragically reassuring in the fact that even looking death in the eye couldn't curb the habit.

"Fuck!" the younger man shouted finally and fell to his knees. His legs—what was left of them—had been mangled and practically shredded.

"Goddamn it," Clarke bellowed and opened fire into the surge of movement around his teammate. A shriek and a splash of blood on the grass beside Jensen confirmed a hit, although he had no idea how much damage he'd caused. He raced forward and kicked furiously to drive the attackers away from the man, then hauled him up.

The smaller man was heavier than he looked, and his lower limbs were all but useless, but Clarke was still able to start moving him. They appeared to have a moment's grace as if the creatures were falling back, most likely to regroup after one of their numbers had either died or taken a bullet or two.

"I won't make it, man," Jensen said and gestured at his legs. "Not...it's a done deal. Leave me and let me hold them off so you can get to the chopper."

"Give it up. Don't think I'll drop your ass, no matter how annoying it is," he retorted, although he struggled under the weight and tried to keep one weapon aimed and ready. He could still hear the creatures, although he doubted he would be able to see them. It was uncanny how they seemed to be able to blend into their surroundings almost to the point of invisibility.

Maybe he could track them by sound. He already knew they bled, and if they could bleed, he could kill them.

He looked skyward and located the chopper as it approached their position on the shortest possible trajectory.

"You have to stay alive to annoy me and many others for a long fucking time, do you hear me?" Clarke told Jensen in an attempt to keep him awake. "Now do something useful with your life and try to help me fight these fuckers off. If I have to do it alone, I swear to God, I will take your money. Understood?"

"Yeah... Yeah, man," the man said and fumbled to draw his pistol. He aimed toward the source of the noises that indicated that the monsters had resumed their advance.

"Only a little longer," he said and managed to keep his wounded teammate upright only through his sheer determination.

"We are approaching the target now," the pilot said through

the radio. "I have a visual on the hunters…setting down now for evac. Standby."

Niki stared down at the radio in her hands and scowled when she registered the ticking in her chest and fingers as she waited for word that her people hadn't died out in the field. She knew their involvement was her responsibility, and damned if she would put them in a situation where they weren't able to get help when they needed it.

"Coming down now… We have a visual—what was that?"

"What was what?" she asked and pressed the button to connect her to the line.

"We're under attack—keep those weapons firing," the pilot said and sounded calm and in control. "Hunters boarding the helicopter now… One wounded. Only two of them."

"Where's the third?" she asked.

"Teller's dead," Clarke called through his connection. "Get us the fuck out of here before they attack in numbers. Don't you fucking die on me, asshole!"

The asshole in question could only be Jensen but nothing could be heard from the talkative hunter, which was alarming in and of itself. Still, a paramedic had joined the rescue flight so she could only hope the man's life was being saved while the chopper rose again. The rotors thumped comfortingly as the aircraft elevated and increased speed.

"What the hell is that?" the co-pilot asked and sounded far less calm than his teammate had.

"A…cloud?" the pilot replied but sounded confused. "Oh, shit!"

Niki winced when the distinctive sound of shattered glass was heard, followed by a sharp screech that hurt her ears. Alarms blared inside the helicopter and voices yelled obscenities beneath the shrilled alerts.

A second later, utter silence replaced the cacophony.

The other men in the tent turned to her as if to ask what her next move would be.

There was really only one. Those men out there were dead, that much was frighteningly clear. If there was anything or anyone to avenge them, it wouldn't be found in this tent.

"Damn those bureaucrats and their fucking penny-pinching, parsimonious assholes!" She hissed a sharp breath and tapped her computer to open a line to Desk. "They didn't want to pay the bill to get this done right. Now, they get to pay the death benefits and get another fucking larger bill. I will approve anything McFadden asks for and shove the invoice so far up their asses they will see the number of zeros on it from the back of their eyeballs."

The line connected.

"Desk, get me McFadden," Niki said into the headset. "And none of this bullshit about driving all the way here. This is an emergency, so tell him to get his ass to Nellis Air Force Base and not give you any shit about it either."

"I'm already on it, Niki," Desk replied.

CHAPTER FIFTEEN

"So, what do you say?" Bobby asked as Taylor climbed out of the mech. "Do you have any complaints?"

He stretched to release a kink in his back. "Not really. Like I said, we do good work. You need to stop worrying about something happening."

"Well, nothing ever does happen until it happens," the mechanic pointed out. "But you're right, we do good work."

Vickie rolled her office chair closer to the two. "When do I get to ride it around? I bet you I could put in some sweet, sweet moves too and show off how agile these things can really be."

"What day is it today?" Taylor asked with a glance at the other man.

"Uh...Thursday?"

"Oh, so never," he replied with a firm nod. "Never times infinity. When you count down from that, the next Wednesday...still no."

"Ugh, you're an asshole." She turned to the desk, muttering something under her breath.

"Believe you me that I'm doing this for your own protection," he told her and scratched his beard idly. "But anyway, the suit's ready to be shipped out and that's supposed to happen tomorrow. Now, we can get started on the next one or we can call it a day an hour and a half early."

Vickie's head raised quickly. "Oh, that doesn't sound too bad. Maybe I misjudged you."

"Let's not reassess our judgments yet, little bean." He laughed. "Remember what we said we'd do when we got off work today."

"Oh…right," she grumbled and looked a good deal less enthusiastic.

"Yes, I'm still the asshole." He grinned but paused when his phone rang again. "People have bugged me constantly today. I swear to God…"

When he pulled the device out his pocket, however, he recognized the number of his caller and his foul mood shifted a little.

"Tanya," he said cheerfully. "It's nice to hear from you again. How's it hanging? Metaphorically speaking, of course."

Bobby scowled and mouthed "Tanya," and Vickie shrugged in response.

"Taylor, nice to hear from you again," the huntress replied. "It's good to know Banks hasn't given you that one job you don't walk away from yet."

"It's only a matter of time, you know. I have no intention of dying of old age. That said, how can I help you? Last I heard, you were heading off to check on that kid of yours."

"Well, it turns out I'm not as important in his life as I thought I was and a couple of days visiting was the limit of my welcome," Tanya explained. "I came back to Vegas. So, Taylor, do you mind if we meet for a late lunch or something? I need to talk to you. It's nothing too urgent, but still, if you're in the mood for food, I could do with a conversation with a redheaded giant."

"Uh, sure," he said. "Do you know Il Fornaio? At New York, New York?"

"Oh, for the love of—seriously?" Vickie shouted.

Taylor covered the phone. "I've never been there for the lunch menu."

She merely rolled her eyes.

"I'm sure I can find it," Tanya replied. "See you there in…shall we say twenty?"

"See you then." He hung up and turned to Bobby. "So, if you guys want to go ahead and start at the gun range, I'll meet you there. Do you mind locking up for me, Bungees?"

"No problem, boss," the man said. "Are you looking to get lucky twice? Because I don't think we can stay at the range that long."

He smirked. "It's a business lunch, I think. She's one of Banks' other hunters and most definitely not my type. And I'm certainly not hers so I shouldn't be longer than an hour. If you guys need to head off early to freshen up for your dates, drop me a message."

"Will do," Bobby said. "You have fun on your date."

"You can go ahead and bite me."

"Kinky."

"Do you come here often?"

Taylor looked up as Tanya approached and slid into the seat across from him in the booth.

He nodded. "I do but not for lunch, though. Their breakfast is to die for, and that's why I usually come. That and the manager is a great guy."

"So, you're not a fan of the lunch manager?" she asked.

"I don't know—never met him." He shrugged. "If he's anything like the breakfast manager, though, I'm sure we'll get along famously."

A waitress came over to them with a welcoming smile and a tablet in hand. "Can I take your orders?"

"Sure." He checked the menu quickly. "I'll have this Piadina Arrotolata con Pollo—although I know for a fact that I haven't pronounced that right—with the side of fries and a beer if you don't mind."

"And I'll have the Linguine Mare Chiaro, with the same beer he ordered," Tanya said quickly without even having to check the menu.

"Coming right up," the waitress replied, noted their orders, and returned to the bar to get their drinks.

Taylor studied the woman across from him, who smiled cheekily. "I might have come here once or twice in the past, although I do have to say I have a preference for their lunch menu."

He chuckled and shrugged. "Well, given how good their breakfast is, I wouldn't hold liking the lunch against anyone."

The waitress returned with their beers, left them on the table, and seemed to sense that they needed to talk and beat a hasty retreat.

"So, why don't you go ahead and talk about this not urgent issue you wanted to discuss," Taylor prompted. "I don't want to press you on your personal problems, and I'll be damned before I get in the middle of family problems that aren't my own. Hell, I steered clear of my own family's problems."

"Now why don't I have any difficulty believing that?" Tanya asked and sipped her beer.

"Because you've met me, that's why," he said. "So, what are you doing in Vegas? Not that you're not allowed to make a trip here or anything. Folks love them some games of chance, after all, even if it is smack-dab right in the middle of the desert."

"Well, I'm not one for gambling anyway," she responded. "I'm actually looking for a job."

He opened his mouth to reply but was cut short when their food arrived. It did smell fantastic, although he knew he had to pay attention to something else first.

"Last I heard, you already had a job," he said once the waitress retreated again. "You know, hunting things and killing them dead. The kind of stuff we were doing when we met."

"I'm not sure if you've heard, but word on the grapevine today is that people in our particular line of work have begun to drop like flies," she explained. "I'm not sure I'm really at liberty to discuss it, but the short and nasty is that I'm done with Banks' task force and I'm looking for gainful employment. I heard you were hiring."

"How?"

"Oh, you know…the grapevine."

Taylor leaned forward. "Banks told you, didn't she?"

She nodded.

He made a face. "I'm not sure how, but she always knows what I need and when I need people to work for me, but yeah. I do happen to need additional hands on deck for the shop. Nothing is really specific right now and it's actually waiting on other matters to resolve themselves."

"I don't mean to pry, but what kinds of matters?"

Taylor gestured vaguely with his fork. "Nothing really important. I took a loan out for the business, and while it's going well, it's not exactly gangbusters. There's only so much work three people can handle, you know?"

"What do you guys do, exactly?" Tanya asked, and took a mouthful from her linguine. "Banks said that you worked as mechanics, but I had a feeling you guys didn't exactly fix cars."

"What did you think we did?"

"I have no idea but I assumed that someone like you getting your hands on a combat mech like the one you used in LA had something to do with it." She spoke around the food in her mouth.

He nodded. "Yeah, we fix mechs for a much lower price than what the folks in the Zoo usually have to pay. It was a business idea I got while I was there, talking to the mercs who complained about how us grunts made less money than them, but at least didn't have to cover the extortionate rates that had to pay to repair their mechs. I realized that it was true and mostly because there's no one else who will help them. After a few calculations, I realized that factoring in pieces, manhours and even shipping, I could undercut their prices."

"Wait, wouldn't corporations take it the wrong way if you undercut their prices?" she asked.

"Sure, if we took away a sizeable chunk of their business," he agreed. "We don't, though. They get most of their money from repairing the mechs the military use and charging the taxpayers an arm and a leg. They don't care if we handle the business from the mercs. In fact, I think they appreciate us taking the complaints away since it means they can continue to overcharge everyone else."

"Wow." Tanya grunted in surprise. "You actually thought this through."

He laughed. "I suppose I should be insulted by how many people say that like it's a surprise that I would actually think a business through before starting it. But I guess I should be happy that they underestimate me so consistently. It makes it more gratifying when I exceed their low expectations."

"I don't know, people figure a big, bulky dude like you doesn't need to use his brains that often," she said. "Do you plan to eat your food, by the way? This is some good shit."

Taylor looked at his plate of fries and a flatbread with a chicken breast, mushrooms, and a mess of other veggies. "Honestly, I thought piadina was some kind of pasta." He shrugged and took a mouthful. His unimpressed look faded as he chewed and quickly took a few more. "Damned if that isn't some good grub."

"Right?" Tanya said. "You really should have looked beyond their breakfast menu and might even want to try the dinner menu too."

"Maybe, but it seems like it would be better to stick to what I'm good at," he replied, his mouth full. "Breakfast foods are my weakness. Besides, I have the feeling this place is much fancier and drunker at night, and that's not really my scene. I like to get my drunk on among friends in a quieter place, not among dumbasses drinking off a losing streak at the tables."

She nodded. "I get that. But you can't deny that the food is good all around."

"I can't deny that, damn right." He swallowed quickly, sipped his beer, and looked at her once again. "So, what do you know about the kind of work that goes into taking apart and fixing mechs?"

Tanya shook her head. "Not a damn thing. I know how to repair my own car and change a tire, though."

He smirked. "You know, why doesn't that surprise me?"

"Because you've met me?"

"I had a feeling you'd say that." He chuckled. "There is a difference between fixing cars and fixing mechs, though. The tech that goes into cars these days is advanced enough, but what they've put into combat mechs is a whole new level. You know how they say necessity is the mother of all invention, and believe you me, we necessitated the hell out of what they've come up with lately."

She nodded. "I'll be out of my element, I get it. Does that mean that I don't get the job?"

"I didn't say that." A short pause ensued while they both focused on their meals.

"You said there were things that were keeping you from taking on any new help?" Tanya said, sipped her beer, and set her glass down.

"Oh, right, so I did. Yeah, it's actually a business issue. I mentioned borrowing money, and it's been a quarter of a year since I took the loan out, so I need to have all my ducks in a row and all the paperwork in order. You know, spending, income, projected income, market research, yadda, yadda, yadda. I have all that ready for a meeting next week and I don't think I can take on any new help before then. Once they approve everything, I can do what they call organic growth— hiring, taking on new clients, that kind of thing. I also need to promote my intern and give my lead mechanic a raise, which leaves me without low-paid help to keep the place running."

She narrowed her eyes at him but simply waited for him to continue.

"I never said it would be a great job," Taylor reminded her. "Not at first, anyway. The salary will be fair, but you have a lot to learn and we have to teach you. Come the next quarter, though, we'll look at your progress and you'll be compensated accordingly. You don't have to take my word for it. Talk to my other two employees and ask them for their opinions. I'll admit, I'm not the best of bosses, but I try to be fair."

She sighed and shook her head. "Look, I'd like to say I'm in a position to negotiate with you but honestly, I need the job and I need it bad. So, if you have the opening, I'll be happy to at least have an interview. I'll take a lower salary and I'm a quick learner."

"It won't only be up to me, though," Taylor said. "The people who work with me are basically my business part-ners—although not on paper, obviously—so they'll need to give you the okay too. But knowing them like I do, it shouldn't be a problem. Bobby and Vickie are good people, and my endorsement will go a long way to recommend you to them."

"You'd do that for me?"

Taylor smiled, finished his food, and leaned back in his seat. "We were in battle together. No matter for how long, that means something to a guy like me. Sentimental, that's me. Anyway, I like to think of myself as a decent enough judge of character, and I judge you a decent enough person. We can do business. The meeting is next Wednesday at ten in the morning. When I get the word from them, I'll give you a call. Deal?"

He extended his hand across the table to her, and after a moment of thought, she smiled and shook it firmly.

"Deal."

CHAPTER SIXTEEN

"I don't get why we have to take one of Tay-Tay's booty calls seriously," Vickie said as she went through the motions of taking the pistol Taylor had handed her apart and put it together again. "Obviously, I get that she needs a job. Everyone does these days with this economy and I sympathize, but giving her a job because she gives you some on the side is a little crude and closer to prostitution than I'm comfortable with."

"Okay, first of all—and we've already covered this—I'm not sleeping with Tanya," Taylor said and handed her the empty magazine to put into the pistol once it was assembled again. "I met her when we worked together on that job in LA. We hit it off and she's a good enough monster-hunter, but we parted ways after that."

"And this qualifies her to work on mechs how, exactly?" Bobby asked.

"She's about as qualified as Vickie was when she started."

"Hey!" she shouted. "I was incredibly qualified and a genius besides. Is this Tanya a genius?"

"Not everyone can be as smart as you, Vickie," he retorted.

"And don't you forget it."

He laughed. "My point is, you'll be upgraded to sales and maybe later to marketing, Bobby will get a raise. We need someone to take on the role of grease monkey, and if she's willing to learn, that's about as good as we can ask for. She's trustworthy and needs work. That's basically all I'm looking for in employees at this point."

Bobby folded his arms and regarded him sternly. "Are the two of you sleeping together?"

"Nope."

"Do you plan to sleep with her in the future?"

"Not a chance."

"Is she hot?"

Taylor looked up from inspecting Vickie's work. "She's fairly hot, yeah."

"Do you mind if I make a pass then?" the man asked.

"Don't you have a date tonight?" he countered.

"I'm merely keeping my options open."

"You two are gross," Vickie snapped acerbically.

"Says the girl who also has a date tonight," Taylor reminded her and scowled at the pistol. "Speaking of gross, this is some terrible work. You'd get a backfire in five rounds or less."

He put it on the table, took the weapon apart again quickly, and reassembled it in the correct order. In under a minute and a half, he completed the process by pushing seventeen rounds into the magazine before he slapped it into place.

"I don't see any difference from how I did it," Vickie said.

"You will," he grumbled. "Now aim the weapon."

She did, and he stepped behind her and adjusted her stance. He almost expected her to make some kind of comment about keeping his hands off the goods, but nothing was said.

"Keep your shoulders set and your arms stiff, but relax the rest of your body," he said when she remained silent. "I chose this one because it has the least amount of kick in the weapons I could find, but it'll still have a kick. Keep your eyes focused on the front sights and leave the target a blur that you can still see. Always aim for center-mass, which means the largest target you can identify."

"How the hell am I supposed to remember all this in a combat situation?" Vickie asked as she tried to follow all his instructions.

"You're not supposed to remember it," Taylor said, took a step back, and put her earbuds in, followed quickly by his own. "It's supposed to be practiced about fifty thousand times until it comes naturally to you. Don't worry. No one gets it on the first attempt."

She nodded, grasped her weapon a little tighter, and pulled the trigger repeatedly until the magazine clicked empty.

"Oh—another thing, although less important, trying to keep track of the bullets you use makes it quicker to reload." He took the weapon from her and removed the empty mag. "Like I said, it's not really that important but it's a cool trick."

They recalled the target from down the range for inspection. Vickie scowled when she saw that only five of the rounds had actually hit the target and only three found center mass.

"Like I said, no one gets it right the first time," Taylor encouraged her.

She sighed. "Yeah, but I wanted to anyway. Should we try again?"

"I think that's enough target practice for the day," he said. "I'm fairly sure folks here at Tropicana's Gun Store don't appreciate us hogging their range for too long. Besides, you two have dates to get to, right?"

"Correctamundo," Vickie said. "I was having so much fun that I almost forgot I have a date. With a cute college guy. Did I mention that?"

"You might have," he said. "I hope you have a great time."

"Okay, I'm headed out," she said and waved to Bobby as well. "See you guys back at the shop?"

"Have fun, kiddo," the mechanic responded. "I think I'll head out too."

They all exited to the parking lot and took their own cars to head to their homes. Taylor paused when his phone rang in his pocket. Bobby glanced back, a questioning look on his face, and he waved him off when he recognized the familiar string of unidentifiable numbers.

"Desk, it's been a while," he said. "Here I was, thinking you guys had enough of me to last at least a couple of months."

"Taylor, it's nice to talk to you again," Desk said in her

comforting almost monotone voice. "I've been instructed to give you a call by Banks. There's a job for you."

He chuckled. "Well, it's about damn time if you ask me. Okay, it's not really the sane thing to say, but there comes a time when a guy aches for another opportunity for action."

"I thought I would give you a quick heads-up," Desk continued. "This isn't what you might call your average job. People have died already."

"People die on every job."

"Hunters, Taylor," she said, her voice still virtually expressionless. "Hunters died on this job. Banks needed to call another team in—something about budgetary constraints, as I understand it, so she couldn't use you immediately. The team she brought in was killed, along with military personnel, so she's been given a blank check to handle it, which means you."

"I can't decide if I'm supposed to be insulted or complimented," Taylor grumbled.

Desk sighed. "Wait until you hear the whole story. This is an emergency situation, so no one will wait for you to drive to Wyoming. People will arrive shortly to help you pack your suit and drive you out to where you'll have a ride waiting to get here quickly. And don't give them any sass—Banks' orders."

Taylor nodded. "Understood."

"Oh, and don't bring your hybrid suit. This is definitely way out of its league."

He slid into Maddie, started the engine, and accelerated quickly to return to the strip mall. A large truck waited in front with a small group of men whose very postures screamed military, even if they weren't in uniform.

"I was told to expect you boys," he said. "Come around back. My stuff's in the garage."

The man who was clearly the CO of the group gestured for his team to move the vehicle to where they could load it.

"You guys are working official business, right?" he asked and the man nodded as they followed the truck at a brisk pace. "Why aren't you wearing your uniforms?"

"We were informed there is an unsavory element in this part of town, sir," the CO replied as Taylor opened the garage. "We intended to attract as little attention as possible. The truck couldn't be helped, though."

"I appreciate that," he said. "And stow the sir crap—sergeant, I assume?"

The man nodded.

"It's been a while since I've worn my uniform," Taylor explained, "and I didn't like being called that even when I did."

"If you say so."

Taylor helped them to drag the crate with his suit to the vehicle, followed by the rest of his supplies in another. There wasn't a huge load, and while he didn't expect to need much in the way of clothes and supplies since he didn't have to drive, there were still things he considered necessary that others might not. Thereafter, he made a few arrangements with regard to the security of the shop.

They were on the move in less than fifteen minutes and out of the city in under a half-hour.

"So, will you boys tell me where we're headed?" he asked and glanced at the young military men seated around him. "Or will we play twenty questions?"

"We're heading to Nellis Air Force Base," the sergeant replied.

"No kidding?" Taylor laughed. "We're going to Area fucking Fifty-One?"

"Well, near there, anyway," the man hedged. "There'll be an aircraft waiting to pick you up and take you to where you need to go."

Instinctively, he grasped the side of his seat a little tighter. He had assumed this would likely involve flying of some kind but that didn't mean that he had to like it.

"Are you okay there?" the sergeant asked, noting his reaction.

"I'm simply not a huge fan of flying, is all," he replied. "I have a handle on it, though."

"I've read your record—what's not been redacted, anyway," the sergeant continued. "You've gone into the Zoo, right? I assume you had to fly around that area of the world."

Taylor smirked. "Well, you're not wrong. There's one way to get over a deathly fear of flying, though, and that's to get yelled at by a drill sergeant until you get your ass on the helicopter and know your platoon will do push-ups all morning if you puke inside. That happens time after time and eventually, you get the hang of it. The fear's still there, of course. There's not much you can do to help that, but there comes a time in a man's life when he learns to control his fears to the point of being able to do what he has to when he has to."

"I can respect that." The sergeant chuckled. "I can't say I've met many Marines who hate flying, though."

"Well, I discovered I'm not a big fan of being out at sea

either," he said. "You go airborne when doing the special forces training in the army and...well, the Air Force is obviously a no-go, so Marines felt like the best bet to me."

The man smirked but said no more.

The sun had already begun to set by the time they pulled into base. There were security checks everywhere, but they rushed through them in record time and finally stopped beside a helicopter. The men exited the truck quickly and loaded his suit and supplies into the aircraft.

"Is something wrong?" the sergeant asked when Taylor hesitated.

"There's only one thing worse than flying in a plane and that's flying in a chopper," he said and turned to face the man. "I guess that must be hilarious to you Air Force guys, right? Someone who's afraid of flying?"

"Ordinarily, yes," he replied and approached the helicopter. "But I happen to know about what you'll go up against and what you have already faced in the past—the kinds of things that terrify me. With that in mind, I have to say we might be on even ground. The folks in charge of ferrying you there also know, and I have a feeling they'll be on their best behavior."

"I appreciate that, Sarge." He shook the man's hand.

"Good luck out there, McFadden."

CHAPTER SEVENTEEN

Fortunately, beautification wasn't something that she did often. For one thing, it felt unnatural, but even she could concede that certain situations called for a little more effort in that department. She wasn't one to skimp on anything when it came down to it.

Still, she had very little to work with. While she really appreciated Taylor giving her a place to stay, the guy didn't have much in the way of facilities, so it wasn't like she could store extra toiletries anywhere. She more or less lived out of the suitcase she had arrived with.

At least the Wi-Fi was great and so was the security, but she could probably find something similar in one of the student living facilities. Well, at least the Wi-Fi. She would have to improve the security herself.

Things being what they were, she would have to settle for the jeans, chains, and black rock band shirt and plat-form boots and hope like hell that her date liked the look of someone out of a nineties *Hot Topic* magazine. Seriously, who didn't like that look?

This reaction was, of course, entirely crazy. It surprised her a little too as she'd never have thought this was something she could see herself doing, but she did want to make a good impression. This was a good opportunity to do that but she honestly wasn't sure how it would work out.

"I hate this." She hissed her irritation and shook her head. "Seriously, I hate it. Why am I stressing out? I'm a genius, and geniuses are sexy. And if the guy is intimidated by how I look or how smart I am, that's his problem right?"

Great, she was talking to herself now. Fucking awesome.

Vickie retrieved her purse when she finally accepted she was as ready as she would ever be and headed down to the garage.

She paused on the stairs when she heard movement in the working area. When Taylor and Bobby weren't around, she received all the alerts for the security. Taylor had set the system up and it worked well, but she had been distracted to the point where she might have missed a few of the warnings. Fortunately, she'd tweaked the system after the last attack. A hacker like her had all kinds of tricks she could implement that her two colleagues probably wouldn't even notice if she didn't point them out. While the men had focused their attention on the obvious, she'd concentrated on a few more subtle layers that provided a deeper level of security she felt was critical. For one thing, she needed to know if they'd been hacked and it had astonished her that Taylor hadn't considered that.

Firewalls and ghost hard drive traps took care of that. She would receive the alerts if and when an intrusion was attempted and forewarned was forearmed. Better still, she'd added a few honey pots here and there, some of them so obvious that they would simply be ignored. It was some of her better work, she thought smugly. Not many people could make the absence of the trap the actual trap, and any hackers would stumble around avoiding the obvious with over-confidence and set themselves up for discovery.

It was, in fact, genius. Of course, it only worked if one actually checked the warnings. Someone was already in the building and she was none the wiser.

"Shit." She muttered irritably under her breath, yanked her phone out of her purse, and checked the security alerts.

Nothing displayed and more importantly, she was no longer in control of the system. Bobby was on the premises, apparently, despite the fact that they'd parted ways a couple of hours before.

She moved on to the garage, still a little anxious about what she would find there, but the big mechanic was alone as he inspected the mechs. He wasn't dressed in his usual work attire and instead, wore what looked like a casual-chic look he somehow rocked.

He appeared to be working, taking a few of the new arrivals apart to inspect them for damages.

Vickie stepped out from where she had lingered. "Hey, Bobby. What the hell are you doing here?"

"Working. What the hell does it look like?" he countered and scowled at her as she approached.

"Allow me to rephrase the question, then." She smirked. "Why the hell are you working when it's after-hours and you look like you're dressed to go to the prom?"

"Well, I got all decked out but I still had a couple of hours to kill, so I came here to see if I could keep myself busy," the large man said and shook his head as he settled into a nearby chair. "If the truth be told, I'm a little uncomfortable with all this dating nonsense. When Taylor talked me into it, nothing seemed complicated, but now that it's here and staring me in the face, I'm a little less confident in my abilities."

Vickie dropped into the seat across from him and leaned forward with her elbows on her knees. "I'll be honest, I have a couple of heebie-jeebies myself. I know I come off as the kind of confident kickass chick everyone else wants to be but—shocker—I have feelings of anxiety sometimes."

The mechanic smiled encouragingly. "I'm not sure why. You look great."

"Don't fall in love with me, Bungees," she warned playfully. "I don't need that kind of workplace awkwardness."

He laughed. "Yeah, well, don't flatter yourself, tiny one. You don't look that great. You look the kind of great that would have college kids all over you is what I mean."

"Oh, well, mission accomplished, then," she replied with a small smile, stood, and twirled on her platform boots. "So, how long has it been since you dated?"

His shrug was a little sheepish. "I'll be honest, I was never much of a dating kind of guy. I mostly had the friends with benefits kind of thing and signed up for military duty early. When you're out there, playing the games civilized people play loses its magic, so it became less about the emotional connection and simply about the sex. And when it came right down to it once I got back, I wasn't ready. Now that I am, I'm not sure how to go about it."

"Here's a little tip," she said and placed a hand on his

shoulder. "Go out there and pretend you're talking to an actual, real person but not a date. Treat her like you would anyone else. Talk, joke, have fun, and if the two of you have enough fun, you can decide to do what normal people do when they like to spend time together—chill if you know what I mean."

"I vaguely recall," Bobby said but shook his head. "And you might be right. I'm overthinking this—and come to think of it, so are you."

"Well, yeah, but it's easier for me to point out that you're overthinking things and not worry about my own problems," Vickie grumbled. "Anyway, are you good? Because I plan to be unavailable for a little while after this, so you won't be able to call me and ask for advice if you fuck up."

"I understand," Bobby said, pushed up from his seat, and grinned. "This guy won't know what hit him." He patted her encouragingly on the back.

It was supposed to be a gentle, affirming gesture, but the power behind it was enough to make her stagger some-what. Vickie still grinned at him, moved in close to wrap her arms around him, and tried to squeeze. There wasn't much of an effect, but it was the effort that counted, right?

"Go get 'em, kid." Bobby ruffled her short hair and she headed to her new car.

It wasn't so much that she felt insecure, of course, but like him, this wasn't her world. When she was in her comfort zone, she was the epitome of cool and collected. Out there dating, trying to see if a cute guy liked being around her enough for another date was entirely different.

But like her colleague had said, she would knock him dead. Hopefully not literally, but it was apt.

The venue Myles had selected for their date didn't look too shabby. It was a local burger joint, the kind that put more effort into what they made than the fast food places, and they made up for the fact that they would be associated with those by creating one hell of a sixties diner vibe.

"It feels like I walked into a freaking pulp fiction reenactment," she said softly as someone dressed like Marilyn Monroe walked over to her.

"Hi there, honey," the woman said. "Walk-in or reservation?"

"I think there's a reservation," Vickie said. "Under Myles Hendricks? Great work on the Marilyn voice, by the way. You really nail it."

"I appreciate it, darling," the waitress said with a small but genuine smile and checked the reservation registry. "I have a Hendricks reservation here for two."

"I'm the plus one."

Marilyn nodded. "Do you have a preference for a place to sit? We have us a slow night tonight, so you can choose."

"Well, in one of the car booths should be fun," she replied.

"Right this way, honey, and I'll let you know when your date gets here."

The woman guided her to what looked like an actual old-fashioned Cadillac that had been converted into a snug yet spacious booth that she slipped into.

"I guess you guys get the order for the five-dollar milkshake all the time, right?" she asked.

The waitress laughed. "Yeah, we do. I never really got

that, but the patrons get a real kick out of it, especially when their friends give them a hard time when they order it."

"It's from a movie," Vickie explained. "A really good movie, mind you. Honestly, I would have thought they would tell you guys you had to watch it if you wanted to work here, but I guess the similarities aren't really the intention."

"I guess not," Marilyn said. "Is there anything I can get for you while you wait?"

She thought about it for a moment. "I'll have a Coke if that's okay."

"Coming right up, honey."

The server headed to the bar as Myles stepped through the entrance. He appeared to have dressed up as well. Although he still wore a pair of jeans, he had chosen a dress shirt and shoes and what looked like a tweed jacket—like he was trying to pull himself off as being a professor but about ten or fifteen years too soon.

He saw her immediately, waved, and indicated to the Elvis waiter who greeted him that someone was waiting for him.

"Hey there, Vickie," he said when he reached the booth.

"Hey, Myles," she replied, leaned in, and gave him an awkward hug. "Sorry, I got here a little early, and I have to say, it looks like fun."

"I know, it looks straight out of—"

"Pulp fiction, yeah, although from what I heard from the waitress, it doesn't seem like that was intentional," she said. "Maybe they simply wanted a bona fide sixties diner and lucked into a demographic of cinephiles."

Marilyn returned with the Coke and placed it on the table. "And what can I get you?" she asked Myles.

"I'll have the five-dollar shake and a menu please," he responded.

"Coming right up," she replied and winked at Vickie before she headed to the bar.

"Anyway, how's your week been?" he asked and leaned on the table between them.

"Oh…you know, getting used to splitting my time between work and studying," she said and took a sip of her Coke. "I think I'm doing it well enough. My boss gives me a fair amount of leeway."

"That sounds great. Have you thought about moving onto the school campus?"

She ran her fingers through her short hair. " I've considered it but I live in the same place where I work, so it'll be six of one, half a dozen of the other as far as travel is concerned. Still, I've thought about it."

"Let me know if you decide to move closer to campus. I'd like to show you around." Myles nodded as his milkshake and their menus arrived.

"That would be nice." She smiled her thanks at the waitress before she opened her menu up. "It's not like I'm a stranger to campus life, though. I dropped out of my first stint in college, so I think some of the experience transferred."

"What made you want to come back?"

Vickie thought about it for a moment. "Honestly, a friend of mine pushed me into it. He said I'll want options later on in life, and those will be made a little easier if I have a degree and maybe a couple of letters behind my name."

"So, this friend of yours," he said. "Is he a good friend? Like a boyfriend?"

"What?" she snapped. "No, nothing like that."

He nodded. "Because it would be okay if he was. What I mean is, I'm not the kind of guy to get jealous. Well, ordinarily I would be, but in this case...well, I actually expected something far less vanilla and more like an open relationship. So again, I'd be okay with that."

She narrowed her eyes at him and took a moment to draw a deep breath and think her next few words through. Despite her instinctive response, she wanted to give him the benefit of the doubt. To simply assume what he was talking about was something gross wouldn't allow her to do that.

Still, he would need to explain himself, and from the way his eyes widened with every passing second, he knew it too.

Good. That meant he would consider his next few words very carefully.

Finally, Vickie had calmed herself enough to speak. "What?"

He didn't say anything immediately but once he realized that the ball was in his court, he nodded. "So, uh, that guy you mentioned...uh, isn't your boyfriend?"

"No, he's actually my boss."

"Oh, well, that changes things."

"How?"

He realized he'd put his foot in his mouth again. "Okay, do you have a boyfriend?"

"No, that's why I'm out on a date with you," Vickie replied. "Why did you assume I had a boyfriend and was willing to date other guys? And you expected something less vanilla and more like an open relationship."

"I think if I say anything more, it'll only dig me deeper into this hole I'm in," he admitted, openly uncomfortable now.

"I'm afraid that ship has sailed, friend of mine," Vickie said.

"It's only…well, with everything else about you being so…exotic, I was open to the possibility that there would be more about you that was exotic too," he continued and spoke slowly. "I'm not really used to anything that isn't strictly vanilla, but I was open to it."

She took another deep breath and studied her Coke for a moment before she looked him dead in the eye. "Is that the only reason you asked to go out with me, Myles? Because I looked like I would be into some freaky shit?"

"Come on. You have to admit you're not really what comes to mind when people think about girls they want to take home to meet their parents," he said.

Once again, he realized it was a mistake as soon as he said it.

"I'm sorry, that's not what I mean," he added quickly.

She closed her eyes and managed to remain calm. "For the record, moms absolutely adore me, so I'm totally the kind of person you bring home to meet the parents. Well, not my mom. I'm still the black sheep in the family, but my point stands."

"I know. I'm sorry."

"Look, this isn't a great first date," she continued. "We're both really nervous and right now, I need time to cool off before I say something I'll regret. Why don't we forget any of this happened and see where it goes when we meet for classes tomorrow?"

"I'd really like that."

She smiled and finished the last few sips of her Coke. "Okay, I'll see you later. And be a gentleman and let me call you first once I've forgotten all about tonight, cool?"

He nodded. "Yeah, absolutely."

"Fantastic." She stood and walked to the register.

Marilyn had watched everything, although she'd likely not heard any of it. Still, she looked like she knew exactly how it had gone.

"Bad date, I take it?" she asked.

"Actually, not my worst first date ever," Vickie said. "Believe me, you don't want to hear what the gold medal in that category was. Anyway, we'll be friends for now and when the jitters pass, we'll see how it goes. I want to pay for my Coke."

"Sure, honey, but I'm sure he wouldn't mind covering that bill."

She shrugged. "It'd be a dick move to make him pay for anything. Thanks for everything, Marilyn."

The waitress smiled again. "Anytime, gorgeous. You have a nice evening now."

"You too."

It was something of a relief to walk to her car. "Fucking evolution needs to stop cramping my style."

CHAPTER EIGHTEEN

Fucking helicopters were even more exposed to the elements than airplanes were, they felt more dangerous, and they were anything but smooth, even the powerful beast he had been ushered into. As a result, Taylor hated flying in the damn things and he knew for a fact that this flight wouldn't improve how he felt about them.

His personal issues aside, it was a long-ass flight from Nevada to Wyoming, which meant his discomfort would be exacerbated by the long, drawn-out, and unpleasant experience.

"Goddammit, I do hate it when I'm right," he grumbled quietly when he saw the open grasslands that indicated they were at least closer to their destination than when they'd started out.

"What's that?" the pilot asked in his headset.

He shook his head. "Nothing, I'm only...uh, talking to myself."

The man made no response to that and they continued in silence. While they had flown at a fairly high average speed, it didn't look like they had made any real progress. It was impossible, but with the mountains to the west and the grasslands that sprawled everywhere else, it almost seemed that they were standing still. Had it not been for the varied patterns of lines of fencing here and there and the odd homestead, he might actually have believed that to be the case.

The sensation of being trapped forever in an airborne tin can only grew worse when the sun set and he no longer had even the few visual indicators of progress. Hours later, he finally identified what he assumed were the lights from a nearby airfield. Given that it was in the middle of goddamn nowhere, it would probably be a military facility like the one they had departed from.

The helicopter decelerated and the entire craft shuddered gently before they landed lightly and the pilots began their post-flight shut-down.

No one would take off immediately, obviously. The chances were they wouldn't go anywhere until the morning. No visible sign of any city lights around him meant that they were at least a hundred miles from any of the larger population centers.

Taylor grimaced at the sense of isolation but reminded himself that it was a good thing, really. Given what he had been brought in to do, having as few civilians in the area as possible was an absolute plus.

A couple of officers advanced on the chopper with their heads lowered and turned away from the rotors that began to slow as they approached.

He opened the door himself, climbed out, and let them

guide him away from the helicopter where an actual conversation could be held.

"We were told to expect you," one of the men—who wore a captain's bars—shouted over the whine of the aircraft behind him. "Unfortunately, we won't run any operations tonight, so you'll need to find accommodation and we'll be ready to fly you out in the morning."

"I had really hoped to put some work in tonight before I turned in." He looked at the two men, the second of whom was a first lieutenant, and both seemed a little uncertain as to his presence in the area. "You do know why I was called in here, right?"

"It was strictly on a need to know basis," the captain said and his scowl suggested that he didn't like that as he walked his visitor toward a couple of the base's buildings. "The two of us are the only ones who need to know, apparently, but we've not been given more than the barest of details."

"Between you, me, and the first lieutenant here, that sounds like bullshit," Taylor said. "Having anyone here who hasn't dealt with this kind of thing in the past simply puts them in danger. I'm surprised this base hasn't been put on high alert."

"Honestly, they haven't shared what the situation up north is with general personnel, only that there's a situation. That said, they only told us to expect you, not why you were brought in." The lieutenant narrowed his eyes and looked as unimpressed as his superior officer.

The hunter paused and shook his head. This could only be Banks doing her thing—which amounted to her acting in the way that seemed smartest to her but could ultimately come back to bite them in the ass. He couldn't blame her for wanting to keep the situation as confidential as possible, but with that said, he couldn't agree that not having the local armed forces in the loop was a good move. From what he'd heard from Desk, they'd already lost a chopper, so keeping a lid on the situation had to be hell for the men who had to do so.

Unfortunately, that was something he would have to take up with the woman herself when he ran into her.

Wherever the hell she was, he thought belligerently.

"I don't suppose you're at liberty to share why you're here?" the captain asked. He at least tried to contain his curiosity about why he had a civilian on his base.

"Well, suffice it to say that I'm here to kill monsters and chew bubblegum," he said and glanced at each of them again. "I don't suppose either of you gentlemen has any gum on you?"

Both shook their heads.

"Damn, and I forgot to bring some myself," he continued. "Anyway, they call me the Cryptid Assassin—it's a stupid code name, to be honest, but it appears to have stuck—and they only call me in when there are beasts of a less than earthly persuasion that need to be dealt with. It's not the best living to make, honestly, but it's a living."

"Wait, you're the Cryptid Assassin?" the lieutenant asked.

"You sound like you've heard the moniker before," Taylor said as they came to a halt beside a military Humvee. "I guess Banks didn't lie when she said my reputation had spread."

"We only really know that you're former military," the

captain interjected and scowled at his comrade. "Marines, from the look of your tattoos. The word is that you were in the Zoo, which qualifies you to deal with a particular kind of threat on US soil on a freelance basis. Obviously, it now makes sense why you're here."

"That's about the long and the short of it, I guess," he agreed. "I went into the Zoo eighty-three times and I came out every time, obviously enough, and that makes me the most qualified to handle whatever the situation is."

"Well, it sounds like they should have called you in at the beginning instead of waiting for the first round of hunters to come in and do what they could," the captain said and seemed both surprised and a little impressed at Taylor's record.

"Yeah," he said quietly. "They could have saved a few lives. I heard none of them made it out."

The base commander nodded, his expression grim. "Together with a helicopter crew sent in to evac the guys. You'll be briefed on the situation, obviously, although that'll probably only be in the morning. Lieutenant Franklin will drive you to a motel a few miles down the road. It's where most civilians stay when they have business at the base and should be up to your standards."

"I don't know, my standards are fairly high," Taylor admitted. "I am a Marine, after all, and sharing a bunk with other recruits does make you accustomed to a certain standard of living."

The captain laughed and shook his hand firmly. "I look forward to working with you, Mr. McFadden."

"Likewise, Captain…"

"Young. Captain Young."

"Captain Young." He grinned. "Thanks for welcoming me."

He climbed into the shotgun seat beside the lieutenant who started the Humvee and pulled out.

"So, they have a lieutenant doing the driving around here?" Taylor asked as they reached the gates and the barrier was lifted to let them pass. "Don't get me wrong, I'm honored, but weren't there any privates who could have been given the menial task of getting me to a motel?"

"Honestly, that would normally be the case, but things have been hectic around here over the past few days," Franklin admitted. "He and I are officially the only ones in the know, but rumors start and spread in a small base like this, and especially when something out of the ordinary happens. Add the fact that we've lost one chopper and the crew, speculation is rife. The base commander wanted to make sure there's some accountability on everything that happens because orders are to keep this confidential. We don't want any privates to take advantage of an order to drive a visitor to the motel and head to a bar or something to either spread or pick up loose talk. Which means I have the duty of driving our VIPs around for now."

Taylor winced. "That can't be fun. Besides, I wouldn't want to sell myself that high. I'm an IP, at the most."

His companion shrugged and accelerated on the two-lane road. "Well, as long as you help to settle things into their normal routine, I really don't mind. Besides, having the opportunity to leave the base, even if it is only for a quick drive down the road and back, is always welcome."

"Why, Lieutenant, you're not planning a visit to that bar you mentioned, are you?"

The man laughed and shook his head. "Nah. Tempted though I might be, certain standards are expected of me and I'd hate to be a disappointment. No, all I'll do is drop you off and return to the base for some shuteye. We might not be on critical alert yet, but it's grown progressively more intense since the situation up north developed."

"It sounds like the kind of situation most folks wouldn't want around their base," he remarked.

Franklin nodded. "You can say that again, but it's not like we can really avoid it. Word is that we still have no real idea what we're dealing with out there."

"And yet they sent hunters out there already?"

"Three of them were called in," the lieutenant said. "They looked like they really knew what they were doing too—armed and armored as you'd expect from people in their profession. They didn't even have time to bunk somewhere like the motel and went immediately into the field. And before you know it, all hell breaks loose and we're three hunters and a chopper and team down. You seem to be the answer to whatever is happening, although I hope they can provide you with a little more information than anyone else seems to have been given."

Taylor scowled for a moment as the lights of the motel drew closer. He didn't know what to say next. His first instinct was to assure the lieutenant that everything would be all right but he didn't want to lie to the man. Besides, he was in the military and was likely used to dealing with bad news without a need to have it sugar-coated.

"Anyway," he said as they came to a halt outside. "Thanks for the ride, Lieutenant. I'm sure the problems will be resolved soon and things will return to normal."

"That's the hope," the man replied and shook his hand. "You have a good rest. It sounds like you'll need it."

He retrieved his bag and headed toward the reception of the motel. They had left his suit and supplies at the base, which made sense as there was no need to ferry them around when they would simply have to be loaded to fly them out again the next morning. He didn't feel overly comfortable about having a mech worth hundreds of thousands of dollars—not to mention what it was worth in earnings—out of his sight but reminded himself that leaving them it was probably the safest choice. There was no telling what would or wouldn't happen at a motel in the middle of nowhere.

The receptionist and apparent owner of the establishment appeared to be former military himself. Taylor could understand the appeal of dealing with customers who were a known kind of risk, and given that his patrons were likely to trust him too was an added benefit, he assumed. Check-in took only moments and he glanced at his watch as he carried his bag to the room. It was a little past ten at night and he would probably have to be up at the crack of dawn.

"I can deal with six hours sleep," he said as if to convince himself of the fact.

He dropped his bag next to the bed and looked through the pamphlets of nearby places that could be called for food as well as a couple of bars in the area.

It seemed almost unbelievable that enough people actually lived around there to support businesses like that. Then again, with a base nearby, a fair number of folks would be off-duty at all times, obviously enough to keep the local businesses open.

Once he'd made his selection, he dialed the number of the nearest pizza place and ordered a meat lover's with extra cheese as well as a bottle of soda—the kind that wouldn't keep him awake.

Not that he really needed any help sleeping. Like most who had been in the military for an extended period of time, he had learned the skill of being able to fall asleep anywhere at any time.

Waking up was the problem, although he could be shocked into instant alertness if the situation called for it.

Circumstances hadn't required that for a while, though. Maybe he was getting soft.

He had the time to take a quick shower before the pizza arrived. Taylor was sure to give the kid a good tip before he settled onto the chair and ate his dinner. It was no Il Fornaio, of course, but after a long ride which also meant he'd missed his normal dinner time, he was famished. It took a considerable number of calories to maintain a body like his, and there was no way to avoid the necessity to get as many in as quickly as possible.

Most of the pizza was finished before he leaned back in his seat. There was enough for a quick breakfast if he needed it, and he slipped the extra slices into the fridge.

"It's weird how cold pizza is almost better than warm," he mumbled as he wandered to the bathroom to brush his teeth before he settled into the bed.

The room was cleaner than most motels—and hell, most hotels. Not that he really expected anything else. It was run by former military men for men still in the service.

It was a little bare and could be described as spartan, lacked conventional decorations, and the walls were painted white with the carpet a drab gray. Still, Taylor had never been one who needed lavish or even elegant décor anyway. He could appreciate it, though, and in Alex's case, he actually respected her taste.

But with that said, he had no inclination to do any decorating himself. As evidence of this, all one really needed to see was the place he currently called home, where a simple collapsible cot and a desk in an otherwise mostly bare room was all he really needed to be comfortable.

He smiled at the thought, turned the lights off, shifted into a more comfortable position, and let his eyes drift closed.

CHAPTER NINETEEN

Loud banging nearby shattered his mostly dreamless sleep and dragged him into a state of semi-consciousness. He muttered a low curse as he began to register that it wasn't a weird dream where something or someone hammered their fists on a piece of wood.

Unfortunately, this was very definitely a real-world irritation. Someone pounded on his door in a way that seemed weirdly familiar. He resisted the idea that a knock could be considered familiar but in this case, it was. There was only one person who could batter a door with that particular brand of ferocity, and she would simply persist until she received a response.

Taylor checked his watch and scowled when the digital screen confirmed that it was only a few minutes past four in the morning. It meant he'd had about five and a half hours of sleep which wasn't nearly enough, but he accepted that it would have to do.

Of course, he wouldn't pretend that he was happy

about that shit. No, he intended to complain about it as much as possible.

He left the door on the chain but unlocked it and pulled it open the inch or so that allowed him to see who was outside. It also let a chilly gust of wind into his room.

Sure enough, Banks glowered at him through the gap. She looked like she had been up for a while and was no happier about it than he was.

With a pointed scowl, he gestured at the sky behind her, which was still dark.

"It's not light out yet," he muttered. "Come back when it is." With that, he slammed the door.

"Not this shit again," Banks said in a voice pitched to be clearly audible to him. He was well aware that he wouldn't manage any more rest for the night, but the least he could do was make her as miserable as he felt.

Unfortunately, his head threatened to throb when she assaulted the door with her fist again. He gave up on being a pain in the ass for a moment, took the chain off, and yanked the door open to wave her in.

"Welcome to my humble abode," he snarked.

She stepped inside with a heavy bag in her arms and he closed the door behind her. As it clicked shut, she turned to look at him and her eyebrow raised when she noticed he wore a pair of tight shorts and nothing else.

"Do you mind getting dressed?" she snapped. "We have work to do today and we should probably get a head start on it."

"Hey, I'm as ready to start working as you are," he said and instinctively began to make the bed. "This is about as dressed as I would be out in the open at the beach or maybe a pool or something. Feel free to join me. Strip down to bra and panties and I promise you that you'll feel more liberated once you do, and we'll be on equal terms besides. Until then, Puritan Patty, you're the one who barged into my room before the sun even came up and demanded entry by waking everyone in a five-mile radius with your racket. So do us all a favor and get busy making coffee."

She bristled at his tone, but he could tell she was already in something of a hurry and didn't want to waste the time it would take for a petty argument with him over clothes.

Instead, she focused on something else. "I'm not your fucking secretary. Make your own goddamn coffee."

Taylor scowled at her as he finished with the bed. "Yeah, because a fucking secretary wouldn't have shanghaied me out of a night of relaxation after a hard day's work, packed my shit, dragged me to Area Fifty-fucking-one, and flown me for most of the night to a God knows if it's even in the middle of the US grassland to tangle with hitherto unknown alien creatures. Oh, and not before I'm dumped in a random motel to get as little sleep as possible before you almost break the door to my damn room down. Did I miss something?"

He was a little out of breath after his short rant and she looked at him, her arms folded in front of her chest and eyebrows raised, her bag now at her feet.

"Are you finished?" she asked.

He nodded.

"Damn, you are grouchy in the mornings," she said and shook her head. "Is it like this every morning? Because in that case, I can see why your lady friends kick you out of bed before they have to get up themselves. That way, they don't have to deal with your whiny ass."

"First of all—since I know you've been staring—we can both say without any embarrassment that whiny is not one of the many words that can be used to describe my ass," Taylor replied. "Secondly, we both know that the reason why they 'kick me out of bed' is because they, like me, are not interested in a relationship that lasts longer than twelve hours and are instead interested in a hefty side of—"

"Don't...don't even say it," Banks interrupted and raised her hand. "It's too early in the morning to find out if the mind can, in fact, throw up. Let's get this started with a compromise, shall we? You get dressed and I'll see if this coffee maker works."

"Fine. That sounds like a plan." He headed into the bathroom without a backward glance.

There were few things that woke him better than a cold shower in the morning. Of course, coffee always helped, but having a jolt of energy when his body assumed he was about to drown in freezing water had the kind of effect that was second to none.

"Okay, the coffee maker's working," she called over the sound of the water. "I'll make us coffee."

Taylor turned to where she looked into the bathroom. He'd left the door cracked in case she wanted to discuss their work while he was getting ready but realized that her gaze wandered and lingered.

She looked up at him when she realized he was watching her in turn and her face turned a bright red before she vanished behind the door again.

"Hey, there's no need to be embarrassed, Banks," he said. "We're all mammals and I suppose it behooves me to ask whether you liked what you saw or not."

"I wouldn't kick you out of bed, I guess," she admitted and continued quickly when she heard him bark a laugh. "The only problem you'd have is getting into my bed in the first place, which I think we both know isn't likely to happen anytime soon."

"Hey, I think we've both established that we aren't attracted to each other in any of the ways that matter," he agreed, turned the water off, and toweled himself briskly before he wandered out in search of clothes. "It doesn't mean that physical appreciation can't be felt and certain... arousal expressed."

She couldn't help a smirk but waited until he had pants on before she handed him a cup of coffee. "Shut up and drink your joe, you enormous pain in the ass."

Taylor shrugged and took a sip of the thick, black liquid. "I'm not generally into back-door action like that, but I'm willing to try it."

"You might want to make sure Bungees is as willing as you are," she quipped. "It's always best to make sure everyone's on the same page with these kinds of things. Otherwise, you have a situation where someone says they like anal but don't specify whether they prefer receiving or giving."

He laughed. "Now who's being a pain in the ass?"

"Still you," she said. "Always you unless stated otherwise. Are you ready to go?"

Banks tapped her foot while he pulled a jacket over his shirt, put his boots on, and closed his go-bag. He was effectively ready to leave the room in under ten minutes and left it almost in the same condition he'd found it in, except that the floor in the bathroom was wet as well as one of the towels.

"Let's get this show on the road," he said with a small grin.

It was quick work to check out and before too long, he joined Banks in an SUV and they raced down the road toward the base.

"You know I'll bill you for this, right?" Taylor asked and showed her the receipt for his stay at the motel. "Oh, and not only for the accommodations but the food too."

She didn't look at him and kept her eyes on the road. "That actually won't be a problem in this case. We've basically been given a blank check to work on this mission."

"If that's the case, why did you call three other hunters before you brought me in?" he countered and tucked the receipts into his bag so he could invoice them later.

She scowled like she'd bitten into a lemon. "I actually hoped you didn't know about that." Obviously, Desk must have filled him in on the details of her own volition. Whatever her reasons for doing so, he decided not to tell Banks and go with a plausible explanation.

"The military folks who greeted me said I wasn't the first freelancer to pass through these parts." He leaned back in his seat, still sipping his coffee. "They might also have mentioned that it was a couple of days ago and they haven't been seen or heard from since."

The agent nodded and took in a deep breath. "First of all, those three weren't my first choice to bring out here to deal with this mess. I would have called you but there were some budget concerns over the past few missions you worked on, so I was told to give you less work. This was one of those times. Either way, they were among the best I've had working with me, and I've counted on all three to get some tough work done over their time with the task force."

He gave her a moment before he repeated a single word to encourage her to continue.

"Were?"

She sighed. "Yeah, were. They ran into trouble out there. One died almost immediately, apparently, and we're still not sure how. They had called for an extraction, which I sent, but the other two didn't make it. The helicopter crew sent out there to pick them up didn't make it either. And to add insult to injury...well, we still don't know what the fuck is out there killing our people."

"Shit." Taylor grunted and shook his head. "I'm sorry about that, although it does explain a few things I've heard."

"Like?"

"Like one of your freelancers cutting ties with the task force and asking me for work," he said. "I'm not sure if this is the reason and if so, how the word spread so quickly, but yeah. Oh, and one of the military guys I talked to stated that things were a little crazy, although they don't have any real idea what we're dealing with. You might want to consider bringing the commander of the base into a more active role since we might need help."

"Agreed, that was the idea," Banks said. "We'll brief the two of you today and hopefully, we'll have helicopters available to support you while you work out in the field."

"Having eyes and guns in the sky is always appreciated,"

he admitted. "And not something we could ever count on in the Zoo, so that's a plus."

"Anyway," she continued. "After the deaths, folks in charge of the task force and even from the Pentagon have contacted me and said I need to get this resolved, no matter the cost or who I have to bring in. The folks running the money side of the operation have loosened the purse strings, and…well, yeah, we had to bring you in. You're still our best man for the job."

He scowled as they pulled up to the base and waited for the barrier to be lifted for them to pass. "You know that if you had brought me in earlier with the rest of the team, the chances would have been better that your costs wouldn't be so high, right?"

"I do know that," she replied and showed her ID to the sergeant, who waved them through. "Of course, I didn't know how bad things were when the first call came in about a problem in Wyoming. If I had, I might have been a little more insistent. The problem, though, was that it wasn't my call to make. I'm technically in charge of the task force, but I still report to people who weren't too happy about bringing you into the fold, to begin with. Results are all well and good, but when they have budget meetings with the Secretary of Defense and have to explain why so much money goes from the FBI to freelancers, people get nervous."

"And it cost them the lives of freelancers as well as military personnel," Taylor pointed out.

She looked at him sharply. "You've been in the military for a while, so I expect that kind of thing is nothing new to you."

"Folks with a shit-load of medals on their chests talk to each other about budgets until the people they command start dying and they panic and throw money everywhere to make the bad press stop?" he asked rhetorically with a small smile. "Yeah, I've seen that movie a hundred times before. And it must be incredibly popular since it spawned so many sequels."

Banks had no verbal response to that as they moved toward the airfield where a team had already begun to fuel one of the helicopters while another hauled the crates with his suit and ammo to it with the help of a pallet jack.

"How many people will be involved in this operation?" Taylor asked when they parked and moved toward the helicopter on foot.

"Almost a hundred," the agent replied. "Only a few dozen will actually be physically involved and the remainder will do the very important job of overseeing the operation. As for actual boots on the ground, though, that'll be a party you'll attend stag, I'm afraid."

"So you won't come out with me?" he asked and scowled when the pilots started the helicopter. "You could put all that mech training to good use."

"I'll join the folks overseeing you while you kick ass."

He laughed. "Fan-fucking-tastic. Well, let's get this show on the road. I have a need to kill me some monsters."

CHAPTER TWENTY

The sun began to rise in the east and a pale glow seeped across the grasslands, although the group in the helicopter had very little of real interest to look at. He wondered why anyone had elected to settle in this area, and given that there weren't too many population centers nearby, it seemed that most people probably agreed with him.

Not all, of course. Ranchers, farmers, and the kind of folks who liked having nice, open spaces around them probably liked this kind of land. He smiled inwardly when he realized that since the point was for it to be wide open space, others weren't encouraged to live on it. It probably worked out for the best, although it did highlight the fact—in his mind, at least—that humans were weird.

The helicopter finally approached a group of field tents set up literally in the middle of nowhere—a forward base, most likely, since they were miles away from the Army National Guard base by now. The only question that remained in his head was what was so important about this particular place.

Within minutes, the aircraft landed smoothly, although it was still a ride Taylor hadn't enjoyed in the slightest. He jumped clear and kept his head down as he and Banks headed toward the tents.

"Wow, you really don't like flying, do you?" she commented with a laugh.

He glared at her. "You want to do this now? Really?"

She merely laughed again. "Come on. I know you said you didn't like flying but I assumed it was one of those icky things where you don't like being in a flying box with another group of humans, sharing the flight with them and their recycled air. But no, it's the flying that gets you."

"Okay, we're doing this now. Fine," he grumbled. "I don't like flying. I know it's not a logical response and that I'm far more likely to be killed on the road than I am in the air. It's not that I can't stand the thought of it, and I have it under control, but it is a phobia, and it'll probably be with me for life. Now, are you satisfied or will we work on this for a while?"

"Oh, if you think I'll let this go, you don't know me at all," Banks said, her grin a little smug. "But I think we'll focus more on the case, for now, so you can relax."

"It's hard to relax," Taylor said and glanced at the heli-copter. "Choppers are worse than planes. It's kind of an instinctive thing and it's not even heights, you know? I can go to the top of the Empire State Building and I'm actually fucking fine. But flying is annoying. It's an actual condition —flight anxiety was what they called it when I was a kid. I even have a couple of pending prescriptions for anti-anxiety medication, but it's not really my thing."

"How so?"

"Well, what the meds do is mostly settle my body and subdue the physical symptoms, but the psychological issues are still there. I still feel rattled after a long flight."

"Do you not take the meds, then?"

He shook his head. "Not really. I don't like them. And I certainly don't want to be dependent on them. They result in sluggish response-times when I need to be sharp and on the money every time, a hundred or two hundred times in a row. When I miss, I get killed, so...yeah. I'll take flight anxiety and avoid flying unless I absolutely have to if it helps me to stay alive."

Banks stared at him and narrowed her eyes.

"What?"

"Nothing," she lied and quickly changed her tone. "No...it's only...I made some assumptions and they weren't correct. I constantly believe you don't think things through and you keep surprising me."

"Yeah, so it's not fun when you realize that the Cro-Magnon has a brain?" Taylor said, grinned, and poked her in the ribs as they reached the tents. She flashed him a warning look as they moved through toward the reason why the forward base had been set up in that particular location.

It wasn't a pleasant sight. Taylor studied the area and tried to assimilate the details in a coherent way. It wasn't that complicated, but it was a little mind-boggling and his brain seemed reluctant to stretch to accommodate it. He looked out over a field of carcasses, some of which had literally been torn to pieces. These remains were mostly bone, but the rest remained largely intact aside from the obvious lethal injuries. Given the amount of meat, it was strange that he hadn't been immediately engulfed by the ghastly smell of rotting flesh or why he didn't see clouds flies as one might expect.

There was really nothing he hated more in the world than the sight of maggots, and while he appreciated the fact that there were none present, it was still curious and a little alarming. The air held a trace of chill that suggested winter was around the corner, but it wasn't cold enough to slow the decay.

Something was entirely wrong with the picture—over and above the sight of what looked like hundreds of dead cattle and a few humans on the perimeter.

"What the fuck?" He looked at Banks.

The agent made a face. "Yeah, and it doesn't get any easier to look at either. I thought I would be immune to it eventually, but not so far. It still gives me all the wrong kinds of chills when I look at it."

"What happened here?" he asked and shook his head, then focused on a few people in hazmat suits who worked on some of the closer corpses.

"Well, from what we've been able to piece together, some cowboys were herding these cattle to a ranch that had recently purchased them when they were attacked by a group of the monsters," she explained. "They killed the previous owner, the hired hands, and hundreds of the cattle. The bulk of the herd panicked, apparently, and must have stampeded, as the new owner located them a fair distance away when he came to see why they hadn't arrived. The monsters disappeared before the corpses were found by him and his guys."

"And no one has seen any sign of them since?" Taylor asked. "Near these bodies, I mean. I know they killed the hunters you sent out to find them."

"Well, no, not around these bodies."

His face twisted in a scowl. "Do you know how these bodies are kept...well, I can't think of a better word than fresh?"

"The lab guys have actually sent a preliminary report on a liquid residue that was left behind on the carcasses," Banks explained as he took a tentative step closer. "It's an extremely complex protein and they're still studying it, but the short version is that from their tests, it basically turns the meat into something indigestible by any other creature that might want it. That applies to anything from scavengers like wolves, coyotes, and vultures to insects and even bacteria."

"Do you think it might be something in the creatures' saliva or that they might have excreted it over the bodies another way?" He dropped to his haunches beside what looked like a horse but made sure not to move too close or get any of the residue on his skin in case it was toxic.

She shook her head. "I have no idea. All we know is that all the bodies are coated with it and the meat isn't decomposing."

"You mean...like they might have done this intentionally?" Taylor asked.

The agent hesitated and stared at him and he could almost hear the cogs turning in her head. "Well...sure. They could have, but why would they leave a field of carcasses covered in goo that stops it decomposing? Most of the creatures—even those out of the Zoo, from what I've heard—tend to be the kind that take what they need from their kills and don't much care what happens to it later."

"Right. But in this case, it would seem they do care."

Banks approached him cautiously where he still studied the corpse and she seemed to make a conscious effort to force herself closer. "What are you thinking, McFadden? That they intentionally wanted all these creatures to be left as fresh as the day they killed them? Why?"

"Well, if there's one thing I know about the Zoo, it's that the goop doesn't decide on something for no reason," he said softly. "The creatures with that running in their veins develop some weird shit, don't get me wrong, but it's always for a reason. I've read that some of the monsters are developed in a kind of experimental way—like the goop is trying to see what would go best with what. We can possibly assume that any creature that isn't repeated, for want of a better word, is a failure. Everything else—like the locusts, for example—may evolve or change but could be said to have worked. Either way, though, their primary drive was to kill us, and every time they died, the Zoo seemed to take back any of the remains so if we didn't take samples immediately, there was no going back for them. The same applied to any human remains. They were simply absorbed as biomass to feed the Zoo expansion."

"Shit. Well, I won't lie, that is a little chilling," Banks admitted.

The hunter nodded, stood, and moved away from the corpses. "You're right, it's chilling, especially when you consider how many people have died there and what the

Zoo does with DNA. Of course, we haven't seen any evidence of human DNA in any of the monsters it spawns, but yes, the whole principle behind how the goop operates is fucking scary."

Banks muttered a low curse of agreement as they headed to one of the tents. "So based on that, we could assume that absorbing the dead is its way of assimilating the DNA and learning from the mistakes of the dead?" she asked quietly after a moment of silence.

They had both had enough of the view, and until he was ready to head out to investigate it further, he needed time to sift through the implications of what he had seen.

"That actually does make sense and it wouldn't surprise me, honestly," he said once they had stepped inside the shelter. "With that said, the researchers haven't yet managed to pin down exactly how the process works. Those who studied the goop from the beginning were at the top of their respective fields and at the cutting edge of biology, chemistry, and hell, even physics. If anyone could find answers, we'd expect it from them, but the reality is that while hindsight can show us some of what the goop has done, it provides no insight into how and why."

Banks nodded and studied him with narrowed eyes. "So, what are you thinking, McFadden? I know you have ideas running amok in that head of yours and while I'd honestly prefer not to, I need you to include me in what you're thinking."

He looked at her and bit the inside of his cheek for a second before he spoke. "Well, like I said, anything in the Zoo seems to be made for a reason. There's some kind of design behind all the monstrosities, even if we don't know what it is or understand it. Logically then, in my head anyway, what they did to those corpses out there was done for a reason."

"What kind of reason?"

"Well, there's only one reason to preserve food, right?" Taylor scowled as the thoughts settled within him. "It's because you intend to eat it later or have maybe saved it for someone else. When I think about it, I'm reminded of how vipers are known to kind of preserve their prey. They keep them fresh by injecting them with venom and relocate them after they die from the poison. Well, I'm not sure that's what they do precisely or exactly how it works, but the principle is right. You keep your food as fresh as possible for as long as possible so you can enjoy all of it without any going to waste."

"Are there any stopovers between here and the fucking point?" Banks snapped.

"My point is," Taylor said and paused to take a deep breath. "My point is that the only logical reason they would have to intentionally preserve their kills like this is if they intend to return to eat it later. They could be saving it for their young to eat, too."

The agent opened her mouth but didn't say anything for a long moment, during which she clearly struggled to remain calm. "I don't want to say it—and believe me, I can feel my tongue turning black even from thinking it—but I've learned to trust your instincts on these things. So... Damn it, what do you think we should do?"

"Well, we have one of two options," he said. "The more optimistic option is therefore the least likely, and that is that the beasts have been scared off their prey by your presence and if you leave, they'll come back for it. They can afford to be patient. The second… Well, I don't like to even think about it because it raises the possibility of the young, but my instinct says this is the answer. They probably killed this many creatures in preparation for a horde of new mouths to feed, headed to safety for their offspring to be born or spawned or whatever, and they'll come back for seconds."

"Which means our people here will be in the way of their larder," Banks said and extrapolated from his train of thought.

"Basically, yeah," he replied. "Whichever option it is—or if there are others I haven't thought of yet—it still comes back to suggesting you get the tents, the researchers, and everyone who won't fight the monsters out of here until we've cleared the area."

The special agent sighed and nodded. "I'll get it done. In the meantime…well, I don't know how many there are, but all things considered, there will be a whole horde of them. What do you need us to leave behind?"

"Leave nothing behind," Taylor told her. "But keep in mind I said until we've cleared the area, not I. While I'm the best there is, there is no fucking way in hell I can do this alone. I don't mind being the boots on the ground, but I won't be able to deliver the kind of firepower needed on my own. I'll probably need extra ammo ready for when I engage the creatures, so have that ready to go. If you want this dealt with conclusively, though, I'll have to have help dealing with them if they're in those kinds of numbers. Most important is having air cover once I'm out there. Helicopters with any guns you can get your hands on."

"Agreed, I'll get the base commander on the horn and let him know you'll need their support," Banks agreed.

He paused and fixed her with a searching look. It wasn't like her to jump on the situation like this without at least giving him some back-sass about how much it would cost.

"Wow, you guys are pulling out all the stops on this one, aren't you?" he snarked.

She smirked. "Are you really that surprised? This is the kind of threat people don't usually fuck around with."

"Fair enough. Now, let's start to clear this place before the monsters come back."

CHAPTER TWENTY-ONE

Taylor had been sure that everyone would want to get as far away from the location as possible when they learned there was a good chance that a small horde of monsters would return. That was more or less the logical response and therefore what was to be expected from people who were usually supposed to be logical for a living.

Surprisingly, they didn't want to go.

"At what other point would people like us be able to study creatures like these up close?" one of the researchers asked with a surprising amount of agreement from her coworkers.

"Being able to see how they interact with their environment would be vital to learning if they might actually be a vital addition to the local ecosystem," another added.

He scowled, irritated by the fact that it had become his job to tell them that they were being dumbasses and needed to get the hell out as quickly as possible.

But Banks was otherwise engaged in the evacuation

process, which left them looking to him since he was supposedly some kind of expert on the monsters they could expect to encounter.

"For fuck's sake." He rumbled his annoyance and dragged in a breath in an effort to restore his patience. "Yeah, if you stay here, the chances are you'll have front-row seats to study what's likely a brand new species and will have all kinds of awards waiting for you based on the papers you'll write on what you saw. All of this is assuming that you live that long. Honestly, I'd put dollars to doughnuts that you guys will be much closer than you'd like to these creatures before you can even say 'science.' In fact, the chances are you'll have firsthand knowledge of these monsters' dietary habits and digestive systems."

The first scientist challenged him with a glacial stare but it didn't help that she was barely over five feet tall and tried to intimidate a massive ginger giant.

Eventually, she gave up and shook her head. "Fine, but I hope you know we're missing out on the opportunity of a lifetime."

"Yeah, and I hope you all know that your lives are being saved out here," he said. "The idea is to leave enough of them to be studied anyway, so I have no idea why you're so cranky."

"Studying them alive is much more conclusive."

"And much deadlier too," Taylor snapped. "Look, no one's forcing you to leave, but if you stay, make sure you sign the paperwork that means no one can sue anyone over any deaths that might and will most likely occur, okay?"

That appeared to get through to them more than any of

his other arguments had, and they were on one of the first helicopters to take them back to the base.

"I swear I think I prefer dealing with Zoo monsters than people who think they're willing to put their lives on the line for science until the moment when their lives are actually on the line," he grumbled and strode over to the crate with his mech suit.

Banks laughed. "Yeah, well, they're the base commander's problem now. All we really need to do is keep them alive long enough to get them out of here."

Taylor began to put the pieces of his armor on, starting with the boots. "I think it simply showed that they didn't like being told what they can and can't do and where they could and couldn't be. It was an interesting sight to see them suddenly change their minds when they realized they were the ones who needed to make the choice about whether they wanted to go or stay. Don't get me wrong, they're smart and it was absolutely the smart decision to head the fuck out of here before all hell broke loose. There's nothing cowardly about not wanting to stick around when monsters come a-knocking."

"So, if they made the smart decision by heading out, what does that make you?"

He grinned at her. "Well, I think we've already established that I'm merely a pea-brained Neanderthal who doesn't know what's best for him, right?"

"True," she said with a small smirk. "But be that as it may, I do need you to come out alive on this one. We've already had too many people die on this mission. I don't need any more dead freelancers so the rest quit on me."

"I'll see what I can do," Taylor replied. "Although I guess

that depends on what you can do. Where are we with air support?"

The last of the helicopters arrived to take the people and tents away and leave Taylor all alone in a field of carcasses. Banks turned to face him.

"I still need to talk to the base commander about that, but I'm certain he won't mind," she replied and picked up one of the pieces of the mech from the crate before Taylor snatched it from her hands. "The way I heard it told, those folks want revenge for their fallen comrades. You'll have your air support."

"Fantastic," he replied as he continued to prepare his armor. "But keep in mind that it's not a request. If you want these monsters gone, the National Guard has to come to the party. If they don't, all bets are off."

"I hear you," she replied, her expression grim. "They'll be here."

He nodded. "And I do believe that's your cue to bug out. I'll take it from here."

"Yeah, I guess so," Banks said and patted him in the shoulder. "Stay safe out there, McFadden. I'd hate to break it to Bungees that you got your ass killed."

"Safe will probably not be an option out there, but I do appreciate your concern for my well-being."

She flipped him off and jogged to the helicopter closest to them as he pulled his helmet on. Within moments, the last of the aircraft elevated and banked away toward the base. When the last backdraft from the rotors stilled, the entire area seemed to settle into a disquieting silence around him.

"I don't know how it's possible but this place is

suddenly a whole lot creepier," Taylor said when he connected to the comms with Desk and probably Banks too.

"Hello there, Taylor, it's good to hear from you again," Desk said.

"It's been a while, Desk. I only wish it was under more pleasant circumstances."

"That is unlikely, given that we only contact each other when business demands it," she replied. "I'm uploading the coordinates where the other team started tracking the monsters to your HUD, as well as some of the footage that was collected before they were killed."

"That should make this walk a little more interesting," he said and easily located the path his unlucky colleagues had left. From the tracks, it looked like the three had gone in with only body armor and weapons. While it wasn't the choice he would have made, he knew for a fact that it was difficult for the average person to acquire an appropriate combat mech unless they had the necessary connections.

The trail led west toward the mountains, but given their travel time before they were attacked, they probably hadn't moved too far. It begged the question of exactly how close the nest he suspected his prey had might be.

The video started to play and showed him the three hunters who had been involved. The quality was questionable but that didn't really matter much as the basics were fairly simple to determine. It was late in the afternoon with some sunlight still available as they walked through the grasslands.

He paused his progress and watched more closely when they obviously realized something had gone wrong. From what he could see, they decided to return the way they had come but something stopped them.

"The creatures circled," he noted aloud. "They set a trap for them. It's not all that unusual in the animal kingdom, but ambush predators generally rely on camouflage."

He still couldn't see any of the mutants, but one of the hunters flailed and fought as massive jaws crushed his head in a single powerful bite. Despite the fact that Taylor focused intently, the creatures were difficult to make out in the footage.

"That there is some good camouflage," he muttered.

Although most of the monster remained obscured, he could roughly make out what it looked like through the motion as it crossed the camera's line of sight. The colors were blurred and hard to differentiate, but the beast appeared to be about the size of a mountain lion. He realized that the perception they engendered of phenomenal speed was the result of their ability to remain camouflaged. From what he could see, it didn't move particularly quickly, at least by his experience of how some Zoo monsters could move.

It was more likely that it sneaked in close and pounced, which exaggerated the sense of speed. While the jaws remained closed around the hunter's head, it delivered a vicious slash down his chest with the claws on the foreleg, which were abnormally long and sharp. It also displayed far more strength than most mountain lions had in their forelegs, evidence of enhancement mutation.

"Hey, Banks," he called on the comms. "Did you see this footage?"

"Yes, and yes," she answered. "What do you see?"

"Well, these critters have some kind of camouflage that I can't really make out." He repeated the attack segment a few times. "But you can pick up the motion. They are big fuckers but not huge and are also smarter than your average monster. It looks like they drew the hunters into a trap and only attacked when they sent word to you for an extraction. It honestly looks like they knew they had the hunters corralled and were studying them and only committed to an attack once there was the possibility of them getting the hell out."

"Do you honestly think they understood that the hunters were calling for extraction?"

"Well, either that or it was one hell of a coincidence that they only became more aggressive once they made the call. Either one is a possibility, I suppose."

He couldn't deny the fact that him reading too much into what they were doing was possible, but he didn't think so. The first hunter was now down and when another was wounded, the man filming opened fire at the area around his teammate in an attempt to drive the attacker back.

A flash of color indicated that a shot had connected and something red splashed on the grass. Taylor couldn't tell whether the rounds had killed it or if it was merely wounded, but what was clear was that he bought time for himself and his fellow survivor. He made no effort to even look at the man's legs which had been severely mangled below the knees. Nothing in either of these attacks indicated whether the odd liquid that preserved the bodies had been excreted by the claws or the saliva.

"What are you looking at now?" Banks asked.

"About twenty seconds before the helicopter arrives," Desk explained.

"It looks like the animals fall back and one of them was wounded or killed," Taylor added. The chopper could be heard approaching in the background as the man with the camera in his helmet dragged his wounded comrade to where it came in to land.

The beasts began to hiss and growl around them again, more intensely than before like they now reacted from a desire for pure vengeance. It wasn't something he'd ever seen in regular animals but it was something Zoo creatures had shown time and time again.

His heart beat a little quicker as the chopper settled. He knew what would happen already but there was a weird fucking hope that somehow, through the video, they would actually make it.

The hunters were helped into the aircraft and a paramedic knelt beside the wounded man as they elevated again. The camera swung quickly to look at something that blocked the light in front of the cockpit and made everything oddly dark. A few flickering images of the chopper spinning out of control were all that was left to watch.

It was never easy to watch people die like that, but the fact that someone had been filming would probably save his life and give him some idea of what to look for. He still had a few details that remained unclear about the monsters, but he felt confident that he knew a little more about what he was dealing with.

What he'd seen merely reinforced the fact that he wouldn't be able to handle them alone. There were too many and they were tough to kill.

He still wasn't sure how they had managed to jump the twenty or so feet to reach the helicopter. They hadn't dragged it down from below although logic suggested they would leap up and grasp the landing skids.

To block the sunlight like that, they were at least as high as the aircraft. It was an interesting thought and hard to imagine. He didn't have the full picture and he didn't like that. Of course, he seldom started out with a full picture but it was always nicer when he did.

"So, you're following their tracks along the same path the other three took," Banks said. "You're on your own out there although we do have helicopters if there's trouble. I have confirmed with the base commander and the teams are standing by. Can I assume you have some kind of plan? Not that I question your judgment at this juncture, of course, but I'll feel much more comfortable if you told me what you had in mind. I've had time to think over the little you mentioned earlier, and I don't much like what it seems to mean."

"As a matter of fact, I do have a plan," Taylor said. "And no, you won't like it, which is why I didn't go into too much detail. In fact, I'd go so far as to say that you would have called it off if you were still on the ground."

She finally ended the long pause that followed with a sigh.

"What's the plan, McFadden?"

"You only call me McFadden when you're pissed at me."

"I always call you McFadden."

"Exactly."

"What's your fucking plan?"

"When I asked you to have air support ready, I didn't

mean them for evac or to simply back me up in a tight situation," Taylor said. "I meant for them to be the cavalry. I'll draw the fuckers into a mass-strike scenario and they come in with rockets, explosives, and guns and wipe the assholes out."

Another pause followed.

"Bait. You mean bait, McFadden."

"Hey, you say bait, I say ground-based assets in an air-based operation."

He could tell she was shaking her head.

"Does your mother know you use that kind of language?" she asked.

"Yeah, I gargle every morning too."

"Fuck it. Fine," she grumbled. "If this works, I win. If it doesn't and you die, I still win."

He laughed. "You say the nicest things. Now quit stalling and get me my fucking air support."

"You're one psychotic bastard, McFadden."

"I keep telling you," he replied. "If you think of me as anything other than that you're already underestimating me. And I don't like it when people underestimate me."

"Why are you doing this?" she asked. "What's the good of money if you don't live long enough to spend it?"

He knew what his answer would be before he said it, but he still needed a moment to think through how to phrase it. "I was serious when I said I didn't want any of those Zoo bastards anywhere on the Continental US where I plan to live a very long and prosperous life. This number of creatures is about as close to a Zoo invasion as I'll allow. If you're worried, remember that I went into the

Zoo eighty-three times and I don't plan to let any dumb mongrels take me—"

He looked around when a low growl caught his attention. It was a fair distance away and sounded more like a whine or a whistle. He wasn't sure, obviously, but it seemed almost like a warning—the way rattlesnakes would make a noise when they noticed a human bumble across their territory.

"What's the matter?" Banks asked, alarmed by his sudden silence.

"If you were serious about wanting me to get out of here alive, you might want to get those choppers in the air," he said and drew his assault rifle from where he'd holstered it on his back. "They're here."

CHAPTER TWENTY-TWO

The low growls and the whistles seemed to transform from a warning to a conversation as he continued to move ahead. It was as if signals were passed from one monster to another while they moved around him and kept watch on his location.

He disliked the fact that he still couldn't see them even more than he disliked the sense of intelligent communication. These creatures were adept at remaining out of sight, but even they weren't the kind that could beat technology more advanced than the human eye.

He called up vision sensors usually required in the Zoo. It was in the middle of the afternoon on a cloudless day but given the late-fall temperatures, the heat vision would probably work fine. Even if it was a little sensitive, the motion sensors would hopefully be a little more help.

The idea didn't bring the full advantages he'd hoped for, unfortunately. Wind whipped across the open grasslands and made things a little more complicated than he preferred. The software struggled to cope with the changes in environment and attempted to provide him with a decent vision of the world around him.

He moved slowly and cautiously now, his senses alert with the very real reality of danger seemingly all around him. Despite the expectation and the inevitability of the upcoming encounter, he was almost surprised when they appeared.

Four of them stood in a wide crescent around him, raised their heads, and uttered the sounds he was now certain were them in contact with each other. Rather than attack, however, they moved farther and farther away as he advanced on them. He tried briefly to look at them without his enhanced visual software but again, they seemed to simply fade into a vague blur against the landscape.

It was difficult to determine what they attempted to do. They possibly wanted to guide him into a trap similar to the one that had killed the other three hunters. On the other hand, they might simply be tracking him to ensure that he stayed away from something they wanted to protect.

On a surface level, the behavior wasn't unheard of among regular animals, but their coordination was exceptional. He wondered if it wasn't something like wolves did while they hunted a moose. They would target the much larger animal, stick close to it, and keep it uncomfortable and moving until it simply ran out of energy.

There was something off about it, though. His unease was triggered by the fact that they didn't attack, which implied a greater purpose.

No, Taylor thought and shook his head firmly as he abandoned all those possibilities. They were scouts. As soon as he continued and it became clear that he wouldn't be deterred, they turned quickly and raced away, deeper into the grassland and out of the range of his motion sensors for the moment. He left the software on anyway. There was no point in letting them sneak up on him again.

"McFadden, your air support is coming in hot," Banks told him crisply. "How are you doing? The lack of gunfire tells me you haven't engaged yet."

"No, but that won't last," he said and sent the data from his motion sensors to Desk, who would send it to Banks. "They didn't try to attack but it was like they watched me and tried to intimidate me so I'd move away from them. When they realized it didn't work, they fell back."

"Fell back where?"

He shrugged and cursed as the whole suit exaggerated the simple motion. "I assume to where the rest of the monsters are. Which means they're in the area and will likely return with reinforcements."

"Why would they need reinforcements?" Banks asked. "Why wouldn't the four of them simply engage you?"

"That's…a fantastic point, actually." He paused and scowled. " They might be heading back to join the rest of their group or maybe even…"

"Even what?"

"I hate to say it, but they might have gone to report on a threat advancing on them." He made a face when he realized how crazy it sounded. "The only time I've seen animals act even vaguely like that was when they had something they wanted to defend."

He received no reply and wondered if they'd lost the connection, but Banks spoke again. "Their young. It's like you said. They're bringing the newborns to the carcasses and the meat they left behind."

"It's as good a theory as any," Taylor answered. He inspected his weapon before he looked out into the field and tried to see something with his naked eye. Technology was useful and very reliable but sometimes, he needed to make sure he could see something with his own eyes before he fell back on the tech.

Trust but verify, as the Russians liked to say.

It wasn't long before he registered movement out there. The ripples that disturbed the grass were mostly from the wind, but something definitely moved faster, against the wind and toward him. The presence of a group was unmistakable, although it was difficult to tell it apart from the vegetation except for the way it moved across the grass. He looked through the sights in his rifle, narrowed his eyes, and focused.

"Shit, still nothing," he complained.

"Don't worry. They'll come for you soon," Banks said.

He scowled and ran a few more checks on his suit. "Oh, I know that and I think I can see them. But it's difficult—like my eyes don't agree with what I'm looking at and are trying to stop me from focusing. It's giving me a headache."

"Like it's an optical illusion?"

"Something like that," he said. "My motion sensors can pick them up so I should be fine."

"What if your suit malfunctions?"

He shook his head. "That won't happen. It can't happen so I can't spend time thinking about that."

Taylor's mind raced as a number of them came within range of his sensors. They likely knew he was there but made no effort to attack him. Instead, they maintained a kind of formation that seemed to blanket the ground. Up closer, he could actually see the grass move as the group passed.

His mind registered a slight trace of alarm when more of them came into view. Dozens became multiple dozens and finally, he had to accept the evidence. There weren't only about thirty of them like everyone had assumed. Instead, there were literally hundreds. He paused and studied them. They acted like he wasn't enough of a threat to even draw them out. While they would attack, it wouldn't be rushed.

That was something in his favor, at least.

"McFadden, your air support is at the checkpoint," Banks confirmed.

He nodded. "Appreciated."

At the checkpoint meant less than five minutes away, which in turn meant that he could begin to act on the plan that slowly formed in his head as he watched the creatures advance. Between him and them stood the monument of why he had been called in. A wrecked helicopter lay with its rotors torn and twisted and the body seared by the flames from the crash.

There were signs of blood outside, where the bodies had likely been dragged out and consumed, but as he drew closer, there was no sign of them, unlike what he'd seen in the field behind him. Either there had been too few of them to leave as meat or the bodies had already been dragged to their lair or nest for consumption.

It didn't really matter. The chopper might be where people had died and some respect needed to be paid, but he couldn't think of a better way to honor the fallen than to soak the ground in the blood of those that had killed them.

Taylor edged closer to the helicopter, increased his pace, and jogged up the exposed side of the downed aircraft. He grasped the top and dragged himself up while he tried to locate the creatures again. They were on the motion sensors but it was still difficult to identify with his own two eyes.

"Fuck."

The comm line pinged, which indicated that someone else had joined it.

"Calling Cryptid Assassin," a man's voice said crisply. "Repeat, Cryptid Assassin, come in."

"This is Cryptid Assassin," he said and primed his assault rifle. He wouldn't admit it aloud—ever—but damned if the nickname hadn't started to grow on him. "I'll go ahead and assume you guys were sent over to save my ass."

"That assumption is correct, Cryptid Assassin," the man replied. "This is Hotel One, and I have three Apaches with me in formation and looking for payback. We simply want to make sure we have your current position so as to avoid having you caught in the fire."

"Roger that, Hotel One. I'm standing on the fallen helicopter, also known as the only cover for hundreds and hundreds of miles," Taylor said. The choppers now faintly audible in the distance. They were still a fair distance away, but that was probably for the best. "Don't shoot at it but feel free to shoot around it. I'll be all over the motherfucker and the chances are there will be a few monsters trying to get a bite of me while I'm there. Your help is definitely appreciated."

"Understood, Cryptid Assassin. We'll avoid shooting you."

"I'd appreciate that."

He could understand that the military men wanted revenge on the monsters that had killed their comrades. It wasn't really any different from how he'd felt back in the day, but after so much time spent in the fucking jungle, he had learned that heading in there looking for payback would always end badly. For one thing, the animals didn't understand the concept, he didn't think, so any attempts at retribution were purely for psychological benefit.

Secondly, heading into a fight with the monsters with a reckless, trigger-happy attitude usually ended badly, exactly like it did with any other combat situation. And people who had been stationed Stateside tended to forget the unspoken rules of combat.

Or, at least, that was what he'd heard. Taylor wouldn't tell them what they could and couldn't do, but he really hoped he could count on them not getting too trigger happy.

For the moment, though, he had other concerns. The rocket launcher on his back came up, and he directed it toward the group of animals that continued to move, if a little slower than before. They were still in formation, and those that advanced a little too quickly suddenly pulled up and stopped to look at the center before they resumed their forward motion when the rest caught up.

His targeting system didn't lock onto their signature at first, but he changed it to lock onto their heat signatures instead. Thankfully, the temperature wasn't hot enough to affect it and the beasts were warm-blooded, apparently—a double-luck bonus he decided was a sign

Were they mammals? From their fangs and claws, he would guess yes, but for the life of him, he still couldn't make out precisely what they looked like.

"Fucking monsters." He hissed his irritation and let the locks coordinate to give him something to fire at. The wind had chilled the air enough that the heat signatures settled further and were better able to coordinate with the motion sensors, which made it easier to locate them since seeing them visually was such an issue.

As he adjusted to the improved sensor information, Taylor realized they were heavily concentrated closer to the middle of their formation. Those in the center actually displayed a higher heat signature than those on the outer edges, and directly in the middle was a signature that was even warmer. The monsters seemed to be focused on that location.

He took a moment to check without the tech help and again with it.

"They have their young with them," he announced on the comm line.

"What's that?" Banks asked.

"It's like a traveling nest," he explained, zoomed in, and recorded a few seconds of footage to send to Banks. "They have what looks like a whole coordinated formation with about fifty or sixty of the creatures pressed together and one hell of a heat signature out there. They're protecting their young and taking them to have what I can only assume is the world's most disgusting Thanksgiving ever.

What's more, it seems like they're intentionally avoiding contact with me to keep their little ones safe."

"Do you think that's a weakness?" she asked. "Something you can exploit?"

He scowled. It was a possibility. "I'm fairly sure I won't be able to exploit them since they will keep me as far away from those baby bastards as possible. It might be something for the choppers to aim at, though, and could collapse their defenses."

"Okay, that seems like a plan."

"Send the imaging to the guys in the choppers to see if they can't target it from a distance."

"Desk is already on it," Banks said. "Good luck."

He nodded. "Thanks."

Ordinarily, he would have said something about how luck was for fools who hadn't prepared and he didn't need it or some badass line like that.

In this case, however, he knew he really, really needed it.

CHAPTER TWENTY-THREE

Vickie could honestly say that games of chance had never appealed to her. Despite this, a casino never failed to offer the kind of temptation she found almost impossible to resist.

For some reason, being able to use her skills with a computer to circumvent both the high-level and low-level security and find the weaknesses in the money-making machines that defined casinos presented the ultimate challenge.

It had nothing to do with the money—although she was honest enough to admit that the extra cash would be welcome if she pulled it off—and everything to do with simply proving she could do it.

Fortunately, common sense and a strong sense of survival prevailed. First, the obvious truth that the security was the ultimate challenge because it was so fucking impenetrable meant she'd be caught, even if she did succeed. Jail time for her meant Zoo time, a remarkably effective deterrent. Second, she'd lose her job with Taylor, which meant losing what promised to be a surprisingly bright future.

Finally, she'd have to face Niki—who might or might not be able to bail her out a second time. Either way, she did not want the woman pissed off with her. Life was too good right now to unleash her.

Still, the temptation would be there every time she stepped into a casino. She hadn't told anyone and never would, but it was the real reason why she avoided them.

Today, however, she had to make an exception. Something was wrong, and she really didn't want to be out of the loop should shit hit the fan. The last time that happened, she and Bobby had been kidnapped and she had no desire to repeat it.

Besides, her date had been a downer and she was in need of company. Taylor had gone somewhere and hadn't been back all night, and Bobby hadn't arrived in time to open the shop either. A quick check on his phone told her he wasn't home and it came as no surprise when she tracked him to Il Fornaio.

The restaurant had begun to fill with people who had spent most of the night drinking and gambling, but it was easy to locate the massive mechanic on one of the seats near the bar. He seemed entirely focused on the stack of fluffy pancakes and a pile of bacon on his plate despite his claims to enjoy the lunch and dinner menus. The occasional sip from a glass of orange juice provided the only distraction.

Vickie moved over to where he sat, slid silently onto

the seat beside him, and picked up one of the nearby menus to peruse the options.

Bobby sent her a sharp glance, obviously wondering who had joined him and elected to sit so close to him instead of giving him the space he wanted.

He saw her and barely nodded before he turned to take another mouthful of a butter and syrup-covered pancake as the waitress arrived with a cup of coffee for him.

"I'll be right with you," the tall woman said to Vickie with a practiced smile before she attended to other customers.

"Take your time," she replied and turned to face Bobby, who simply maintained a steadfast focus on his food. "So, what's the problem, Bungees?"

"I have pancakes, bacon, OJ, and good coffee," the mechanic said and slurped the coffee for emphasis. "Why would there be a problem?"

"Because you usually have your breakfast at the shop, for one thing," she replied. "You tuck into the doughnuts and coffee you grab on the way there, and honestly, so do I. When you failed to show up, I was worried. And given that you've chosen comfort food of the highest order, it's very obvious something's wrong. Take it from someone who's done that a fair amount over the years."

The large man smirked and nodded. "You're wise beyond your years, Vickie."

She nodded. "It's a blessing and a curse, honestly."

"I'm not sure I want to talk about it, though," he said.

"Fair enough," she answered as the waitress returned to take her order. "I'll have what he's having—the pancake, bacon, OJ, and coffee combo looks, smells, and probably tastes good."

"Coming right up," the woman replied with a small smile and tapped the order into her tablet.

"By the standards you mentioned, you're probably in need of comfort food too," Bobby pointed out. "Do you feel like talking about it?"

"Only if you'll do the same," she countered.

He nodded. "Fair enough, but you go first."

Vickie sighed and gave him a disgruntled glance. "Fine. Well, for starters, my date last night was a total bust."

"I thought you were happy to go out with a cute college guy."

She shrugged and ran her fingers through her hair. "Well, he's definitely cute and I think we'll hang out together. He's a TA and has helped me adjust to being on a university campus again. He's nice enough and again, cute."

"So, what was the issue?"

"He made assumptions about me based on my looks," she said and scowled at the countertop. "We didn't go into specifics but...well, he assumed I had a boyfriend and was seeing him on the side. He thought he was being really nice by saying he understood and didn't have a problem with it."

"Wait, so he thought you were—"

"Into something called polyamory, according to the Internet," she said bluntly. "And he went on to say that he had expected me to be into things that were much kinkier than seeing two guys at the same time."

Bobby laughed. "And you'll still be friends with this guy? Why would you do that?"

"I think we were both a little nervous going into the

date and he tried to overcompensate by being cool about everything, even if he wasn't really," Vickie explained. "I walked away before he put his foot in his mouth again and said something truly offensive. We'll be friends for now, mostly to keep the fact that we still need to interact on campus from getting too awkward. If he manages to redeem himself in my eyes, we might look into another date sometime in the future."

Her companion studied her curiously and was distracted from saying anything when the waitress brought Vickie's food and drinks. The woman put them on the bar, nodded, and turned away to her next customer.

"I have to say, you handled it with much less...uh, violence than I would have," the mechanic said with a small smile. "I'm fairly sure I would have clocked him in the jaw and walked out."

"Well, I walked out, spent most of the rest of the night trying to decide what was wrong with me—or what was wrong with him—until I decided fuck it and went to bed."

"Honestly, that story kind of makes my date not seem that bad," he said and took a bite of one of the bacon strips.

"Oh, shit, you're going to make me feel terrible, aren't you?" Vickie muttered and attacked her pancakes with a vengeance.

"Okay, so it started out well but it quickly became apparent that we had literally nothing in common," Bobby told her. "She's a personal trainer and I'm a specialized mechanic. When we both realized that, she told me flat-out that she wasn't interested in having a long-term relationship with me."

"Ouch." She growled around a mouthful of pancake. "Well, at least she was open and honest about it."

"Sure, and she said that while a relationship wouldn't go anywhere, it was obvious that we were physically attracted to each other. Then she asked if I wanted to go back to her place," he continued gloomily.

The hacker scowled at him for a moment. "Well, yeah, that's far better than how my date went. How the hell do you call that a bust?"

"Well, I left after we were finished and spent the night at my own apartment," he said. "I don't know how Taylor does it. He talks about it like it's not a big thing, but I felt dirty, you know? Kind of like we had both used each other and for some reason, were worse off for it."

Vickie sighed and nodded. "Taylor's his own kind of guy. The Zoo affected him more than he's willing to admit."

"You have no idea," Bobby replied. "I've done this song and dance with him for a long time—far longer than you. He would come out, having lost people, and would look shattered like he had been reminded of his own mortality or something. The first time he went in, only he and a couple of others made it out. I'm sure that's what broke him the first time. And then... Well, the last time was very similar. Only he and a few others made it out, and he had enough."

"I guess after being faced with how quickly he could lose people he relied on to stay alive, it began to feel a little pointless," she conceded thoughtfully. "But you went into the Zoo a few times too, right? Why aren't you the same kind of broken?"

"I faced the issues I had head-on and realized I wasn't

cut out for that place," he told her without hesitation. "I got help for my issues and things worked out. He...never got there. He's been in that broken state of mind for so long, I don't think he sees it as broken anymore. It's like a survival instinct more than anything else."

She nodded and looked at her plate in surprise when she realized she'd demolished the pancakes at a surprising rate and only had the bacon left. "Taylor didn't come back to the shop last night. He was gone when I got back from my date and he didn't come in all night. There was no word from him when I opened this morning. Not from you either, but it was easier to find you."

Bobby glanced at her and shrugged. "Well, like I said, it's like him to be out with his one-night stands all night and only come back in the morning, right?"

"Well, yeah, but in the end, he usually comes around home sometime." She frowned. "Honestly, I assumed he would be here with you but apparently not."

He took a sip of his coffee. "The guy's a grown man with a business to run. He was probably getting business done or something."

"Well, there's the fact that he transferred the security of the shop to my phone last night and hasn't taken it back yet," she pointed out and raised an eyebrow.

The mechanic paused, replaced his coffee cup on the saucer, and studied her phone when she showed him she was still in charge of the strip mall security.

"Huh." Bobby grunted and rubbed his chin. "That is unusual. Did you try his phone? He had it with him as I saw him take a call when we left the gun range."

Vickie nodded. "It went straight to voicemail."

The mechanic nodded. "Okay, the only other time I've seen him do something like this was when he was called away to do his side job for Banks. That was in an emergency, though, as he usually has me check his mech before he loads it into his vehicle. But if he had to leave in a hurry, he could have forgotten to message me. He's human, like any of us."

"Both Maddie and Liz were in the garage when I got there."

"It must have been one hell of an emergency," he grumbled. "Either way, there's not much we can do except wait for him to contact us unless you want to get hold of your cousin to see if he's working a job for her."

The hacker raised her hands to bring that train of thought to a halt. "I think we should hold off on going amber alert here. Like you said, Taylor's a grown man and can go where he pleases. Although, with that said, we're still his employees and we're still on a schedule, so what do you say we head to the shop and get some work done?"

Bobby nodded and finished his coffee. "You're not wrong. I don't feel much like working today, but we do have things to do, whether Taylor's around or not. Are you finished?"

Vickie held a finger up as she drained the last drops from her glass of OJ. "Almost."

"Great, let's get a check," he said. "By the way, did we not oversell this place or did we?"

"You did not. The food is great," she replied with a small smile. "I can see myself coming for lunch but not today, though. Taylor pays me well but not that well, and I still have my car payments to take care of."

He pushed up from his seat and gestured for the waitress. "So, split checks."

She nodded. "Cheap-ass date."

"I'm not your type, remember?"

CHAPTER TWENTY-FOUR

The choppers were close enough now that the steady thump-thump of their rotors intruded into the eerie silence that had settled over the grassland. Even the growls and calls of the monsters had subsided like they recognized the calm before the storm. He was unsure whether the mech simply improved his hearing or if the National Guard Apaches were actually less than a minute away. His instinct said that was the case and he made no effort to second-guess himself. A second or two either way made no difference in the bigger scheme of things.

Taylor once again considered his plan and his options. The best time to engage the monsters was when they were close enough that he could open fire on them without having to worry about wasting ammo. He could select his targets and use the secondary assault rifle he had brought with him. It was still difficult for the targeting software to find the creatures but he could see them using his sensors so he could shoot them himself.

Besides, if he could hear the helicopters, so could they.

Not only that, they were intelligent enough to recognize the incoming threat and take steps to avoid it—their first choice if they were, in fact, protecting their young. With their camouflage and canny tricks, they could very easily vanish once again and move safely out of what he'd carefully selected as the best killing field. He needed to act and draw them in to fully commit to an attack.

"Knock, knock, motherfuckers!" He growled and launched two rockets from his shoulder.

The explosives powered into the massed mutants and five or six of them fell. The others recoiled from each explosion and focused their attention on him. The low whistled growls erupted immediately from the entire group and now contained real fury and vicious intent that he could almost feel like a shock wave.

Those on the perimeter surged into a concerted assault while the group in the center remained steady and moved forward slowly, still babysitting from the looks of it.

Still, he had to be grateful for that as those that attacked were more than enough. He opened fire and the assault rifles kicked in response and delivered a fusillade at the approaching ranks. He had seen them back away in the video when one of their number had taken a few hits but this time, evasion was not part of their plan.

He had seen the reaction before, of course. This kind of raw ferocity revealed that they were more than willing to watch their own cut down by the dozens if it meant he was killed in the process. It was a classic Zoo response and clearly identified these mutants with those in the alien jungle

Victory wouldn't come easy. Taylor bellowed a challenge and watched them circle the fallen helicopter. He remained alert for the right moment to strike and when a few bounded up, launched two rockets from his shoulder. The missiles drilled through them and shrapnel savaged their bodies as they were driven back while the assault rifles reloaded.

Bobby's upgrades had made sure the tracks that brought the new mags in were extra slick in their operation. It wasn't much longer than a second before he switched to semi-auto and pulled the trigger again, choosing his shots rather than simply spraying around him while he waited for the rocket launcher on his shoulder to reload.

The mutants would clearly not give up easily and showed no signs of slowing either. Those he'd only injured continued to limp forward and gnashed their knife-sized teeth at him as they tried to climb the fallen helicopter. They weren't successful and only served as a stepping stone for those that weren't wounded. He needed to keep moving as they swarmed onto the wreckage, but he didn't want to give up the high ground unless he was forced to do so.

"We have a visual on you, Cryptid Assassin," the pilot said. The choppers had moved significantly closer while he'd been focused on the battle. "It looks like you could use some help."

"Any fucking time now!" Taylor yelled in response and plumes of smoke issued from the aircraft in the same second as his statement. The explosives shook the ground hard enough to make him almost lose his footing on the metal. Massive, smoking craters appeared around the wreckage, followed quickly by the low, steady drone as the machine guns opened fire.

The National Guard teams showed no inclination to be sparing with their ammo and simply obliterated the monsters as quickly as possible. The enemy made no effort to fall back or even try to escape. A group of them continued to try to attack Taylor's position, but the others turned toward the group pressed in against the young. The mass of creatures seemed to bunch even closer than before as if to create a meat shield.

He paused, his head tilted as he studied their behavior. It was very evident that their sole priority was to protect the younger creatures to the point where they made no effort to protect themselves. An idea began to form in his head.

A few of them drew away from their attack on him, looked at the helicopters that delivered their deadly barrages, and growled and whistled as if in a hasty discussion. A group suddenly pushed up from the ground and uttered what could only be described as a shriek.

The unexpected motion finally revealed what they actually looked like. Their bodies were the size of mountain lions, and while they vaguely conformed to the mammalian build of that breed, they didn't resemble the larger cats at all. Nor did they move like them either and traveled across the open ground a little differently, but nothing he'd imagined prepared him for what came next.

Taylor gaped as they vaulted vertically with their forelimbs spread wide and almost impossibly large. Skin extended between limbs and body to form enormous wings that caught the wind as they flapped, and the creatures gained height. They seemed to have abandoned any attempt at camouflage and he was able to study the elongated jaws, the long, fang-like teeth the size of daggers, and their even longer claws that appeared almost stiletto-like and were most likely used for slicing.

"Fucking bats," he mumbled in disgust. "Camouflaging, foraging, meat-preserving bats. We'll have a fun time coming up with a name for that one. Hey, Hotel One, do you see this?"

"See what?" the pilot asked.

"The creatures are flying toward you," he shouted and maintained his own stream of fire although he was effectively unable to help them out even if he didn't need to deal with his own attackers.

He reminded himself grimly that they were the ones with the firepower, after all.

"What?" the pilot asked and sounded skeptical. Their sensors had apparently failed to pick the monsters up, and it was only when they could physically see them that the aircraft banked sharply to the right in an attempt to avoid the swarm that approached.

"I won't panic," he told himself and dragged in a few deep breaths. "Nope. I'll calm my ass down and focus on killing these bastards. Think about the money, McFadden. All the money you'll make. Blank check, that was what Banks said."

He didn't like bats and never had, and now that he could actually see them, his jaw clenched and teeth gritted in an instinctual response. He'd never encountered anything quite like this in the Zoo and to see them there seemed almost like adding insult to injury. Even more than the other mutants he'd fought on US soil, these did not belong there, dammit.

The choppers appeared to have avoided the group of flying beasts, but the one on the left suddenly pulled hard to the side and struggled to maintain altitude. A mutant had latched onto it and dug its teeth into the Apache's armor to tear it off and reach what was inside. It was a terrifying reminder of what the monsters would do if they got their fangs into him.

Especially since his mech's suit was nowhere near as thick as what the chopper was protected by.

The helicopter banked and jerked in an effort to shake the beast, but a few more joined it and their combined weight dragged it lower until it tumbled and careened across the grasslands to leave a barren swath of destruction behind it. The crash killed the monsters that had held on to the end, but there were more where those had come from.

Hundreds more, he reminded himself when he glanced at the large mass that still huddled and attempted to move forward while the battle raged around them.

"Fuck!" The pilots shouted to one another as the monsters that were still in the air continued their efforts to destroy the aircraft.

"Shoot them!" Taylor shouted.

"Our weapons can't lock on!"

Taylor cursed and looked around the wreck he was on. The beasts had paused somewhat in their assault on his position, possibly because the greater threat in the sky needed to be dealt with for the moment. Once they were finished there, they would be able to kill him at their leisure.

He needed a way to draw them away from the choppers and ground them. The National Guard would need to fall back, regroup, replenish their ammo, and return. Hopefully, they would be able to get a lock on those that took flight before they became a problem now that they knew what to expect.

"Shit, this isn't a good idea," he told himself acidly and fired a few shots at the creatures that had reached the top of the chopper he was on. He drew a few deep breaths before he jumped clear of it.

It wasn't a good idea to give up the high ground but it had to be done. There was no other way to distract them and if they destroyed the choppers, he stood no chance at all. He could go out with a big enough bang that he took a good number with him but go out he would. This, crazy and reckless though it was, at least carried marginally better odds.

He landed on one of the monsters and the weight of his suit crushed the bones surprisingly easily. It made him wonder if they had hollow bones like birds but he pushed the thought aside. That was something for the researchers to look into once they had an abundance of bodies to study.

Taylor rolled over the creature and the suit almost completely flattened it before he pushed to his feet. Those that hadn't taken flight immediately attacked. They were still difficult to see with the naked eye but his motion and heat sensors compensated and he was able to select his targets once they got close enough. If they were too far, he lost them but for now, he could work with what he had.

Entirely focused, he continued to shoot and eliminated

the creatures that targeted him until the mags clicked empty. His ammo had begun to run dangerously low but that wasn't the main concern right now. The mutants still harried the three choppers overhead and would soon have the upper hand. He turned quickly and jogged toward the large mass of creatures still huddled to protect their young, forced a lock on the location instead of a single target, and fired three of the rockets.

They streaked away ahead of a trail of white smoke as they followed a direct trajectory to where the group continued to move slowly. He'd overshot them slightly and caught the front line, but when a number of the creatures dropped and shrapnel sliced through their ranks, it had the desired effect. A chorus of loud screeches ensued like a frantic call for help, and those overhead suddenly cut away from the aircraft and swooped in as protection.

"You guys should be clear now!" Taylor called.

"Thanks for the assist, Cryptid Assassin!" the pilot for Hotel One responded. "We need to pull back, get more ammo, and prepare for another strike. How do you feel about surviving until we get back?"

"It's not like I have much choice," he said and noted that the enemy had mostly given up attacking him for the moment and seemed focused on those that had been wounded on the perimeter of their mobile nest.

"True," the man admitted. "We'll drop ammo for you. It should be a ping on your HUD. Sorry we can't do more at the moment."

"Don't worry about it." He had already moved away from the creatures. They looked like they had begun to regroup and reassess, and he had a bad feeling that once they were finished, he'd have their undivided attention. That in itself was a daunting thought, and he wouldn't have any air power on his side this time. Not for a little while, at least.

"Actually, I think I have something of a plan," Taylor said and jogged quickly to where the ammo drifted earthward attached to a parachute.

"We're open to ideas here, Cryptid Assassin," the pilot replied. "Anything that doesn't force us to deal with those fuckers flying close again is good."

He winced at even the thought of it. "Yeah, that's my bad. I should have been able to call that from the video that survived from the other attack. They didn't try to jump over the chopper but they flew up to meet it. I feel a little stupid at the moment."

"We can save the self-deprecation for later," the man said. "Why don't you talk about that plan you mentioned?"

"Right." He snapped out of his momentary distraction. "The long and the short of it is that when you collect more ammo, you need to load up on one of those big booms— you know, the fuckers that are just shy of being nuclear. Do you guys have any of those at the base?"

"Hey, McFadden," Banks said and intruded quickly into the conversation. "What the fuck do you think you're planning out there?"

"Banks, get back to overseeing the operation," he snapped, absolutely in no mood for interference.

"This is me overseeing the operation. What are you planning?"

"The plan is for them to get the biggest fucking boom available," he said and ignored the burn in his muscles when he pushed the mech into a run it was not designed for.

"We can load rockets with thermobaric payloads," the pilot said. "But in order for us to be able to come in close enough to get a lock on the fuckers, we'll be caught in the blast radius too."

"Don't worry about that," Taylor said. "I'll give you the targeting system. You only need to bring the biggest fucking boom you can find."

"McFadden, I feel like they should worry about it," Banks protested. "Your being close enough to laser-target the rockets they'll launch will leave you inside the blast radius."

"I can give them a target and get the hell out before the explosion," he said. "I can do it but don't worry about me. Worry about what happens when you can't stop these monsters before they make it into the nearest population center. Once they reach all those corpses, they won't stop breeding. If you think this is a problem, imagine what will happen with them on the loose in the closest town with schools and old age homes in the mix. We'll never have a better chance to stop them than now."

A long silence from the other end of the comm indicated that they were most likely arguing about whether or not they could authorize the strike with him still near the blast radius.

"Look, I'll do this, one way or another." He reached the ammo dump and began to peel the crate off and add the new rockets and ammo mags to his suit. "I intend to stay here until either they're all dead or I am, so you might as well take advantage of that."

More silence followed but he ignored the implications. He'd made his mind up, and if she knew nothing else about him, Banks knew only death could change it.

"We appreciate your work, son," a man said over the comms, likely one of the others who were overseeing the operation. "Give them hell."

CHAPTER TWENTY-FIVE

"I don't like this," Rod said and shook his head.

"You didn't have a choice in this matter," Luca replied quietly. "Well, you did have a choice and you made it. There is nothing that can change that now. We all have our battles to fight. This isn't yours."

The plane turned on the tarmac and eased in closer to where the two men stood.

"But simply killing people like this feels...wrong," he protested. "I know there's nothing to add to this that will make a difference, but killing the guy feels like it'll maybe have the wrong kind of reaction from the locals. I'm not sure I want them to feel like we simply kill the people who don't agree with us. Fear is a great motivator but only when there's some kind of meaning behind it. Killing people might not send that message."

"You don't need to worry about what they'll do," his companion said placidly. "These men are professionals. This is about sending the kind of message that these people understand. Pay up and you'll have protection. Don't pay and you won't. You can try to bring protection in from outside but it won't work out for you. People in this business don't get into it because they feel you can get them what they want. It's because you can get them what they need, and that has nothing to do with the fear of being killed. It has to do with needing to run and operate a business. If they have faith in us, they pay. If they don't, we don't get paid. It's about inspiring faith in the kind of people who might start to doubt."

"Yeah, I know but—"

"People doubt your ability to lead," the capo continued and simply spoke smoothly over him so he was forced to end his protest. "You still bring in the money and more money than before. Others get rich and fat off your efforts, but they think what you do are the kinds of things they can do for themselves. They did this, so why should they have to listen to you? They feel like you're the silent partner who is starting to profit off their hard work."

Rod nodded reluctantly. "Look, it's not that I don't understand why this is necessary. People will ask questions about those who are dealt with and they'll fear you for that."

"Not me," the man reminded him. "You. They will see McFadden dead and realize what happens when they cross you, when they don't pay you for protection, or spit in your face when you offer it again nicely. They'll see you enforce the will of the families in Vegas, and they'll respect you for it in the same way the family respects you."

"I appreciate that." He ran his fingers nervously down

the lines of his suit. "Murder is one hell of a line to cross, though. I didn't realize I would cross it so soon. For about ten years, my dad operated without having to make any decisions like this. People knew he was good for the threats and so it never needed to be said or even alluded to."

"Everyone merely needs to be reminded that the family is not to be trifled with." Luca patted him on the shoulder, the gesture a little condescending. "And you need to be reminded of it. I don't need to tell you that I'm here to help you establish control. The family likes your management style and the fact that you know how to make them their money. Now, they want it to be something that lasts, and that only happens if people respect you like they did your father. I'm here to make sure of it."

Rod looked at the plane as two men hurried down the steps. They wore the same kind of look his companion appeared to prefer. The costly but understated suits were only offset here or there by an expensive watch or ring that had been given to them by someone they couldn't afford to insult by not wearing them.

Neither looked like the capo. He came across as a man who hadn't been involved in the dirtier side of their business, while the newcomers definitely did not. There was a powerful look about them, physical rather than psychological. From the first glance, he could tell they were military men, the kind who had been in the heat of battle instead of giving orders and when those days came to an end, they chose to fight another war.

There was no battle they would turn away from, and

that was useful to certain people. Whether they had been members since before their time in the military or were recent additions was irrelevant. Either way, they were the kind of men who would be brought in when a serious message needed to be sent.

This was, of course, merely supposition. He'd seen similar men enter his father's house from time to time and had always been told they were there on business. He'd never really understood who's business or even what it entailed and had felt no inclination to curiosity and simply accepted it at face value.

What he did recall, though, was that he had been terrified of them and had always hidden away when they'd tried to engage him. A couple had brought presents like a new phone or a tablet or video games, and they always bowed and kissed the ring on his father's hand.

Respect, Marino senior said. The family respected his ability to hold their business interests in Vegas secure and funnel the money they needed to Sicily. He reminded himself that respect was all that was important and that he intended to keep earning it.

It was why they were giving him the chance. It wasn't something he felt he deserved, but that wasn't really an issue. He had already made his mind up to earn it. They liked having the money in their hands and would be sure to put him in a position to win.

"Mr. Marino, these are our delegates in this situation," Luca said and gestured first to the man with short black hair and then the one with the beard. "Bruno and Romano have been with the family for a long time and built a reputation as men who will settle situations like these."

"*E un piacere conoscerlo, Signor Marino,*" the bearded man, Romano, said and bowed his head.

Rod remembered the gesture his father always made—a simple extension of his right hand that held the ring with his family's crest. It had been expected, clearly, as Romano moved forward almost instantly, took it, and pressed his lips to the crest on the ring, followed quickly by his comrade.

While it was an old-fashioned tradition, the people in Sicily were suckers for the old ways. Even though the Marino family hadn't been nobility in the area for a long time, they were still treated like it.

Respect, as his father had said. Nothing was more important. It was where the money came from, where everything else did too, and there was no business without it.

"*Come possiamo aiutarlo, Signor Marino?*" Bruno asked.

Rod couldn't tell if they spoke Italian because it was all they knew or they knew how to speak English but thought he should know enough of the mother tongue to be able to communicate what he wanted with them.

He disliked the idea that they might actually question him in any way, no matter what recommendations they brought to resolve his problems.

His expression schooled carefully into quiet confidence, he merely shook his head and gestured for the capo to step forward. If these men didn't want to deal with him on his terms, he would definitely not be intimidated into acting according to theirs.

Luca understood that, of course, and inclined his head

slightly to him before he turned to the hitmen who had been summoned.

This wasn't a favor he wanted done. He wanted them to do their jobs and that was the message that needed to be sent.

"There's a businessman in the city who needs to be dealt with, and Signor Marino defers to your judgment regarding how," the capo told them in English, which confirmed Rod's suspicions about their intentions. "The details should be waiting for you on your phones. The target is former military, well-armed, and connected with the FBI, so don't underestimate him. The situation is to be resolved. Understood?"

"Of course," both men answered at the same.

"Excellent," Stefano said. "You have reservations at Signor Marino's hotel, where your equipment will be waiting for you. Rest, recover, and get to work as quickly as possible."

Both men bowed deferentially as their car drew up to take them to the hotel, which gave him and Stefano some space to talk as they walked toward their own vehicle.

"Well played," the man said with a small smile.

"They're employees," he said. "They're not doing me a favor so they need to understand that. They're doing their job. Nothing more, nothing less."

The capo nodded. "They're the best in the business. There should be no trouble."

Banks shook her head, took a deep breath, and rubbed her

temples to ease a growing headache. She was the one in charge of the operation and so had to make the call about whether Taylor was being too reckless with his own life. One option was to make the call and send a chopper in to lift him out of the area instead of bombing the shit out of it. They would have to risk a few things—which he'd pointed out in no uncertain terms—but to save the life of her best hunter instead of sacrificing it, wasn't it worth the risk?

In this case, however—and she was sure every man on the base would agree—it was customary for anyone overseeing the operation from afar to defer to the judgment of the people who had boots on the ground. It wasn't a traditional gesture of respect but because they were the ones who were present and therefore actually knew what was happening. Their lives hung in the balance, and if they had any insights as to what could be done next, their contribution mattered.

What Taylor had suggested was, without a doubt, the best idea. Everyone agreed that they had to deliver as much firepower as they could in the shortest possible time. The peculiar issue that they weren't able to lock onto the monsters was the problem. Her hunter had to stay close to do it for them. It was the best option available, one that would end the threat the monsters posed.

A very unique threat, she had to admit, and one she knew had to be handled right there and right now. He'd been absolutely right when he'd pointed out that they would risk a disaster of greater proportions later once the mutants were able to feed on the corpses they had left. The repercussions of that were unthinkable. To avoid them, the only option was a definitive strike with everything they had while they were vulnerable and out in the open.

He was right, dammit. Even if it did risk his life, it was the right call to make.

So why was she so hesitant about it? She knew he'd made the right decision, dangerous though it was. Did she really care enough about keeping him alive that she was willing to risk the potential worst-case scenario? Thankfully, she didn't have to dig too deeply into that as the helicopters returned.

They were in a hurry and there were only three of them left. The other had been dragged down by the monsters that, apparently, could fly. She wondered belligerently how many more fucking surprises the bastards had in store for them.

"We have four fresh Apaches lined up and ready to go," the base commander told her without preamble as the comms crackled to life. Obviously, the Army had now escalated the situation from monster problem to fucking unacceptable monster problem. She restrained a brittle laugh. "The three who returned will use the time to prepare and will launch when the first wave reaches the target area, together with a fourth to fill their numbers. I also have a third wave preparing."

"Thank you, Captain," she said and forced her mind from the fact that Taylor was out there and alone for the moment. It seemed she was the only one who needed to get her head right and regard this as the critical issue it really was.

"Ma'am, what's the call?" a lieutenant asked her, his tone edged with impatience.

She took a deep breath, shook her head, and wanted to say no, but that didn't feel right.

"Load the choppers with those thermobaric rockets," she said and closed her eyes. It wasn't supposed to feel this bad. She tried to convince herself that she didn't want to lose Taylor because she'd put so much into bringing him onto the task force.

But what he was doing right now was the whole point of it.

"Right away, ma'am," the man replied and called the pilots on the radio. She was an Agent with the FBI—a civilian, technically—but she ran the operation. Somehow, that made her outrank virtually everyone on the base, at least where the operation was concerned.

Except for the base commander, of course, and the people who were overseeing the mission as her superiors. Still, it was her call. She was the one who had to decide the course of so many lives.

"Shit," she whispered, scowled, and turned to the screen that displayed what they could make out of the action. It was essentially only the satellite feed that revealed where Taylor currently stood and the fact that he was still breathing but not much else.

"Niki?" She startled when the private line that only she could hear activated. "Niki, you listen to me. You can't let Taylor do this."

The voice was clearly familiar and it took less than a second before she realized who had listened in on the call. She really shouldn't have been surprised that her sister wouldn't let her crush go, given the amount of work she put into making sure Taylor was a part of the task force. But seriously, talking like this during an operation?

She'd crossed the damn line.

"Jennie, this is a secure fucking line. How did you get on it?" Niki struggled to keep her voice low and not draw the attention of the people who might become suspicious.

"Yeah, tell me about secure lines," her sister said and laughed dryly. "You can't let him do this. He'll get himself killed for no goddamn reason."

"No, goddammit. There's a horde of monsters out there wanting a piece of him and they will tear through here—"

"You're in Wyoming, which is literally the state version of a tumbleweed," Jennie pointed out. "A quick military intervention is all that's needed. Bomb the crap out of any area they're in and boom, you're done. There is no need to risk any lives."

"It's not that simple and you know it," Niki whispered sharply into her microphone. "These creatures need to be dealt with here and now and we have that chance."

"You'll kill him."

She paused and dragged in a deep breath as she thought about those words for a moment. While she wouldn't actually pull the trigger herself, in authorizing the strike, she might as well have killed him. Maybe that was why she was hesitant. If Taylor died, Jennie would never speak to her again.

The agent sighed. "This was Taylor's call, Jennie. He's the one on the ground and knows the situation better than anyone else here. We have to defer to his judgment and that's final."

"Yeah, well, you didn't have to agree with his call," her

sister grumbled. "Taylor is a crazy bastard and you know it."

"No shit. He kills monsters for a living," she snapped, her tone impatient and even slightly angry. "Now get off the fucking line!"

CHAPTER TWENTY-SIX

Taylor reloaded hastily using what had been left for him. The rockets had been a staple of his onslaught and he'd used them any way he could, so he definitely needed more of those. He was also running out of spare mags and bullets. None had been used from the sidearm yet, but he had a feeling he would need every bullet available out there, so he found places to stash as much as he could.

The ammo dump was left mostly empty as he reset the software on his HUD to provide an updated view of what he now had to work with.

Thankfully, they had dropped him enough to deal with a small army, which was precisely what he was up against —a small army of mutant monsters bent on destruction.

He no longer had the high ground and the beasts would be able to run him down if he gave them the chance. The only elevation close enough was the second chopper they'd brought down as the original one was already overrun.

If he wanted to reach the relative safety this would

afford him, he had to move before the enemy began to advance in earnest.

"Banks, you'd better oversee the choppers loading those big fucking missiles!" Taylor yelled over the radio. His heart thudded almost painfully in his chest and sweat collected on his skin and inched down his spine. Everything in him wanted to strip out of the armor and scratch that particular itch but it would have to wait until later. He didn't want to think about the reality that he'd soon forget about it when the shit hit the fan.

His assault rifles were primed and the reticles displayed on his HUD to reveal the mass of creatures that advanced relentlessly.

It was still hard to see them, the fuckers. The damn creatures were unsettling with the way they blended into the landscape around them like that, but he wasn't as worried about them anymore. They were horrifying but they were warm-blooded and he could pick them up on the heat sensors and also on the motion sensors when they were close enough.

Those in the sky would still have trouble, being too far away to lock onto their heat signatures or their movement. Unfortunately, that was why he needed to stay on the ground.

That and the fact that he wasn't done with the fuckers, not yet.

He moved to the second downed chopper and studied the perimeter. It seemed realistic to give himself about three minutes before the wreck would be swarmed by monsters, enough time to get himself situated again for another round of fighting.

It would take seven minutes for the choppers to reach him, hopefully with enough firepower to level a small city. He grasped his rifles a little firmer and strode around the area to assess how he could use it to his advantage.

A low whistled growl caught his attention and he turned quickly toward the sound. One of the monsters that had attacked the aircraft thrashed under the weight of it while it hissed and spat at him like a cat. The camouflage still worked but its eyes were visible. They were small for the size of the body and certainly when compared to the teeth and jaws, which opened almost to a complete ninety-degree angle and snapped at him. He shook his head at the almost primal hatred and rage. Even with its internal organs crushed under the weight of the helicopter, the fucker tried to kill him.

Taylor strapped the right assault rifle to his back, drew his sidearm, and fired three rounds into the open jaws of the creature. The round punched through and left a spray of blood on the metal above it as he holstered his weapon.

"These fucking monsters won't lay down and die," he muttered as he scrambled to the top of the chopper and pushed the broken rotors out of the way as he settled into his elevated position.

It wouldn't last, unfortunately. Already, a group of the mutants surged toward him and broke away from the main force to attack. They moved incredibly quickly across the grassland and while he was again confused by their ability to blend with their surroundings, he estimated that the group comprised at least three dozen of the creatures.

As if choreographed and meticulously coordinated, they took to the skies. They simply vaulted skyward and their massive wings spread into the air around them to catch the wind. Once they had gained sufficient altitude, they flapped their wings and resumed their approach.

It was an awesome sight or would have been if it weren't terrifying. He drew his second rifle and raised his weapons to aim at the mutants. The heat sensors told him that others moved along on the ground, most likely a second line of the attack, but he didn't need to pay attention to those yet.

Manually aiming the rockets would always be a pain in the ass, even with the heat signatures, and it was easier to do if he had the targeting reticles to work with.

Taylor narrowed his eyes and took a deep breath as he selected his targets in the middle of their formation. They moved like a group of trained pilots and homed in on him with every intention to strike with all kinds of deadly force.

A moment's fear gave way to the determination to not allow their purpose to succeed. Calmly, he took his shot and delivered a stream of the rockets from his shoulder-mounted launcher, four in a quick series, as the white plumes drifted behind them. They streaked into a perfect strike in the center, positioned to cause as much damage to the monsters as possible.

The mutants that were hit were almost turned into a red mist and those close to them began to plummet as the shrapnel erupted, and a massive hole was created in the ranks of those that could still fly. Whistles and growls immediately followed the attack and he opened fire on full auto at those that remained. Three more plunged earthward and their fellows decided to abandon that avenue of attack.

"Yeah, that's right, motherfuckers." He hooted in satisfaction and reloaded the rocket launcher on his shoulders before he turned to fire at the creatures below him. "You're dealing with a real hunter this time."

The inane one-sided conversation was simply a way to release tension and while he knew for a fact that the monsters couldn't understand what he said, it did wonders to keep his spirits up. Of course, his ongoing assault and the gratifying results when the beasts were annihilated and smoking craters left where they had been also boosted his morale significantly. If he didn't allow himself to dwell on the fact that his attackers only represented a small portion of the overall numbers, he could almost believe he'd make it out of there.

The mutants seemed to have decided to maintain a ground assault this time and he couldn't blame them for that. Their air attack had failed spectacularly, and there was little else they could do until they could be sure he was too engaged with those below him to defend against those that attempted another strike from above.

Taylor could only hope the helicopters would have returned by then.

"McFadden, are you still with us?" Banks asked over the comms.

"I'm a little busy right now!" he shouted and let one of the rifles reload as he fired the other. He needed to maintain a consistent barrage to prevent them from reaching the helicopter.

"Oh, well, I thought you might want to know that the

helicopters are on their way to you, armed with the biggest fucking rockets they could spare. Now, Taylor, you fucking tell me that what you've planned isn't some crazy kind of suicide mission and I'll believe you."

It was a surprisingly deep question and full of all kinds of hidden meanings, but he doubted that she meant any of them. It wasn't like she cared enough to try to convince him to stay alive. She needed his hunting skills, of course, but as the folks running the money of the operation had already made clear, they were ready to look beyond him, no matter how skilled he was.

Was it a slap in the face? Definitely. Enough to get himself killed trying to prove himself? Not a chance.

"I fully intend to survive this mission and many others," Taylor assured her while he used the rockets on his back to cover for a quick reload on both assault rifles before he resumed the fight. "And that'll only happen if they put their best foot forward and time their launch at precisely the right moment, do you understand me?"

"I understand," she said. "I'm relaying your message to the pilots now. If you get yourself killed, I will surely kick your ass."

"You'll try," he said with a small grin and narrowed his eyes to focus on a few of the creatures that rushed toward the helicopter. They repeated the process, then did so a few times more and seemed to make no effort to actually climb it. It took him a while to realize what they were doing.

"Oh…right. For fuck's sake," Taylor grumbled as the aircraft shifted when three dozen or so of the monsters combined their efforts to shove the wreckage back.

Rolling it would be enough to knock him off. The damn

things had obviously worked out his plot to keep them at bay and now tried to reverse it and push him off his high ground.

"I really wish we'd installed magnetic clamps on the boots!" he shouted, followed the movement of the helicopter as it tipped, and vaulted clear when his footing slipped.

He landed hard, once again on one of the bat-like creatures, and crushed it under the weight of the suit. His momentum carried him onto his shoulder and he rolled quickly to regain his feet.

It went about as well as he could have expected it to but he hadn't been able to avoid a couple of painful tweaks in his back and shoulders and a sharp stab in the side of his head when he landed. Ruefully, he acknowledged that it could have gone better.

"Anytime you assholes feel like showing up!" he shouted into the comms. He still had no idea where the choppers were and had somehow lost track of the timing in all the fun. They could be seconds away or minutes, and he would still have to fight for his life.

A couple of the beasts realized that he was now clear of the helicopter and charged. The first was easily eliminated by two rounds through the head, but the second wasn't so easily deterred. It pounced viciously with its jaws wide and ready to tear into him.

He leaned forward, hammered his forearm into the dagger-long fangs as it collided with him, and knocked it back a few steps. No matter how strong it was, it wouldn't be stronger than a mech.

The mutant darted back and then forward again in an

attempt to catch him off-guard using the same attack. Its jaws split almost down the middle to catch him.

He fired and it fell back when three rounds powered through its mouth and out the back of its skull. It was weird how he could see the inside of the mouth and flecks of bone and blood better than he could see the outside of it.

Not unexpected, of course. Merely weird.

"You're smart," he said with a soft chuckle and reloaded hastily, "but you ain't that smart. It's good to know."

"Cryptid Assassin, this is Hotel Five. Do you copy?" a man called over the comms.

"I read you loud and clear, Hotel Five." He laughed. "What happened to Hotel One? Did he decide the party was no fun?"

"He'll be back, Cryptid Assassin. We didn't want you to have to wait too long and we were fueled and ready. They'll be launching as we speak."

"Well, it's good to have you boys in the mix. I was afraid I would have to kill all these fuckers on my own out here."

"No need to worry about that, Cryptid Assassin. This is Hotel Six. We are forty-five seconds away from your position," another man interjected. "Be advised, we will maintain a higher altitude for this run. For any directed rocket strikes, we will need you to provide laser guidance from the ground."

"Understood. I think I can do that but our timing will have to be perfect," Taylor said. "The creatures converge on the center of the nest every time it's hit, so when I target it with a few rockets to draw them in, you need to already have your finger on the trigger up there. That's our chance to wipe them the fuck out."

"Understood," the pilot replied. "What should we look for?"

He took a deep breath and steeled himself for what was now his reality. "Well, you'll see a few explosions and the laser will go hot. I'll hold it for as long as I can."

"Roger that, Cryptid Assassin. Good luck."

Taylor pushed forward, focused and alert as the creatures turned to attack him. He still had no real idea of how many there were. Their mass seemed to blend together in the motion and heat sensors, which made it difficult to identify them individually.

Another deep breath helped to settle a brief flurry of doubts. There really was no other choice.

"You got this, Cryptid Assassin," he said and opened fire. The good thing about them being massed together was that they were hard to miss. The bullets drove through them easily, found the mutants behind, and dealt considerable damage to them too.

The plan and its logistics scrolled through his mind as he paced forward slightly. They seemed to know that they were on equal footing with him this time. He lacked the higher ground for the battle but they had lost their comfortable advantage of being difficult to see. He had no idea how they would know this—or even how he knew they did—but their behavior had changed subtly, which seemed to confirm it. They now used rushed attacks in an attempt to distract him while a few others moved to try to catch him along the flanks.

A few fangs lashed out and one managed to rip a chunk

of his armor off. Taylor shoved them away and continued to shoot and reload as quickly as he could, alternating his guns.

The right assault rifle ran out of ammo first. He dropped it and drew his sidearm out of its holster in a practiced motion.

The rotors of the helicopters thumped above him before the commlink pinged again.

"We are in position," Hotel Six advised him.

"Roger that."

He pushed forward another few paces and used the weight of the mech to crush a couple of the wounded monsters underfoot. A few seconds later, he stopped close to the rolled chopper and within the necessary range, lasered himself a few targets at the center of the mass of creatures, and fired the rockets upward. They arced lazily toward their destination.

The monsters seemed to realize their nest was under attack when the missiles were still in the air. They abandoned their assault on him and had already moved to cover the nest before the rockets struck home.

"Target is live. Repeat, target is live!" Taylor yelled.

"Dropping ordinance."

Four rockets launched from the helicopters, dropped quickly, and moved even faster once the propellant kicked in.

His entire existence was now counted in seconds. He held the laser on the target for as long as he dared. They needed that to maintain their trajectory, but they would stay on course once they were close enough.

He gritted his teeth and held his position for a few

more seconds before he deactivated the laser, spun, and flung himself desperately behind the helicopter that had been rolled and was still the only option for cover in a hundred miles. Thankfully, it was also one he could reach in the time he gave himself, and he decided luck had indeed played a part to position the crashed aircraft so close to where he needed to be.

Instinct drove him now and he curled into himself, locked his hands around the back of his helmet, and closed his eyes.

The ground shuddered when the rockets detonated, almost like the foreshock that rippled before an earthquake. The roar of the explosion followed and made his ears ring even through the filters of the mech. He realized he was screaming before the blast wave struck. It rolled the helicopter over him and the weight turned his entire world black.

CHAPTER TWENTY-SEVEN

Neither Bruno nor Romano had ever questioned their place in the family. They had both spent years and years putting their lives on the line to make sure the men who had run the kind of criminal syndicate that spanned the planet could continue to make the inordinate sums of money they considered their right.

The mob had been a part of their lives since they were born and had seeped into the culture of the city they'd grown up in. When they had been asked by the local caporegime to join the military to gain experience to prepare them to serve the family, they had agreed without question.

Now, there was a very real possibility that they might be killed overseas, but that sure as hell beat being killed in their homes for resisting orders.

The two men had both had similar dreams. They had wanted to leave the military and be feared members of the family. That part, at least, had come to fruition. The training and experience earned them a position that could not be lost as killers and enforcers, to the point where even those who outranked them were fearful lest they be sent to kill them.

And the dreams, of course, flew ever higher. They were of pure Sicilian blood and therefore in a position to be raised even further in the family once they were established in their position. Blind faith in their superiors and following every order to the letter had brought them this far.

These considerations made it especially difficult to have to bow and kiss the ring of a man who hadn't technically been a member until circumstances had forced it on him after his father's death. It seemed unacceptable that two men who had served the family faithfully for decades had to follow the orders of a frat boy who held a high position simply because he'd come from his father's dick.

It was the culmination of meritocracy versus nepotism, and they would have to follow orders until their death.

The kid, on the other hand, would more than likely lose his position once the family found someone better suited to running the Vegas investments.

Still, it was a reason to visit Vegas. Marino had put them up in decent rooms, gave them credit in the casino, and supplied them with virtually anything they could need or want, whether it was for the job or simply to keep them happy while they were in the country.

The man might not have earned his current position but damned if he didn't know what it meant to be a good host.

And all they needed to do was kill one man and level his place of business. It wouldn't have been considered a challenge except for the fact that they had been brought in. People didn't bring Bruno and Romano in if they had other options. The two were famous as the last resort, those who were called when someone needed to be dealt with without delay.

And that was what they were ready to do. The men had already been warned as to what to expect from the man known as Taylor McFadden. He was apparently a former military man, with most of his history in the armed forces already having been blacked out. That usually meant the kind of operations that wouldn't sound good to the international community, but in his case, it meant years spent in the one place in the world the two had refused to go.

Alien monsters in alien jungles were the kind of thing anyone sane stayed well, well away from. Given the time McFadden had spent there and the kind of money he walked away with, it seemed entirely logical that sane did not apply in his case.

Based on that, they wouldn't assume this would be a smooth operation. From what they'd been told, underestimating him had been the problem from the beginning. The whereabouts of the last freelancers was still unknown, despite extensive efforts to locate them using contacts even at government level. It seemed prudent to learn from the mistakes of others.

"*Cazzo*," Romano said softly and looked at his partner. "Our friend has managed to crack the security system."

"Are you sure?" Bruno asked and fixed the youth with a hard look. The hacker the family had provided seemed unperturbed, however, and returned his stare with a smug smirk that looked almost sinister with his sallow features and spiked black hair. He tolerated the kid because he needed him, but he did wonder how anyone with Sicilian blood could stoop so low as to encrust his ears with so many piercings it was difficult to tell whether the appendages were actually still there. "Earlier you said it wouldn't be easy to do."

"Well, of course it's not easy," the kid replied with a chuckle. "That is why you needed someone with my skills."

For not the first time, Romano intervened between the two. "Yes, we needed hacker skills. I've seen top-of-the-line systems and this takes the goddamn cake. I don't think it's even on the market. This guy apparently built it himself with shit he brought back from the Zoo."

"Are there any weaknesses?" Bruno asked and leaned closer to see what his partner had on his laptop. "Can we disable it? Cut the power or something like that?"

"He probably has a generator in place," the young man said scornfully. "Either way, you have to assume he does. I suppose you can try to turn the power off, but if he has something in place to counter that, it'll be enough of a warning that the element of surprise will be lost."

Bruno scowled. The kid had a point and on principle, he wished he could dispute it. Maybe when the job was done, he could discreetly teach him a lesson or two about respecting his elders.

"All we need to do is get in there," Romano said quickly. "McFadden is out of town so we can eliminate the mechanic and the woman without interference. Once inside, we have two choices. We can either wait until he returns and provide a little welcome home party for him.

He won't suspect a thing and won't have time to mount any kind of defense. Once he's dealt with, we simply burn the bodies in the building and leave."

"We don't know how long he's away for," Bruno reminded him. "No one has even been able to confirm where he went."

"That is true, but his employees will know. If he's scheduled to return within a day or so, we wait. If not, our second option applies. We kill the woman and the mechanic and burn the building. That will pull him back in a hurry but we can catch him in the open. He'll have no one on the premises to help him or any defenses, which would make him vulnerable. We finish the job and leave. Simple."

"Like you said, all we need is to get in there," Bruno said derisively. "And you pointed out that his security system is top-of-the-line. It makes Fort Knox look like a piggy bank. So I'm not sure what you mean by simple."

"Hel-looo," the kid said before either of them could say anything more. "You've missed the point. I found a weakness in their software. I can adjust the alarm system using the way they have it set for people who are known to enter. That way, it won't register you as intruders until you're already inside."

Romano regarded him with a thoughtful expression. "That could work. But wouldn't that alert them?"

"Please." The young man snorted disdainfully. "This guy might be all kickass or whatever, but he's not a computer specialist. I can see he's tried to put in a few traps and firewalls and whatever, but it's basic."

"How much time do you need?"

"Two seconds. You can go in any time you're ready."

Bruno regarded him for a moment, still openly suspicious, but simply shrugged and turned to his partner. "Okay. McFadden is out of town so we don't need to worry about his interference. What about the other two?"

"What about them?" Romano's smile was cold. "One is a woman—a college dropout, based on the information we have. She has probably also been in trouble with the law, as there is a sealed file still pending, which means this job is probationary. I doubt she has any combat experience beyond the odd cockroach or two."

"Let's not forget that they work on those mech suits. The man in one of those could pose a problem."

The other man laughed. "They repair them, which means most of them will not be functional and so aren't anything to concern ourselves with. Besides, he's a mechanic. Until recently, he worked on cars and although he was in the military prior to that, he was merely a Motor Pool mechanic. He might be able to fix the suits, but it takes training to be able to use them without injuring or even killing yourself. Those two are sitting ducks, especially if we have the element of surprise."

"Perfecto," Bruno said decisively as his frown cleared. He drew his weapon out of its holster and deftly applied the suppressor. The kid closed his laptop and slid out to wait at the driver's door, ready to move the vehicle to a different location to avoid attracting too much attention. "Make sure you wait in one of the rooms at the hotel where you won't draw attention to yourself," he told the hacker, who nodded.

"I have a burner phone, as we agreed, but which isn't

turned on," Romano added. "Once we are ready, we'll activate it and call you for pickup."

"And if you don't call?" The young man didn't sound sarcastic but both men resented the implication that they might fail.

"If we haven't contacted you within two days, assume we are dead and get the fuck out of there. Someone from the family will dispose of the vehicle—and you if you don't keep your mouth shut." Bruno fixed him with a hard look.

The kid grimaced but made no protest. He obviously knew it wasn't an empty threat.

Both men conducted a weapons check before they stepped out and the hacker slid behind the wheel, started the engine, and turned to return to the hotel. The hitmen walked the rest of the way to the strip mall, keeping their gait rapid but casual. It was a practiced walk that suggested people who were in a rush to be somewhere but without any suspicious indications that they might be on the way to kill a man in his place of business.

Vickie eyed her phone, tilted her head, and scowled at it for a moment.

Bobby glanced at her a couple of times before he realized that the girl wasn't doing her job and fixed her with a stern look. "What's the matter? Did your date text you, asking if you could go out?"

"Please, he...didn't seem that desperate, anyway," she said. "No, nothing like that. Did you add any new names to the security exempt list recently?"

"I don't know enough about the system to try anything like that," Bobby said. "Did you? Maybe you added the name of some fuckboi while you were drunk."

The hacker snorted "Do you really think I would invite anyone I might be physically attracted to over to this place? While I respect the fact that Taylor's trying to build something here, as it is, it's like the building version of a purity ring."

"You make a fantastic point," Bobby grumbled and wandered over to see what she was looking at. "Could Taylor have added them?"

"Nope, it happened after he left," Vickie replied, rolling her seat over to the desk where the computer was stationed. "Actually, the time stamp puts the addition at... five minutes ago."

"What does that mean?"

"Okay. I guess it's confession time."

"What, so you did add a fuckboi?"

"Come on, this is serious. I might have...uh, well, tweaked the security system a little." She grimaced when he opened his mouth to speak, his expression indignant. "Hear me out, would you? After Taylor was shot at and we were kidnapped, I realized we needed a little extra, which included the hacking side of things which of course, neither of you two know much about. I simply added a little encryption and a few firewalls—nothing illegal and nothing weird either."

"And?" He at least seemed willing to give her the benefit of the doubt.

"Well, part of that kind of security is adding traps—the proverbial honeypot—to fool any hackers into thinking they got into the system undetected. The obvious one was our approved entry list. For anyone to get in, they'd have to use that or bypass it, but either way, I'd get the alerts and we'd know about it. Well, Smith and Green were added to the system and whoever did it has no idea we know."

"Smith? Green?" Bobby snorted. "Like that's not suspicious or anything. Couldn't they have come up with better names?"

"Cut it out, Bungees. Yes, they're dumb and I totally agree with you, but the point is that someone's trying to break into our fucking place," Vickie said sharply.

"Right," he said after a pause. "I wish you'd told us about—"

The hacker scowled at him. "Look, you can get as pissy as you like about me wanting to give us all a little extra protection when this is all over. My tweaks have worked, which should tell you something—unless you'd like to discard the obvious and...fuck, I dunno, run with the Skynet scenario? After all, you guys are working with AIs around here, right?"

"Only the one AI and it's tied to Liz."

"Or maybe it only wants you to think it's tied to Liz. Have you thought about that?"

Bobby stared at her for a long moment before he finally shrugged.

"Yeah, someone's trying to break in," he conceded. Are they already inside the perimeter?"

"No...oh, yeah, there they are," Vickie said. "Two take-no-prisoner dudes, both armed with what looks like silenced pistols and a backpack."

"Okay, you go upstairs and get your gun, exactly like we practiced," he said.

"I only practiced how to put it together, not how to shoot it at someone!" she protested.

He scowled at her again. "Exactly like we practiced. Come on, get going. We are under attack here. Get up there and have your gun ready, but maybe operate the defenses from the safety of your room."

"Right, and what will you get?" she asked, already off her chair and headed toward the door.

"Something considerably bigger than a handgun," the mechanic said and studied the camera feed as the two intruders began to attempt to break in through the front door.

For someone who was supposedly such a pain in the ass for the local talent, a simple padlock certainly didn't make much of a statement about security. It took Bruno only a minute or so before he was able to pick it and open the door.

"You know, for a guy who has a security system that some military installations would probably kill for, his locking system really needs an upgrade," Romano whispered. He was the first inside and covered the corners on his entrance before he gestured for his partner to enter.

"Maybe he didn't think he needed it," the man suggested and followed the man quickly to check the corners with his suppressed pistol ready before they moved deeper into the room. "Again, he put work into that system. He might have run out of money and was waiting for more to come in."

"Whatever." Romano shook his head.

He turned, ready to fire, when he caught movement out of the corner of his eye. For a moment, he simply stared as the door closed swiftly behind them. He crossed toward it and yanked on the handle.

"It's locked."

Bruno shrugged, unperturbed by the oddness of it. "Maybe it's one of those automatic-locking doors."

"Then why wasn't it locked when we got in?" Romano asked and tugged the handle again. "There was only the padlock outside but the door wasn't locked. What changed?"

His partner paused for a moment but shook his head. "It's not important. We need to find the woman and the mechanic and interrogate them before we kill them. If McFadden is away for a while, we set the charges to blow this place the fuck up. There's no need to create unnecessary distractions."

The man had a point, of course, and they proceeded carefully through what appeared to have once been a grocery store or something similar. Old shelving rusted in place and the structure seemed to be in general disrepair, so McFadden obviously hadn't put anything into construction in this section of the mall. Maybe the previous owners ran out of money and merely needed to get rid of the property to pay back the loans, which was what allowed an enterprising businessman like McFadden to purchase it. He had done some renovations, so perhaps he planned to do it section by section as he needed them

Either way, this particular area looked like it had mostly been left untouched after the purchase, which meant their targets were likely in another part of the building.

"Shouldn't we simply plant the explosives and be done with it?" Bruno whispered, and peered into the gloom when they paused to make out the way ahead. "It seems a waste of time to find these people when leveling the premises would kill them anyway and bring our target back quicker."

Romero shook his head. "We discussed this. We need to interrogate those two so we know exactly what tricks McFadden might have up his sleeve. While it's unlikely, he might be part of a secret task force or something and could call them in if something happened here."

The other man hissed a couple of curses under his breath and tightened his grasp on his weapon as they crossed the seemingly endless abandoned space and negotiated the racking as carefully as they could.

"I hate these fucking night vision goggles," Romero whispered. "They disorient me, and I can't see shit."

"I'd use my phone, but you told me not to bring it," his partner snapped.

"We both know that even a GPS signal pinged off a nearby tower would be enough to incriminate us, and we're better than that. Now calm the fuck down. We're alone in here, so don't let your nerves get the better of you."

"But you're really, really not," a voice said from ahead of them.

Both men raised their weapons quickly and professionally and pulled the triggers three times each. Their experience had proven that to be the perfect number to ensure a very dead target.

Romero squinted into the gloom to where the bullets ricocheted off a solid but indefinable shape. A few bright sparks were created but the body—if that was what it was —showed no sign of injury.

He frowned when he caught the unexpected whir of servos as the figure took a step forward and resolved into the semblance of a man. The weight of the step was enough to make the floor shake, and while the Sicilian had met large men in his day, none had ever been that heavy.

His mind overcame his momentary shock and clicked into an assessment of the situation. The weight plus the sound of mechanical parts moving over each other told him the unlikely scenario they'd so easily discounted had become the reality. Simply put, they were in deep, deep shit.

"Fall back!" he shouted and instinctively pulled the trigger again and again. His effort brought no results, however, and more footsteps echoed and the floor shuddered. Something moved in the near darkness a little above his head and he tried to step away, but it swung faster than he could move.

He tasted blood as he fell and heard Bruno fall beside him and cough like he'd had a broken rib puncture his lung.

"*Cazzo!*" Romero hissed in fury and stared at the mech that towered over them.

Vickie munched on the bowl of popcorn she'd prepared and watched the fight through the security cameras.

Of course, it proved to be less than a fight and more like an ass-whupping that would only have one result. The two were good and she didn't doubt that without the advance warning and the availability of a borrowed mech, she and Bungees might well be prisoners at best and dead at worst. This team certainly seemed way more professional than the duo that had managed to kidnap them frighteningly easily. Thankfully, no man, irrespective of how well-trained and experienced he might be, had any chance against a mech.

Once it was over, she turned the lights on in the room and grimaced at the bloodstains on the tiled floor of the empty grocery store.

"How do you feel, Bungees?" she asked over the radio.

"I'm good, actually. except for a little cleaning, I'd say Mech suit one-two-one-two is ready to be shipped out," Bobby replied and the shoulders of the mech rolled dramatically. "Who the hell said we need Taylor to test these babies out, anyway?"

"Absolutely no one," she replied. "I've asked to try to ride in one of them."

"And the answer is still no," he told her firmly.

The hacker ran her hands through her short hair and pouted at the screen in front of her. "I'm actually a little pissed that these assholes dared to make another attempt. I thought we made it very clear that we were not to be fucked with."

"Except with Banks involved, no actual message was

sent," Bobby pointed out. "So maybe they're not too good when it comes to reading between the lines."

"Obviously not. The fact that their hitmen simply vanished should be plain enough," Vickie grumbled. "But maybe they did get the message and simply don't care. Either way, I'll see if I can backtrack these assholes and get a better idea of where they came from. We might be able to nip any other attacks in the proverbial bud."

Bobby turned to return to the shop, moving the mech carefully. "That sounds like a good idea. I think Taylor would probably like to meet whoever's sending these dumbasses too. You might want to contact your aunt as well and let her know there is cleaning up to do. "

"She's my cousin!" she corrected him.

"Whatever."

CHAPTER TWENTY-EIGHT

The weird repetitive beep that intruded into his fuzzy brain wasn't fast enough to be an alarm clock. Besides that, it wasn't the kind of noise he usually heard. Maybe he'd tripped some kind of alarm in a house and he needed to disarm it before the cops were called?

No, that didn't sound like him. He didn't even know of a house he might be in anyway, so it made no sense.

The darkness was everywhere and it was thick enough that it seemed to swarm around him so it was impossible to move. He gritted his teeth and tried again but nothing happened—like he was stuck in a tar pit, he thought blearily.

Beep... beep... beep...

The infuriating tone increased speed. Maybe it was an alarm.

Taylor's eyes finally opened and he turned, still in darkness. Something moved. He couldn't see it but somehow still knew it was there. Images snapped into focus and vanished as quickly—large claws, large wings, fangs, and a mouth that opened to utter a low whistled growl directed toward him. He raised his hands defensively as the creature lurched forward, its fangs aimed at his throat.

Beep, beep, beep...

The world changed suddenly from black to white, his eyes opened, and his body lunged forward to fight the monster.

It took a moment to register that nothing was there. His eyes were blinded by the light that seared the world around him, and a shock of agony consumed his body as he fell onto the bed. He coughed and the paroxysms wracked his body with more pain.

"Fuck." He gasped. "Mistakes were made. So much regret…"

His eyes adjusted to the light which, as it turned out, wasn't even that bright. He lay in a hospital bed, alone in the room where two IVs were plugged into his left arm. Sensors attached to his chest and heart transmitted to the monitor, which was where the annoying beeping originated.

The noise was as irritating as it had been when he had been unconscious. He looked for the painkiller button and knew if he could only tap it gently, the aches and pains that ravaged his body would recede to a dull ache instead.

"Nurse?" he mumbled and looked toward the door as it cracked open. "Nurse! Where's that fucking button?"

He fumbled for it but stopped when the door opened fully and a familiar face looked in.

The damn woman wouldn't leave him alone. He had the feeling the last thing he looked at would be that annoying face of hers.

"Nurse?" he asked again and pretended not to recognize her. "Nurse, I think I'm ready for my sponge bath."

She stepped in and closed the door behind her. "Welcome back to the land of the living, McFadden."

"Thanks," he replied. "About that sponge bath?"

"Ass." She chuckled.

"Well, that too but let's not start there," Taylor retorted, and she punched his shoulder lightly. It still triggered a shock of sensation. "Ouch! Watch it!"

"Sorry, I didn't know you were such a sensitive little bitch," she said, although she looked a little repentant and rubbed his shoulder gently. "How are you feeling?"

"Like I was hit by a truck, which then reversed and backed over me and ran me over again," he admitted. "What happened, anyway?"

"Very nearly death by idiocy," Banks replied and drew a chair up to sit next to his bed. "I wish I could say it was the first time."

"Did my idiocy pay off?" He inspected the IV in his arm. "Emphasis on pay, of course. Like, how big is my paycheck for this job?"

She gave him what looked like a genuine smile. "Big enough that the bean-counters in Washington squealed like stuck fucking pigs. When they realized how many animals you killed out there, they managed to stretch beyond their assholes and reached a cap they could approve, which ended up at a little over two hundred and fifty thousand dollars. Plus expenses, of course."

Taylor nodded and tried not to let his eyes widen at the amount. "Out of sheer curiosity, how many creatures were actually killed?"

"They stopped counting at a hundred and twelve," she replied and leaned back in her seat. "Well, that's the number of whole bodies that were recovered. The rest were in pieces and burnt beyond recognition. I'm talking deep-fried for a couple of hours in burning oil kind of burnt. I can only assume that the researchers who hoped for study material weren't too happy about that."

"Fuck them. If they wanted all of them as whole bodies, they should have helped me to kill the sons of bitches." He coughed again and groaned as he clutched his ribs. "Not that they would have been able to do much, of course. Although they might have been useful as meat shields."

She smirked. "And do you want to know what the best part of it all is?"

"Wow me."

"Your paycheck won't even come out of our budget," Banks said and laughed. "Since this was technically a military operation, the Pentagon will foot the bill from their freelancer budget. So you'll be paid a fucking shitload, I don't lose anything from my budget, and they even took responsibility for what will be paid to the families of the three hunters who died in round one."

He shook his head. "Now who's being an asshole?"

She shrugged. "Maybe you're rubbing off on me."

"In your lonely, pathetic dreams," he replied and turned her own quote on her.

Banks raised an eyebrow at him. "You know, you should be nicer to me. It took them a while to clear the area of the bombing for a potential rescue mission, and many of the higher-ups were willing to write you off as dearly departed. Once they cleared it after five hours, I went in there myself to make sure they found you and dragged you out."

Taylor raised his eyebrows and relaxed into his bed with a soft sight. "Yeah? I honestly saw those explosions—well, felt—while I cowered behind that fallen chopper and prayed for my life and I really thought I was a goner. Seriously, it felt like a fucking earthquake when they dropped not one, not two, not three, but eight of the fucking things."

"I guess they really didn't want to risk the possibility that any of the fuckers might live," she said. "Honestly, I don't blame them. They got payback for their fallen brothers and they were actually adamant that we go back and get you out, whether or not you were still alive. I guess they thought you being stupid was rather you being heroic or some shit. You military types are such clichés."

"Yeah, well, we got the job done, so maybe being a cliché isn't such a bad thing," he pointed out.

"Sure, you're effective. Anyway, I joined the cleanup team on the ground and they pointed out that you had probably taken cover behind one of the choppers. It took us a while to find you, though, since they had been moved in the blast. I personally made sure you were airlifted out. Asshole you may be, but I put too much work into getting you onto my task force to let you die yet."

He laughed, then coughed. "Fuck, it hurts to laugh."

"From what they told me, your suit's closed environment system stopped the change in pressure from the blast tearing your lungs to pieces, plus all the other internal organs. It took a beating but it kept you alive. Those are damn good suits you guys work with."

Taylor nodded. "Bungees is the best in the business. I'll

have to buy him lunch for this shit. And I know where he'll want to go. Not only that, I'm sure I know what he'll order."

"Oh…" Banks grunted, looked at her chair, and toyed with the armrests.

He narrowed his eyes at her. "What?"

"Nothing."

"It didn't sound like nothing."

"It's only…" She sighed. "Well, you need to focus on your recovery. Nothing's more important."

"Bullshit. Lay the news on me." Taylor growled a warning.

She scowled at him. "Well, not that it really matters, but a couple more dumbasses paid your shop a visit."

Taylor tried to push himself up from the bed but groaned in pain and sank down again. "This whole being injured business is such a literal pain in the ass. Fucking hell. Are they okay, though? Bobby and Vickie weren't hurt, right?"

"Do you think I would hang around with your dumb ass if my cousin was hurt or in any kind of danger?" she retorted and raised an eyebrow.

"I guess not." He sighed. "They're okay, then?"

"Yeah, and you can deal with that once you're done recovering." She patted his arm placatingly.

"Speaking of recovery, what kind of injuries am I looking at?"

"How much time do you have?"

He raised his hands in frustration.

"Oh… Right, all the time in the world," she said with an embarrassed chuckle. "Well, from the initial report of the doctors who stabilized you, there was a severe concussion and a few cracks in your skull, but the damage wasn't as bad as it could have been. Your shoulder was dislocated and they reset that shit. You have five broken ribs from when a literal helicopter rolled over you, and there were a couple of problems with internal organs being displaced by the shockwaves. The good news, though, is they said everything should heal on its own without any surgery. They do want you to remain under observation for a couple of weeks. All in all, you could have had it far worse."

Taylor nodded. "You'd think I'd regret calling in the strike, but honestly, these injuries are probably nothing compared to what those motherfuckers would have done to me without help from above."

"Hey, if you say so," Banks replied. "I still think it was an idiotic move on your part."

"Idiotic, but effective," he retorted.

She laughed. "If that doesn't describe you to a T."

He nodded. "That's fair enough."

Her phone rang as she opened her mouth to offer a rejoinder. "Sorry, I have to take this."

"Take your time," he replied as she exited the room and stepped into the hallway, leaving the door cracked as she answered.

"Jennie, why the fuck are you calling?" she asked without any kind of greeting.

The memory of a certain phone call stirred, and he recalled that Jennie was Banks' sister. He had seen her in Portland but they had never actually been introduced. It irritated him now that he'd never managed to find out why she'd called him and tried to pass herself off as a member of the task force.

For some reason, he vaguely remembered her saying Banks was in trouble before she'd ended the conversation in a panic.

Damn. It made no sense but given the timing, she might well have called about her sister's presence in Wyoming. Maybe the hit on the head had been a little harder than he realized and he was simply imagining shit now, but he was sure she had called.

"He's fine!" Banks said and spoke a little louder than necessary. The shadow of her pacing up and down the hallway was visible through the doorway. "Okay, yeah, he's not fine, but the doctors' consensus is that he'll survive. I'm not sure why you think you know better than the doctors, and why the hell did you hack into the hospital's files anyway?"

Taylor's eyebrows raised in real surprise. Maybe Vickie wasn't the only hacker in the family.

"Well, given the fact that he's on mandatory bed rest and recovering from a literal list of injuries that would have killed most people, I don't think you coming over and giving him a quote, 'good humping,' unquote, will make him feel any better," the agent said snidely. "Did I mention that he was run over by a literal—not figurative, literal —helicopter?"

Taylor would have disagreed with her opinion on the recovery potential of a good humping, but that was probably only the painkillers talking.

"You know what, if it'll get you off my back, fine. I'll think of a way to let you meet him officially, okay?" Banks continued. "But only once he's fully cleared from bed rest. The guy took a fucking beating out there and I need him up and ready to go if something like this comes up again. Okay, b—yeah, I love you too. Bye."

The phone call came to an end and she returned to the room and the chair she'd sat in before, a little red in the face.

"Is everything okay?" Taylor asked, trying to break the silence.

"As right as rain."

He nodded. "Who was that on the phone?"

"Nunya," Banks replied simply.

He made a face and nodded again. "You...uh, you know you left the door open a smidgeon there, right? I heard everything. Well, at least from your side of the conversation."

She sighed, closed her eyes, and rubbed her temples gently. "Yeah, I realize."

"And you're standing by 'Nunya' as your response?" He rolled his eyes and fixed his gaze on the ceiling.

"Yep."

Finally, when it was clear she wouldn't be drawn out, he sighed. "You know, Jennie called me while I was still in Vegas. She ended the call in a hurry before she actually told me why she called, but she did say something about you being in trouble. When I think about it, I have the feeling she wanted to get me involved in what was happening in Wyoming while you were still dealing with the other three hunters."

Banks sighed and nodded.

"Cool. I simply thought you should know," he said. "I don't want to be a rat or anything but thought you should know that…uh, Nunya is getting involved whether you want her to or not."

"I get that." Banks pushed from her seat. "I need some sleep. It's been one long fucking day."

"Do you mind sending the nurse in on your way out?" Taylor asked. "I still need that sponge bath."

"I'm sure I saw one of the male nurses out there," she said with a small smirk and squeezed his arm gently. "Get better soon, Taylor."

"Thanks."

Have you read *The BOHICA Chronicles* from C.J. Fawcett and Jonathan Brazee? A complete series box set is available now from Amazon and through Kindle Unlimited.

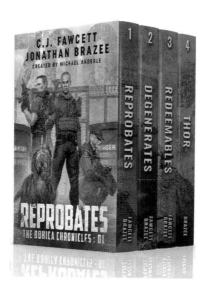

Kicked out of the military for brawling, what can three friends from different countries do to make some needed money?

Grab your copy of the entire BOHICA Chronicles at a discount today!

Reprobates:

With nothing in their future, Former US Marine Charles, ex-SAS Booker, and ex-Australian Army Roo decide to give the Zoo a shot.

Without the contacts, without backing, without knowing what they are getting into, they scramble to get their foot in the door to even make rent in one of the most dangerous areas in the world.

With high rewards comes high risk. Can they learn on the job, where failure means death?

Relying on their training, they will scratch, claw, and take the most dangerous jobs to prove themselves, but will it be enough? Can they fight the establishment and the Zoo at the same time?

And what the heck's up with that puppy they found?

Degenerates:

What happens when you come back from vacation to find out your dog ate the dog-sitter?

And your dog isn't a dog?

The BOHICA Warriors have had some success in the Zoo, but they need to expand and become more professional to make it into the big time.

Each member goes home to recruit more members to join the team.

Definitely bigger, hopefully badder, they return ready to kick some ZOO ass.

With a dead dog-sitter on their hands and more dangerous missions inside the Zoo, the six team members have to bond and learn to work together, even if they are sometimes at odds with each other.

Succeed, and riches will follow.

Fail, and the Zoo will extract its revenge in its own permanent fashion.

Redeemables:

NOTHING KEEPS A MAN AND HIS 'DOG' APART...

But what if the dog is a man-killing beast made up of alien genetics?

Thor is with his own kind as they range the Zoo, but something is missing for him. Charles is with his own kind as they work both inside and outside the walls of the ZOO.

Once connected, the two of them are now split apart by events that overcame each.

Or are they?

Follow the BOHICA Warriors as they continue to make a name for themselves as the most professional of the MERC Zoo teams. So much so that people on the outside have heard of them.

Follow Thor as he asserts himself in his pack.

Around the Zoo, nothing remains static, and some things *might converge yet again if death doesn't get in the way.*

Thor:

The ZOO wants to kill THOR. Humans would want that as well, but they don't know what he is.

What is Charles going to do?

Charles brings Thor to Benin, where he can safely hide out until things calm down. Unfortunately for both of them, that takes them out of the frying pan and into the fire.

The Pendjari National Park isn't the Zoo, but lions, elephants, and rhinos are not pushovers.

When human militias invade the park, Thor and park ranger Achille Amadou are trapped between the proverbial rock and a hard place. How do you protect the park and THOR Achille has to hide just*what* Thor is...

Can he hide what Thor is when Thor makes that hard to accomplish?

Will the militias figure out what that creature is that attacks them?

Available now from Amazon and through Kindle Unlimited.

AUTHOR NOTES

FEBRUARY 13, 2020

Thank you for reading our Cryptid Assassin stories!

Wow, I'm sitting down in the Aria's Five-50 Pizza restaurant (at the bar) about to work on OpusX 5 and (hopefully) the beats ideas for Cryptid Assassin 05. This book publishes in about twelve hours or so, and I'm typing my fingers off to bring you just a little of what happens Behind the Fiction (Podcast: https://lmbpn.com/category/behind-the-fiction/).

Thank you all for making Cryptid Assassin a success! If you have a person who needs to bring Taylor McFadden and his merry crew into their lives, don't hesitate to mention his stories to them!

Diary, February 9th – 15th

So, it's Monday the 10th at the moment, and I'm already up to a few shenanigans that are cool.

At least, *in my opinion.*

A few weeks ago, we did a model shoot for one of our series. During that shoot, we took some special headshots of the model to allow us to see if we could map a real face to a 3D head. Now, that doesn't seem like anything special.

Except, we are a publishing company (trying to become an entertainment company.)

We type—a lot—and edit and publish and all sorts of things related to putting out books. Having said all that, we have been working towards 3D bodies / heads / video clips for three (3) years, and recently, Reallusion (https://www. reallusion.com) has released a way for us to use our modeling images / cover shoots for a bit more.

Take a moment (or twenty) to see the product Reallusion has released (link above) to map a face to a 3D model. I think you could have fun with it. Imagine taking a picture of your grandparent, or mom, or friend and placing them in a short animated video.

Can you *IMAGINE* the mischief you could get into? It would be *FANTASTIC*.

Now that you have the power, don't do anything evil. (I can't say "don't do anything I wouldn't do" since we all know I'm an author. *I'll absolutely do something you shouldn't do and laugh maniacally as I do it.)*

Even if you don't have the time right now, use your phone to capture the images of your friend/loved one/person you hate ranting about a subject. You will be able to use the voice to match the lips of the 3D character in the future. You just need the photos and audio at the moment. Use them when you get time.

Or, someone on Fiverr (www.Fiverr.com) will eventually offer it as a service for $50.00, I believe.

Consider it the not-very-fake deepfake (https://en. wikipedia.org/wiki/Deepfake) – the cheap version.

I'm so happy to be back in Vegas!

I'm back from the #Superstars Writing Seminar in Colorado Springs, Colorado. The people were fantastic, the relationships I formed spectacular.

The lack of oxygen was suffocating. (PUN, PUN! Wait, is that considered a pun?)

(*Editor's note: No.*)

(Author's Reply: *Damn.*)

It might surprise you to know that Las Vegas is about a half-mile above sea level. So, while I came down from on high, Vegas isn't exactly brimming with oxygen. This might also explain why some casinos (rumored?) pump oxygen into the casino area itself to keep people awake.

I think I might go visit the Aria to work. Maybe I'll be pumped full of oxygen.

Dammit, I need a nap, and it's only 10:30am in the morning. This jetlag is STILL kicking me in the ass.

Do enjoy your week. I'm going to go pretend to be an old man who needs his late-morning nap.

Ad Aeternitatem,

Michael

P.S. – It is Thursday the 13th. Yes, I did buy my wife something for tomorrow – I'm an author who is *not* suicidal. The purchase includes candy, not a hair dryer or washing machine because I don't want my intelligent wife to focus on devious shit for my future. Plus, I'm going to take her to see the movie Knives Out. I don't want her to consider it research..

THE BOHICA CHRONICLES

Printed in Poland
by Amazon Fulfillment
Poland Sp. z o.o., Wrocław

58457529R00190